Snow Deer
and
Cocoa Cheer

ALSO BY JOANNE DEMAIO

The Winter Novels
Snowflakes and Coffee Cakes
Snow Deer and Cocoa Cheer
Cardinal Cabin
First Flurries
Eighteen Winters
—And More Winter Novels—

The Seaside Saga
Blue Jeans and Coffee Beans
The Denim Blue Sea
Beach Blues
Beach Breeze
The Beach Inn
Beach Bliss
Castaway Cottage
Night Beach
Little Beach Bungalow
Every Summer
Salt Air Secrets
Stony Point Summer
—And More Seaside Saga Books—

Summer Standalone Novels
True Blend
Whole Latte Life

Novella
The Beach Cottage

Snow Deer and Cocoa Cheer

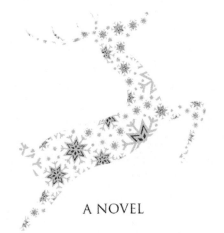

A NOVEL

JOANNE DEMAIO

Copyright © 2015 Joanne DeMaio
All rights reserved.

ISBN: 1515120775
ISBN 13: 9781515120773

Joannedemaio.com

To Jena and Mary,

for always making the season special

one

FRESH SNOWFALL GLISTENS ON THE old maple tree beside the red barn. A soft layer of it clings to the tree's outstretched branches reaching skyward. Someone once told Jane March there's something special about New England snow; it's different from other snow. So she looks closely at the painted planks of the barn walls, at the snowcapped roof and pale gray clouds above. It's true; there's no denying it. Maybe it's the hush of it all, or the gentleness to those twirling, spinning snowflakes that seem to waltz in a wintry breeze. As they fall in front of the red barn, it becomes perfectly clear. A simple balsam wreath hung over the barn doors would do it, would say Christmas in that quintessential style that stirs the heart.

She sits back for a moment before touching her brush bristles into the green paint and adding a wreath shape onto the barn wall. Overlaying a drop of water gives the delicate pine needles a sense of motion in the wind. Later, when the paint dries, she'll speckle white snow on the wreath and finish it with a burgundy bow.

"Done." Jane gets up carefully, still favoring her newly broken left wrist. She adjusts the sling around her neck and walks to the windows. At least it's her left wrist that's broken, leaving her free, somewhat, to continue her designing. Her mother set up a temporary office space in the farmhouse's sunroom, with its wall of paned windows overlooking the carriage house and field beyond. It's a spot where the deer often graze, where they blend in with the sweeping brown and green wild grasses of autumn.

Outside, the scene that meets her eyes is a far cry from the December image she just painted for her latest greeting card. This window view is one of her favorites, though, this palette of gold and red and yellow October foliage, the copper weather vane on the carriage house glinting in the sunshine.

But autumn views won't help her artwork. If she's going to hold onto her job, she has got to find a way to channel *Christmas* during these brief weeks recuperating at her childhood home in Addison. It would really help if the vintage holiday cards she ordered would arrive. Their charm and whimsy from years gone by might inspire her to capture the spirit of the season, with a Jane March modern-day twist. Not needing a repeat of yesterday's front-door incident, she hurries back to the large table covered with her computer and paints and images, and grabs a blank sheet of paper. In a friendly cursive, she jots *Hello!* to the mailman, then asks if he might bring the mail up to the front stoop and leave it on the milk can there.

Hoping it's not too much to ask, Jane folds the note in half and heads to the door. With her good arm, she drags a brass umbrella stand over and props it in the doorway to stop the front door from locking shut behind her. Maybe those vintage cards will finally arrive today. She walks to the mailbox at the curb and tucks the note inside. Halfway back to the house, she looks over her shoulder, returns to the mailbox and flips the red flag up.

⟡

Something about the country music playing on the radio suits him just fine. The way the singer's voice slides, it gives a sort of woeful rhythm to his stops, to the opening squeak and closing snap of the mailboxes. Until a car is idled, parked right in front of the next house and interrupting the sadness he's been channeling in song. Must be someone talking on their cell phone, pulled over to the curb oblivious to the necessary, and anticipated, approach of the letter carrier. Wes gives his mail truck horn a toot to move the driver along, then steers over to the curbside mailbox. He lifts a few letters from the side tray and tosses them in, giving the mailbox's loose door a good slam when it flops open as he puts the truck in gear.

Further down the road, the truck tires thump across the wooden planks of the covered bridge. Wouldn't he love to pause right there and look out on the babbling brook beneath it? Instead, he finishes delivering envelopes and sale flyers to the Brookside Road rustic Cape Cods and gabled-roof colonials, before turning onto Old Willow Road.

First stop there? Beautifully suited to the historic ship captain's house at the end of a long driveway is a shiny black mailbox mounted on an elaborate white post with a scrolled-metal vine displaying the house number. But the second box on the street is bungee-corded together, the cord wrapped around and around the box and post. Really, would it be too much to replace these shabby boxes barely attached to their dilapidated roadside posts? He opens it with a sigh, and the door wobbles on one hinge as he puts a padded envelope in the mailbox, then aligns the door and presses it shut before pulling away from the curb. All while some lonely cowboy wails about his heart, singing words he might as well have borrowed from Wes.

The air is cooler here in Olde Addison, which is closer to the water. The Connecticut River snakes off in the distance, a silver ribbon winding around the curves of the river valley, beyond the red and gold trees. He maneuvers past a weeping willow with branches cascading alongside the curb. At the March house, the flag is up on the blue-painted mailbox, and he's surprised to find that the note is for him. Surprised at first, then annoyed. Another delay interrupting the rhythm he and the country crooner have pieced together, Wes slamming mailboxes in beat to the song's bleeding heart.

So he flips up his non-postal-approved bomber jacket collar, checks his reflection in the rearview mirror to be sure he doesn't look too haggard, not having shaved for two days now, and slides the truck door open. A brisk wind flaps his regulation side-striped trousers, so he quickly walks along the stone path, up the stairs to the matching blue-painted porch, and sets the March mail on the milk can.

Right when he starts to turn, a gust of that October wind lifts one of the envelopes and flips it onto the floor, so he picks it up and knocks at the door with a few sharp raps. When no one answers, he glances around and sees an empty clay flowerpot perched on the porch railing. That'll have to do, because he can't waste any more of his meticulously scheduled time waiting to hand-deliver to finicky families on windy days. He drops the envelope on the milk can, sets the dusty flowerpot on top of it, turns and dashes down the porch steps, pushing up his leather jacket sleeve to check his watch as he goes.

"Wait!"

Oh, the thought crosses Wes' mind, so briefly, to keep hurrying to his truck and his now-behind-schedule mail delivery. The way her voice gets lost in the wind, she might think he missed hearing it. But instead he stops halfway down the walkway and turns back. He does a slight double take, expecting to see an apologetic Lillian March standing on the farmhouse porch, maybe waving an envelope she's hoping he can take. Not expecting to see who he believes might be her daughter, wearing a knitted shawl over jeans and leaning out from the doorway, sandy blonde hair swinging over her shoulder. He squints a moment, satisfied it is the daughter—Jane, he thinks her name is—and heads toward her.

"Did you have something to mail?" Wes asks.

"Wes?" Her right hand shields her eyes from the glare of sunshine as she stands in the open doorway. "Wes Davis? Is that you?"

"Guilty as charged."

"Well, how nice to see you. It's been so long."

"It has, Jane. It's Jane, right? How've you been?"

"Okay!" she says, nodding. "I'm doing okay. You're the … mailman?"

As she says it, he sees it: the wide grin and slight tip of her head that he can't really read. "Just got my ten-year pin." Without thinking, he lifts the lapel of his non-regulation bomber and flashes the official pin on his shirt collar, before hiking up the leather jacket around his neck again.

"How do you like that! Very nice, and so is this valet mail service. Thank you."

He notices that Jane doesn't leave the house, but rather leans against the wood-paneled door, half in and half out. "No problem today. But it's a one-time deal, I'm on a schedule. Only the package companies do regular door delivery." His mail truck idles at the curb; it's where he itches to be, listening to that lonely heart singing his sad calamity—twang and all. And the way Jane's standing, still partially inside the house, it's clear she doesn't want to chat about mail routes, or the way packages are sequentially lined up in the rear of the truck. "Plus it's a busy road. Too much traffic to be parking the truck curbside."

Jane looks down to the—wouldn't you know it?—now-quiet country road. "It's just that my mother has the only key. She must have misplaced the extra, what with the past year she had," she explains. "And yesterday? Gosh, what a fiasco! I got locked out when this temperamental door closed behind me when I went to get the mail. Sat stranded on the porch all morning."

Wes checks his watch. "Sorry to hear that, but you're all set now." He turns to leave, and when she starts to ask something about handing her the mail from the milk can, he waves his hand without looking back. Seriously? She can't take a step outside for her mail? "Nice seeing you, Jane," he calls. As he trots down the blue-painted porch steps and along the stone walkway, he hears her dragging something across the floor. When he approaches his truck, he glances her way and sees an umbrella stand propped in front of that temperamental wooden door. As Jane steps out and bends for the mail, her shawl swings to the side—and he also catches sight of her left arm in a sling, leaving him feeling pretty much like a complete heel.

two

TOO BAD SHE CAN'T CAPTURE scent in her greeting cards. It evokes such nostalgia, and oh, what comfort. Sitting at the kitchen table that evening, where her mother placed a small pillow so she could rest her broken wrist, Jane inhales the aroma of pork chops and onions simmering on the stovetop.

"Mom, you're making it really hard for me to ever leave here." Her mother stands at the stove in a long paisley-print skirt, a sage-colored cardigan loose over it, a turquoise pendant around her neck. Her thick silver hair is pulled back in a twist. "I'm going to miss these home-cooked meals," Jane adds, wistful already.

"I'll make up some frozen care packages, okay? But it's still a ways off before you go. How long did the doctor say the cast would be on?" Lillian asks while stirring the potatoes.

"Six weeks, minimum."

"That's lots of meals here." Lillian checks the sizzling pork chops and shuts off the flame before scooping a serving onto Jane's plate. "How was your day today? Get much designing done?"

"Some. Technically, I really don't have to work, being that

7

I'm out on short-term disability. But greeting cards are a tough market right now, with so much DIY going on."

"DIY?"

"Do-it-yourself. Which is making things very competitive. And at our last weekly meeting, my boss mentioned that I needed to up my game. My cards have gone stale, I guess. So this will definitely be a working medical leave. Thanks for getting a studio area set up for me, I forgot how much I loved that sunroom."

Lillian sets down Jane's plate, heaped with chops and mashed potatoes and green beans, caramelized onions drizzled over it all. "Anything to help. Maybe that view of the field will inspire you. I even saw a red fox out there the other day! And once the leaves fall, you can see a sliver of river in the distance." She turns to the kitchen window, framed with star-print curtains, and motions to the twilight sky. "And don't worry, if you ever need to go to the office, I can drive you. Or I'm sure your sister could, too."

"Chloe? To Cobblestone Cards? But she's so busy with the kids. And that's really nice of you, Mom, but I'm good here. I scan my designs into the system and email them off, no problem."

"Well, thank goodness for technology." Her mother sits across from her and sprinkles salt on her meal. "It's still unfortunate about your wrist. Things like that happen, of course. An unexpected slippery floor and down you go."

"Believe me, Cobblestone takes full responsibility. It rained so much that day last week, and with everyone in and out, one little puddle on the floor did the trick."

"But that puddle should've been mopped up right away. Even though it *is* nice having you here to recuperate. The house has been so quiet with your dad gone." Lillian reaches over and pours a splash of wine into their glasses. "I'd been overseeing the carriage house construction, which kept me plenty busy. But that's done now. I'll tell you, when that old carriage house burned down a couple years ago, I never thought I'd love the new one even more. Too bad Dad's not here to see it."

"I know." Jane takes a mouthful of the sweet onions and beans mixed together, knowing how her mother's deeply missed Edward since he died last year. "Did you get that extra key made yet?" Jane asks around another forkful of food. "The mailman is so crabby. I left a note asking him to bring up the mail, and he didn't seem to appreciate it."

"Wesley? Oh, he's just tense, I'm sure. His wedding's in a few weeks, so things must be busy for him. Didn't Greg tell you when he checked your arm? They are brothers, after all."

"Wedding? Huh, that's odd. No, Greg didn't even mention it." She leans close to the table, resting her arm-in-a-cast on the soft pillow. "But the waiting room was packed, so he was very busy."

"Greg's still available, dear," Lillian says as she lifts her glass for a sip of wine. "Orthopedic surgeon, well established, nice family."

"Mom! Greg's the same now as when he was my high school prom date—a confirmed bachelor." When Jane takes her plate and starts to stand, Lillian snatches it and motions for her to sit. "He's a nice enough guy," Jane continues, setting her casted arm on the soft pillow again and thinking of her doctor appointment the other day, all while her mother loads up her plate with seconds. "But Greg Davis seems happy enough being single."

Brown cartons are lined up two-deep in the hallway, ready to be carried out to the moving van this weekend. So like working along an assembly line, Wes methodically rips off piece after piece of packing tape and presses each strip along the top of the successive boxes: towels and dishes and framed pictures and most of his clothes, neatly folded and wrapped and secured for the trip to their new home. He glances around at the empty walls and swigs his beer. A few more boxes of very last-minute items and he'll be good to go, to leave this one-bedroom apartment behind.

Not that he really wants to; he always liked the rustic feel of this refurbished mill factory. The brick accent walls, the waterfall and small pond outside, the beamed living room ceiling ... it suited him with its casualness. But he didn't renew the lease, with the wedding and all, so now he's got to move.

When the timer beeps in the kitchen, Wes pulls his dinner out of the oven and sets the pre-made lasagna on the top burner, letting it cool while he turns on the countertop TV.

"Glorious days are coming up, folks," meteorologist Leo Sterling announces as he points to his Addison weather map. "Get out in that crisp Connecticut air. Great for pumpkin pickin' or scarecrow stuffing."

"Or moving." Wes grabs the Italian dressing from the refrigerator and sets it beside his salad and carefully placed silverware.

"Autumn gold, it never gets old," Leo concludes.

Which gets Wes to consider his ring finger with a passing thought of wedding-band gold, then to look over at his black tuxedo hanging on the outside of his bedroom door. The answering machine blinks on the granite breakfast island he'll also miss when he moves out, so he hits the button as he brings over his plate of lasagna and sits on a stool. His father's voice offers to lend Wes cuff links for the wedding, the same ones he wore when he married Wes' mother. He goes on about how the cuff links will go great with the tux on Wes' big day.

10

Then comes the message from the community boathouse alongside the river, its grand water-view hall reserved months ago for his wedding reception. The banquet room manager asks for a final head count as soon as possible.

Nothing else comes after that, except a long beep and silence.

With a wave of his hand toward the hanging tuxedo, the answering machine, the scrawled to-do list on the pad on the countertop, he turns away from it all and digs into his lasagna, looking back at his black tux only once.

three

WES TURNS OFF MAIN STREET onto Birch Lane and carefully maneuvers the rented moving van Saturday morning. He manages to pull the bulky vehicle into the narrow driveway, back it out to turn it around and park it at the curb. The lawns are still covered with misty dew, the foliage rich in color beneath the rising sun's rays. He gives a look at the small Victorian home, at the clapboard siding with fish-scale shingled accent, much of it fading and needing a fresh coat of paint. The front peak with its sunburst gable will be no easy feat to get to. Even with those fine architectural details, the house has lost some charm with its recent neglect. Of course it'll be up to him to haul out the ladder and paintbrushes to tend to it, once and for all. No amount of pestering his father to hire a contractor has worked.

But still, home is home. Yet he's finding it hard to open the door and actually get out of the moving van. It's quiet at this hour, the traffic light with only a few people headed out for a coffee to-go, maybe before hitting Saturday tag sales or getting a head start on leaf peeping. The house is the first one on Birch Lane, so a glimpse of the cove is visible further down Main Street. When a pickup drives by with fishing poles and a cooler in the truck bed, Wes knows just what kind of a lazy day the driver has in store.

What he wouldn't give to be having *that* day. But his father, Pete, appears in the front doorway, coffee in hand, so Wes hesitantly steps down from the vehicle and heads to the front stoop, the one with the top spandrel trim—each turned-spindle painted two complementary colors—also needing a coat of paint. Pete swings the storm door open for him, and Wes walks into the house, back home again.

"What's going on?" his father asks, turning and watching as Wes sets down a black duffel bag in the front foyer.

"I'm moving in."

"What?"

Wes sets a hand on the stair banister, glances up the steps, then looks into the living room where lace curtain panels hang in the bay window. "You heard me. The wedding's off."

His father does it then, he chokes on a mouthful of coffee with that piece of news.

"That's right, Dad. Even better? I lost my apartment in the whole mess, and since you never moved out to somewhere smaller and easier to manage, I'm moving in."

"Wait, back it up here. Called off? You mean your wedding's *cancelled*?" His father somehow gets the words out while still sputtering through the choking.

Wes takes off his fleece vest and hangs it on the banister before heading to the kitchen while saying over his shoulder, "In the process."

"What the hell did you do?" his father asks from behind him.

"*I* didn't call it off." In the kitchen, Wes walks around, feeling a little lost with everything going on. Finally, he opens one of the glass-front cabinets lined in white lace and grabs a coffee cup. "Sheila did, so you'll have to ask her."

When he turns, Pete is leaning in the doorway, coffee mug cupped in his hands, squinting at him. And Wes figures sure as hell his father sees the circles beneath his eyes now, the unshaven scruff on his face. And what it all is, is this: the truth—plain and simple—that no way did Wes see this breakup coming.

"Okay. I guess you can move in upstairs."

"No." Wes lifts the coffeepot and pours a steaming mug. "I'll just take my old room down here, right off the kitchen. It'll be easier that way, and it's only temporary, until I get myself situated."

"Suit yourself, but I still cannot believe this. The wedding is weeks away, Wes."

"Was, Dad. *Was* weeks away, believe me." He pours cream into his coffee, takes a long drink and turns to his father, noticing the corduroy slacks and button-down shirt beneath a threadbare cardigan. Glaringly apparent is that he's not in his postal uniform. "What are you doing home, anyway? Not delivering mail today? You feel okay?"

"Personal day. Got a ton of them to use before the year's over. Planned on doing some whittling out in the shed."

"Seriously, Dad? First of all," Wes begins as he opens the refrigerator, his work boots heavy on the floor, "have you even eaten anything? You look pale." He pulls out a carton of eggs. "And shouldn't you be getting this place into shape? You told me you'd start scraping the porch trim months ago."

He notices it, the way his father pulls out one of the straight-back farm chairs and sits at the table, turning up a worn cuff of his sweater with a slight smile on his face.

But Wes keeps fussing with the food, finding a frying pan in the cabinet, turning on the flame and dropping a slab of butter in the pan, folding back the cuffs of his own thermal-weave shirt, tipping and moving the pan as the butter melts.

"Don't you know breakfast is the most important meal of the day? It gives you the energy you need." He cracks open a couple eggs into the sizzling pan. "And today you'll need a lot, helping me move boxes. Greg's on his way over, too, to give a hand with the furniture and heavier stuff." He checks the edges of the sunny-side-up eggs. "And be careful lifting things. Remember to bend at the knees and keep your back straight."

❧

"I've got one of those scarecrows on a stick, from the nursery, Jane. I bought it last year. It's in the front closet."

Jane knows, being the true Yankee her mother is, that the scarecrow will be cleaned up and freshened, ready to stand sentry beside a hay bale and pumpkin for many more autumns. She opens the closet door and steps inside. Someone, back in the day, had the foresight to build deep closets in this old farmhouse, particularly the front closet. She figures its intent was to hold the boots and coveralls and jackets and hats when the farming was done at the day's end.

Now, suburban storage replaces farm gear: scarecrows and a vacuum cleaner and a bristle broom to give the front porch a tidy sweep. And, she sees while sliding a box from the corner with her good arm, a carton of watercolor and oil paintings. She kneels down right then and there and brushes through the canvases: countryside Addison near the cove, the town green, the old Christmas Barn on a snowy day, white picket fences in front of imposing colonials, winding stone walls. The artist's name is written in the lower corner of each— Lillian March.

"Schmaltzy." The word comes from behind her, but she can't turn away from the images of small-town Addison. "I

15

submitted those to a juried show in the city years ago, but they were never accepted. Schmaltzy. I seem to remember that's how they described them."

Jane looks up at her mother in disbelief. "More like charming! You captured Addison beautifully."

"I guess they're too good to be true," Lillian tells her. "That's what your father said back then. The judges simply didn't believe a town could be that lovely." She nods down toward the paintings. "It's a good thing I taught art at the high school, because I could never find a way to make a living with my painting. Like you do," she says with a warm smile before grabbing a quilted jacket from a hanger. "But never mind those, they're ancient history now. Let's go, we've got Operation Pumpkin going on!"

Oh, it's been years since her mother used that word. Operation Pumpkin or Operation Shoe Shopping or Operation Beachcombing. *Operation* always meant a day chock-full of fun. And from their morning stops at farm stands buying mums and fresh jams, to a lunchtime hayride under golden October sunlight—sitting on a horse-drawn wagon pulled over packed-dirt trails to the finest pumpkin patch Jane's ever seen—to standing in line afterward waiting for warm apple fritters dusted with powdered sugar, the day doesn't let her down. Well, except maybe for the waiting-in-line-for-fritters part.

Because standing in line, everything stops when Jane's cell phone dings with a work message and Lillian asks about her job.

"Mom, I'm really afraid they'll replace me, especially now that they're getting used to me *not* being there. You know, while I'm recuperating." She lifts her slinged-and-casted arm from beneath her fringed poncho. "So I need to use this time to find a new design angle for next year's Christmas cards."

16

"Angle, schmangle. Everyone's got some sort of angle going on these days. Do you think the answer's as easy as that?"

Jane considers the crowd of families and couples and random pumpkin-pickers around them, people wearing fleece jackets and hiking shoes, chatting happily—and wishes she could only do the same.

"It's worth a shot, Mom. Because what I know is that …" She pauses to check the email that just arrived from Cobblestone Cards. "After reviewing my latest drawings? Well, in their words—" She flashes her mother the cell phone screen. "They think I may have lost my jingle."

◦◦◦

The padded red booth at Joel's Bar and Grille is plenty spacious for the amount of food they order. Wes sits across from his father and brother, all of them tired after a day of moving furniture and boxes. The streetlight outside shines through the blinds of a side window, which Wes shoves open a few inches to let in some of the cool evening air.

Greg reaches for a melted-cheese nacho while their father orders his dinner.

"Give me the meatloaf sandwich, with a side of onion rings." Pete sets his menu down. "A draft beer, too. Nice and cold."

Greg gives a last look at his menu. "I'll have the same, but make it a soda instead."

"On call tonight?" Wes asks.

"Yup, got to keep things straight."

"What's the buffalo chicken wrap come with?" Wes asks their waitress as she jots down Greg's order.

"Chips and a pickle."

17

"Great, make them the baked chips. Add a draft and I'm good, too."

"Really?" Greg asks when the waitress leaves. "You're having a wrap?"

"Healthy choice. You should appreciate that, Scrubs, being a doctor and whatnot."

Greg leans back in the booth. "We burned enough calories moving you in today to go all out with the food. I'm famished."

The waitress returns with three tall glasses of drinks and sets them on paper coasters. "Here you go, boys."

"Dad," Wes says when she breezes off. "You on any medication?"

Pete squints at him suspiciously. "Why?"

"Liquor can counter the effects of some prescriptions. You taking anything for cholesterol? Nerves?"

"Nerves?" Greg asks. "How bad can his nerves be as a career letter carrier?"

"Hey," Pete warns, setting his elbows on the table. "Yesterday, I had a dog run out and try to sink its teeth into my hand when I delivered the mail. One wrong move and I'd have been in the ER. You ever have someone try to bite you in your line of work?"

Greg tips his glass to his father's. "Just giving you a hard time, Dad. I could never do what you and Wes do."

"I'm glad someone followed in my footsteps. Or truck tracks, I should say." Pete tips his glass to Wes'. "My pop would've been proud, you being a third-generation mailman after all."

"It's not forever, so don't get hung up on it," Wes assures him. "Even though I won't be giving my notice yet, like I planned. But someday."

"Still can't believe you almost gave up the post office to

18

work in a private security firm." His father says this while scrutinizing him over his beer.

"It's a family business, Dad. Sheila's family. And very lucrative."

"What do they do, hire out those rent-a-cops?" Greg asks.

"No. Well, maybe. They handle security for private gigs, corporate businesses. And I *would've* been family, moved up to management. Now that's all scrapped, right along with the wedding."

"So it's really not happening? For sure?" Pete asks.

"Absolutely." As he says it, Wes sees how his father still cannot believe that Sheila nearly left him at the altar. Changed her mind at the last minute and hightailed it home to her family in Indiana—where she and Wes were supposed to go together, after the honeymoon. Wedding here, home there, new life set to begin, trading in a postal uniform for security threads.

Wes grabs his beer and hitches his head toward the back of the room, beyond the half wall where a garland of red and gold leaves hangs entwined with tiny orange lights. "And I'm done discussing it. Quick game of darts before the food's here, Scrubs?" he asks his brother. When Greg takes his soda and heads over, Wes turns to his father, who's already pulling out his pocketknife and a small stick of wood. "Dad? What about you?"

Pete raises a partially formed deer in answer, so Wes winds his way around the tables, past the bar anchored with illuminated twig pumpkins on either end, waving hello to a few familiar faces before setting his beer down near the dartboard.

"What's riding on this?" Greg asks with a grin. "Ten bucks this time?"

"Nothing. I'm done being a betting man for a while."

"After gambling on the wrong woman, I guess you would be. What are your plans, guy, now that you're unattached again?" His brother takes aim and throws his dart.

"Keeping things open. Give Dad a hand around the house for the time being."

"No shit," Greg says, picking up another dart.

"At least until my luck changes, with a new job maybe, an apartment. Not sure what's next."

"You know something?" Greg throws his third dart. "I never liked that Sheila, anyway."

"Really?" Wes stops, right as he's about to take aim. "Why didn't you ever tell me?"

"She was your girl, so I didn't say anything." Greg taps off his buzzing pager. "But she was always a little full of herself, seemed to me. Hey," he says, checking his watch. "I'm going to catch the waitress and ask her to wrap my dinner. The hospital's calling."

When Wes settles back in the booth, he leaves Greg waiting at the bar for his take-out dinner, talking with the bartender. An evening news anchor delivers the headlines on a flat-screen TV mounted on a paneled side wall. All the while, his father continues whittling a deer's head.

"I swapped my honeymoon ticket for a trip to California, Dad. End of the year." His father's fingers pull at the knife blade as he shapes the deer's side profile. So Wes reaches into an inside jacket pocket and sets his new airline ticket receipt on the table. "The holidays are coming up. And I don't feel like sticking around and answering annoying wedding questions from aunts, cousins."

"What's that, your flight ticket?"

"Looks it, but it's not. This is my receipt, which includes the detailed itinerary. Modern technology, Dad. The airlines use e-tickets now, it's all done online."

"That right?" his father asks while slicing off a thin piece of wood. "No more nice paper tickets?"

"Nope. But this receipt shows the same thing. Dates, times, departures, airports—it's all on here. So I just *call* this my ticket, while I count down the days."

"Yo, Wes." The bartender approaches with two shot glasses.

Something's up; Wes can seriously tell when Kevin places a shot glass in front of him. "Kevin, what's happening?"

"Thought maybe this was your stag night, seeing you come in with Greg and your father. But the good doctor mentioned your *former* bride-to-be and, heck, sorry to hear the wedding's off. It's tough, I know."

"Yeah, well. It happens." Wes sits back uncomfortably, his beer and a shot in front of him.

"So allow me to upgrade your drink to a stronger brew." Kevin slides Wes' shot glass closer. "A toast to better times?" He holds up his own glass, waiting for Wes to raise his.

Which he does, throwing the concoction down his throat and setting the glass, hard, on the table.

Kevin downs his drink and pats Wes' back before heading to the bar. "Something to numb the pain, my man," he calls over his shoulder as the waitress sets their platters on the booth table.

Pain might not be the right word, but numb definitely is, after that potent toast. Wes snags a few chips while his father still whittles the wooden deer's head, leaving his food waiting.

"You're honestly going west for the holiday?" Pete finally asks.

Wes lifts his wrap, considering his whittling father at the same time. "That's right. For about a week." He takes a bite of the wrap overstuffed with breaded chicken pieces and tomato and shredded lettuce and blue cheese dressing, wiping a dribble of sauce from his chin. "You know how family is. They'll want all the nitty-gritty wedding details, lay on the sympathy. And I really don't want to hear it." He picks up his airline ticket and carefully tucks it in his jacket pocket. "Figured I'll be in the sky Christmas Eve, safe from any prying on the plane."

His father pulls his plate closer, takes a taste of the meatloaf sandwich, then carves a little more. It's his way, Wes has seen it over the years, this focusing on a difficult whittling area instead of arguing. His father gently scoops out a groove in the center of the deer's ear.

Wes bites into his chicken wrap again, not saying another word.

four

CHLOE PRESSES A KNIFE THROUGH a thick slab of cake. "Whoops," she whispers when cinnamon crumbs drop onto Jane's worktable and she brushes them into her open hand.

"I miss mornings like this, hanging out with my sis," Jane tells her. Holding two delicate china plates, she walks across the wide-planked floor, a slant of early morning sunlight shining across it.

Chloe sets a hunk of cake on each plate, grabs the travel coffee mug she'd brought along, and takes her pastry and java to the overstuffed white rattan chairs in the corner nook. "Me, too. It's fun sneaking over here for a visit when Bob's at work, the kids in school. Mom makes the *best* food, and it's like the good old days, being home again with you. But I can only stay a bit, my Tuesday To-Do meeting is at nine."

Before Jane joins her sister, she drags over the box of their mother's countryside paintings. "You have to see these," she says. "They're such a visual history of Addison. Look at this one." She hands Chloe a painting that is mostly of a white picket fence, with a corner of a colonial house visible behind it. Their mother obviously wanted to capture the picket-fence vibe that purely says home sweet home. "Now if I could paint something like this, but add swags of green garland and maybe twinkling lights, a pretty snow flurry, and add a snappy verse to modernize it, can't you see a Christmas card?"

"Definitely," Chloe says around a mouthful of cake. "Oh, this is so good. Get your plate and try some!"

Jane grabs her dish from the worktable, forks a chunk of cake and closes her eyes with its delectable taste.

"Now what's this I hear from Mom about you losing your jingle?" Chloe asks while thumbing through the paintings.

What Jane wishes with that question is this: that she could simply linger with the sweet crumb cake her mother baked, bask in the sunlight warming the farmhouse back room, maybe gaze out the paned windows to the fall foliage. But that kind of easy lingering won't keep her job secure. "That's one way of putting it," she tells her sister. "Lost jingle, writer's block, creative drain."

"How hard can it be? I mean, can't you start with a catchy rhyme … ho ho ho, snow snow snow?"

"Huh. Easy for you to say. Try coming up with jingles after you've designed thousands of greeting cards, at the same time the boss is pressuring you for something fresh. Not to mention the cubicle pressure. You know, being surrounded by shelves of research books and painting instruments, and tins of pencils and pastels—and other designers you suspect might out-design you."

"I think I'll stick to booking travel reservations." Chloe stands then and slips on her corduroy blazer, flipping her brown hair out from under its collar. "Listen sis, whatever it takes, you have to try. You're thirty-three years old. Do you really want to start over with some other job?"

"Absolutely not. I love what I do."

"So take advantage of the situation. You've got this

gorgeous scenery here at home while healing that arm. Just breathe, slowly, and take it all in. Because you've *got* to get your jingle back—it's what you do!"

Jane stands, and using her right arm, opens one of the windows. Unseasonably warm air wafts into the room. "I'm trying. I broke out my snowman socks, cued the holiday music, ordered vintage Christmas cards." She opens a drawer in a painted end table. "I even bought candy canes to hook on my cocoa mug. And wow, check it out! There's a deer outside."

"Where?" Chloe walks closer to the windows while buttoning her blazer.

"There!" The way the sun shines low on the autumn wildflowers, it plays tricks on Jane's eyes as she squints to see it. "It blends right in with the grasses."

"I must've missed it, and I really have to run. The travel agency is putting together a singles' tour to Italy, and our To-Do meeting this morning plots the stops." She scoops up her coffee mug and grabs her purse from the worktable, browsing Jane's latest sketches as she does. "This one's nice, the horse-drawn wagon ride to a Christmas tree farm?"

Jane steps beside her, remembering the wagon ride with her mother the other day. It *is* nice, the way the painted scene captures those wonderful hours together; she merely substituted snowcapped pine trees for the pumpkin patch.

"Gosh, look at the time!" Chloe gives her a hug and rushes through the house to the front door. "For now, you just take care of that arm. I'll call you later, Jane, after the girls' tap-dance lessons."

When the surly, one-key front door slams shut behind Chloe, Jane sees her older sister's striped chambray scarf on the chair and runs to the window waving it. But it's too late; Chloe's car is already pulling out of the long driveway. So she drapes it around her own neck before returning to her mother's white picket fence painting and scanning it into the computer.

"Let's see," Jane muses as she creates a snow flurry with her image-editing software, adds a swag of pine garland to the fence pickets, then drops on a couple of red velvet bows. "Not bad, if I do say so myself."

If her boss agrees, she'll gladly paint a similar image, maybe a series of them. It can't hurt to email it off to Cobblestone Cards, which she does, asking if something like this would fit into next year's catalog.

Making now the perfect time for an inspiring cup of cocoa. So she heads to the kitchen and adds cocoa powder and sugar to a mug, stirs in milk and places the mug in the microwave. Right as she sets the timer button, someone knocks at the front door.

"Chloe," she whispers while sliding the scarf off her neck and rushing to give it to her sister. "I hope you won't be late for work," she begins while pulling the door open and stopping short. "Oh!"

"Jane," Wes Davis says, standing on her stoop in his mailman uniform and pulling off a pair of dark sunglasses.

"Wes! I thought you'd be Chloe. My sister?"

He nods. "I know Chloe, sorry to disappoint you."

"No. It's just that I have her scarf." Jane lifts the chambray scarf with her good arm while her foot props open the temperamental door. "Wait. Is that my mail?" She tips her head and waggles a finger at him. "I thought you didn't deliver to the door."

Wes hands her a small stack of envelopes. "I noticed your cast yesterday, and well …" He pauses as he drops an envelope and bends to pick it up. "So what've you been up to, Jane?"

26

Jane reaches for the mail he holds out. "You mean besides breaking my bones?"

"Take a fall somewhere?"

"At work. Cobblestone Cards, over in Eastfield."

"The greeting card place?"

"That's the one. I'm a designer there. But my mother wouldn't hear of me living alone in my apartment and fending for myself." She holds up her arm-in-a-cast. "So I'm back home for a few weeks, recuperating. Mom set up a nice office space, and I'm working from here, too." Jane shrugs then, pausing as Wes checks his watch. "That's why I'm anxious to get my mail. I'm waiting for an order of vintage cards that I really, *really* need." She thumbs through the envelopes. "Hmm, nothing."

"Well, Jane," Wes says with a glance at his idling mail truck.

"And here I am, rambling. Sorry." She steps outside a little, while certain to be leaning against the door that wants to spring closed behind her. "Because hey, how about you! I hear you're getting married."

Wes looks off to the street, then back at her. "You heard right, but there's been a—" He stops as Jane turns toward a sharply beeping timer from inside the house.

"Hold that thought?" she asks. "Pretty please? I'll be back in a sec."

She hurries to the kitchen and quickly stirs her hot cocoa, then rushes to the front door holding her Christmas cup with a mini candy cane hooked on the edge. And watches Wes drive off in his mail truck, already approaching the house next door.

"Well. How do you like that?" she asks herself, leaning out and watching this testy Wesley Davis drive off. "With not so much as a wave goodbye."

The two mail trucks are parked side by side, the driver windows perfectly aligned, with Wes' truck facing the cove waters beneath the noonday sun. His lunch is emptied out on a tray beside him, and he lines up the sandwich, apple, chips and bottle of water. Finally he opens his side window to talk with his father as they eat together.

"What do you think of these?" Wes passes a handful of paint swatches over through the open windows. "Picked them up at the hardware store when I delivered their mail."

His father reaches for them and spreads the colors like a deck of cards, arranging each painted tab neatly in his fingers.

"They're from the historical paint section, since we're talking a Victorian. See anything you like?" Wes lifts the top half of his roll, straightens the cheese, then bites in. "That Woodstock Putty looks good, maybe with a brick-red trim."

"I'm not sure." His father carefully fans the paint colors on his dashboard. "It's the kind of thing to consider from various angles, under different light." He picks up half of his grinder and takes a large bite.

Like always, that's all that happens. They have lunch while silently pondering some mundane thing in life. This time, it's paint chips, which Wes glances over at before taking a long swallow of his water. "Jeez, it's warm today, especially for October. Won't be too many more lunches like this, with the windows down."

"Indian summer, feels like." Pete extends his hand outside the window. "Just for a day, forecast says a cold front's coming in tomorrow."

"Well, I bought a few of those mini paint jars. I'll brush sample colors on the side of the house later, before the weather changes, to give you a better feel for them." Wes leans out toward his father's truck, watching Pete unwrap and slice something in two. "And what the heck is that?"

"Raspberry-chocolate shortbread bar." He hands Wes a neatly cut half on a paper napkin.

"Where'd you get this?"

"Snowflakes and Coffee Cakes." His father nods over toward the brown barn sitting on the far sloping banks of Addison Cove. A maple tree towers beside it, ablaze in red foliage. "That Christmas barn has the best pastries. Everything homemade, like Mom used to make." With that, he takes a bite and holds up the rest in a pastry toast to the skies above. "Oh man, heaven."

Anything that looks this good can't be good for you. Wes takes a bite of his piece, then wipes a bead of perspiration from his forehead. "You know your metabolism slows as you age, Dad. Got to watch your calorie intake."

"That's why I like my route, lots of walking neighborhoods on it. Keeps me fit."

Wes considers the rest of the chocolate-raspberry swirled goodness in his hand before putting it all in his mouth. "You keep eating like this, you'll be wearing the Santa suit at Aunt Connie's on Christmas."

His father wipes his fingers on a napkin and turns to look over at Wes sitting in his mail truck. "She's planning a big holiday shindig this year. It'll be fun, you'll see."

That's all it takes to spike Wes' blood pressure, and so he shoves his food wrappings into his lunch bag. "I already told you, Dad. I'm not sticking around for Christmas and I don't want to hear endless questions from the family." He slides his door open, gets out and pulls off his blue knit sweater, regulation—eagle patch included. "Truth is, I don't know how much longer I'll stick around this town. The wedding's off, but that doesn't mean that it's still not time for a change, you hear me?"

His father glares at him, then slides open his own driver

door. "I'm going to walk this off, the raspberry bar *and* your attitude. You coming with me?"

Wes leans back into his truck, drops his sweater on the seat and locks up the door. They walk close to the water and head in the direction of a patch of woods at the far end of the parking lot. A mallard duck waddles along behind them, pecking at a stone or two on the packed-dirt. At the edge of the woods, a thin fallen limb leans against a tree. Wes steps over a stone wall, picks up the branch and turns it in his hand. "Not bad for whittling, still has some moisture in it," he says as he slightly bends it.

Pete takes it from him, his thumb running along the bark. "Good piece, nice and straight. I'll cut it up and put it in the freezer tonight. Helps keep the moisture in."

The duck moves closer behind them and stops then, settling on a tuft of dried grass in the sun. Wes walks along the cove shore, the water lapping gently, the sky above it pale blue. The cove parking lot is filled with workers like him and his father, having lunch waterside in their cars this warm day and walking a bit as they take in the serene sight. A man strolls along the dock and gets into a rowboat, unhitches it from the pier and slowly paddles across the water.

"Look!" His father's voice is nearly a whisper. "Over there. A little buck." He points to a distant cluster of trees.

A lone deer stands at the water's edge, head lowered to drink, big eyes ever wary. Its tawny color nearly blends in with the trees. As Wes steps closer, his boot snaps a stick. The deer raises its antlered head, then bolts into the thicket.

"Gone, just like that," Pete says, watching the deer disappear.

"Damn, he moved fast. Like he was never even there."

"It's what they do." His father picks up another twig and inspects it closely, this one from a birch tree with peeling white bark on it. "They're solitary animals. It's their speed and agility that help them escape danger. Must've spooked it when you stepped on that stick and he hightailed it out of here."

They head back to their mail trucks to finish the day's shift. And all the while, Wes gets it. He totally gets that deer bolting without any thought. It's what he did earlier, bolted from any of Jane's dangerous wedding questions before she even had a chance to ask. He couldn't get himself off her porch fast enough, not wanting to be trapped by her inquisitiveness, by her gentle eyes watching him as she tipped her head and tucked her blonde hair behind an ear.

When he starts his truck and waves his father off, Wes throws a knowing glance toward the thicket, to where that young buck is quietly keeping itself alone, and safe.

five

A ROW OF PENDANT LIGHTS hangs from each side of the arched ceiling, illuminating the cavernous space in the community center's back room. Large windows at the gabled end let in even more light, the sun leaving a pool of white on the work area.

"Really, Mom," Jane persists, seeing the kitchenette off to the side, near a few round snack tables. The storage part of the room is filled with stacks and stacks of folding chairs, a podium, and very long tables with their legs snapped closed beneath them, leaning against the wall. "Can't your paint class do this?" She lifts off her shawl and sets it on a table.

"No," Lillian says, taking Jane's right arm and giving a tug. "We're painting scenic landscapes, not cut-out snowmen and basic pine trees. And since it was so nice of Chloe's husband to deliver these from the high school woodshop class—"

"Wait, Bob brought these over?"

"Earlier today, on his way to work at the fire station. He used that big pickup truck of his. And I thought it would be good if you pitch in, too. Get you out of that house a bit."

Jane walks over to the tree cutouts. The high school students shaped them from pieces of plywood, then attached easel backs to stand them. They're rudimentary, she thinks while running her hand along one, which gives them their own charm. "What are these for again?"

"My students are exhibiting work in an art show here, during December. Their best watercolors and oils will hang in the lobby, and the pine trees and snowmen are decorations for the event. So if you can paint them with a mystical, wintry feeling, it would be perfect. Just give them that Jane March spin, okay dear?"

In a nutshell, that's her dilemma—figuring out precisely what the Jane March spin might be. As she walks around the plywood cutouts, her cell phone dings in her jeans pocket. It's a message from her boss, which she reads while her mother chatters about how excited her students are to display their framed landscapes.

But Jane barely hears her, being so engrossed in the email typed in urgent caps: LOVE IT. WHATEVER YOU'RE DOING, SEND MORE. ASAP!!

The problem is, it's her *mother's* painting they love, the one that she enhanced with her image-editing software, adding snowfall and balsam garland and twinkly lights to the white picket fence scene. "Mom, it's work," she says as Lillian moves one of the plywood trees to the side. "I seriously have to get home."

"But you're on medical leave!"

"Do you know how cutthroat the greeting card business is these days? I could be here today, gone tomorrow."

"What about these snowmen? I was going to set you up before my class begins."

With a beseeching look, Jane waves her phone. "Please?" she whispers. "Urgent request from the boss."

"Well, and did you forget the house key? You were going to walk over to Cooper Hardware and get a spare while I was teaching."

"Can you get it made, after class?" Jane lifts her knitted shawl from the table, and her mother rushes over to help. "It would mean a lot," Jane says while Lillian straightens the soft shawl fabric on her shoulders.

"Fine. At least you got out for a little while. But I'll have to hurry you home, I can't be late for my students."

Once in the car, Jane reaches into her tote and finagles a pen and paper scrap from among notepads and markers and tubes of glitter and sequins, and a manila envelope filled with sample greeting cards, and her camera and journal and hand cream. Finally, she drops her tote on the floor near her feet and jots a note, folding the paper in half when she's done.

"Mom," she says, tucking her hair behind an ear as her mother turns the car onto Old Willow Road. "Stop in front of the mailbox for me?"

Her mother throws her a curious glance and stops as Jane leans out the passenger window at their blue mailbox, puts the note in and flips the red flag up.

He's not sure about holding her tight, all through the night. Not sure about her missing his kiss. Wanting his touch. Saying his name.

What he *is* sure of is that he doesn't want to wonder about love today, and so he slaps the radio off. Enough of that. Does he really need to hear his sad story in every country song that comes on? It's got him so distracted, he almost misses his next delivery and stops just beyond the mailbox. So he puts the truck in reverse, snaps open the box in front of the newly sided Garrison colonial and tosses in a handful of bills, bills and more bills. Everybody owes someone something, it seems. Everyone except him. Not anymore.

Nope, he doesn't owe anyone anything. Not one damn thing. And he plans on keeping it that way, with no payments due from his heart to some woman wanting him beside her, wanting dates, wanting him to plan a wedding, find a house, move, love, change.

He pulls away from the curb, nearly clipping a car passing him. At the L-shaped ranch house ahead, after dropping a letter on the street while filling its box, he maneuvers the truck up a couple feet, gets out and retrieves the letter, walks to the mailbox and sets it in the box.

"Now stay there." The words come under his breath as he gets back in the truck, slides the door shut and heads further down Old Willow Road, driving straight through a few branchlets of an overhanging willow tree. After rounding the curve in the road, his eyes see it—oh yes they do—right away. So okay, does that mean he was looking for it? Hoping for it?

"You think too much," he tells himself while glancing to the March mailbox several houses ahead, with that red flag straight up, practically calling his name. Best to put the radio on again, anything to keep his thoughts distracted by, well, by women. He switches it to the all-news station and carefully fills each mailbox before Jane's.

But his eye is constantly drawn ahead. Because the thing is, the March farmhouse magically has that greeting-card ambiance, with those paned windows and the way they look out onto the front porch, littered now with fallen leaves scattered around potted mums and a fat orange pumpkin. After flipping down the mailbox's red flag, he reads Jane's earnest request asking him to bring the mail up to the house, just one more day. *Please.* So he gathers the March mail off his tray, checks his reflection in the mirror and brushes a shadow on his face, gets out of the truck and trips on the curb.

"Smooth," he whispers as he heads up the stone walkway.

He notices the pale yellow color of the farmhouse shingles, since he's considering house colors for his own place now. The yellow suits this home, with its contrasting blue porch, with the scarecrow propped against the black lamppost, with the country swag curtains in those big windows. Before knocking, he clears his throat.

"Hey, Wes," Jane says as she opens the door. "Oh, thank you for delivering the goods!"

"No problem."

"Now before you hurry off," she warns with a slight wink, "I've got something for you, so you wait right here. Okay?"

He nods.

"Promise?" she asks. "You won't leave again?"

He laughs and turns up his hands, giving the porch a once-over when she disappears into her house. A twig-and-berry wreath hangs on the wood door, and someone laced a string of Halloween lights through the porch balusters, weaving them in and out of each spindle, below the top rail. At the far end of the porch, past those floor-to-ceiling windows framed with slate-blue shutters, a cushioned porch swing sits idle. Wouldn't surprise him if this house actually showed up on a Jane March greeting card, the way it portrays that kind of welcoming life. He turns when the door swings open again.

"Cream or sugar?" Jane hands him a mug of piping hot coffee, much to his surprise.

"Jane," he begins, looking away, then at her again. "Okay, a quick cup. With cream."

She leans over to a hall table and hands him a pewter creamer through the door propped open with her foot. So he adds a splash of cream, then sets his mug beside a green-and-yellow gourd on the antique milk can. "Here, let me get the door for you."

"That'd be great. It's so cantankerous, it always wants to

36

close behind me." She holds it open so that he can reach in and prop the umbrella stand in front of it. "Much better," she says while stepping outside with her coffee and taking a deep breath of the crisp air. "Aah, I think I smell a woodstove burning."

"It's getting to be that time, definitely." Wes sips his coffee, standing near the porch railing. One mini-pumpkin sits on the side of each porch step.

"I'm so glad you came to the door because, well, I wanted to have a coffee toast for your wedding." Jane holds up her coffee cup with a wide smile. "Cheers?"

"About that ..." Wes begins, running a hand back through his hair. If the post office had a haircut regulation, he's sure his own hair recently outgrew it, the way it hits his collar now. There was no point in keeping it trimmed once the wedding was nixed.

"Did I say something wrong?" Jane asks with that tip of the head she favors.

He sips his coffee, taking a long swallow of the brew before setting the cup down on the milk can. "I won't burden you with the details, but the whole thing's been called off."

"Good heavens! Your wedding?"

He shrugs. "Yup."

"Oh my gosh, I'm so sorry! I didn't know."

"Word hasn't gotten out much yet, but I'm sure it will." He glances at his watch, then over to his truck. "Listen, I'm on a tight schedule the post office is really strict about. People get worried if they don't see me right on time. Mrs. Crenshaw, down the end of the street, well, she's probably itching to call nine-one-one already."

"Of course, I didn't mean to keep you. I just thought ..." she says, then gives him a sad smile. "Sorry."

"Thanks for the coffee." Wes turns and sees the whole

Jane March greeting-card setting before him, all bucolic and serene. "Hey, let me straighten your scarecrow," he tells her. Anything, any excuse to extricate himself from those darn sympathetic eyes, that sad smile. He hurries off the porch, sidesteps another potted mum near the lamppost and lifts the scarecrow beneath the arms to pull it perfectly upright.

"Really appreciate that," Jane calls out, and when he looks back, she gives a little finger wave while watching him go.

❧

And it's like some floodgate opens then, on this perfectly sunny Thursday, the foliage at its mid-October peak, the sky crystal blue—the floodgate into Wes' woebegone story. At the Lombardos' Tudor-style house, Frank runs out the front door and gives a sharp whistle as Wes is pulling away. So he stops and waits, Frank breathless when he catches up and hands him a letter to be mailed.

"Sorry about the wedding, man." Frank stands there in his sweatpants and a tee, and there it is, that sorrowful face. When Wes turns up his hands in question, Frank admits, "I stopped at Joel's for a beer last night. Kevin mentioned it."

Seems Kevin isn't the only one mentioning it. Apparently Sheila began the tedious process of cancelling everything, too. After lunch, when Wes walks into Circa 1765 with the mail for Sara Beth's antique shop, she waves to him from the far end of the room where she's dusting a mahogany pedestal table. "Hang on," she tells him before setting a massive vase of silk flowers on it and hurrying over. "I am so sorry to hear about your wedding, Wes," she says. "Nice guy like you, what a shame."

"I guess word's getting around." Wes scoops her outgoing mail off the main counter near the door.

"Kind of. Those packages you delivered here yesterday? They were actually from Sheila, returning things she'd bought for your new home in Indiana." Sara Beth tsks and shakes her head, sending him off with a quick pat.

Can't get much more pathetic than that, being the recipient of a shoulder pat. When he drives through the covered bridge beyond the antique shop and heads toward the western side of town, he passes The Green, where potted mums of yellow, red and white circle the stone wishing fountain spraying a plume of water droplets skyward. Where his wedding party— it was small, his best man Greg and a couple ushers and bridesmaids—was scheduled to be photographed after the church ceremony, right before the grand, rustic boathouse-on-the-river reception, choice of chicken parm or filet mignon entrée. He can just imagine it, everyone in tuxes and gowns, smiling into the sunshine, maybe a late-autumn breeze rippling his bride's veil.

Near the end of his route, he parks the mail truck to deliver to businesses on foot, walking along the cobblestone sidewalk in the center of town. He wraps a bridal gown catalog around a few pieces of mail for Wedding Wishes; a bell above the door jingles when he walks in.

"Oh, Wesley," Amy says, pausing while adjusting some 1960s mod-looking, knee-length wedding dress on a mannequin in the display window. "I heard the bad news," she tells him. "Sheila called to cancel her fitting and gave me the details. It's unfortunate, the way these things happen sometimes. Everything okay?"

"Okay? Yeah, you know." Wes stands there in the showroom, trapped in the middle of a wedding kaleidoscope, from photos of just-married couples on Amy's wish wall; to a birdbath overflowing with satin gloves and pearl necklaces and silk flowers; to the white and cream gowns, gowns,

gowns. He hikes up his mail-pouch strap. "Sheila's taking care of the particulars, cancelling things."

"Good! That's good. I mean, that *you* don't have to." Then it comes: that smile, downturned. The classic sad smile of sympathy.

six

JANE LIFTS A SILVER ORNAMENT from the dusty attic box her mother left on her worktable, then loops a wire hook through the glass ball's filigree top. All of the Christmas ornaments are silver—some shiny, some glittery—and family treasures. She hangs them from the framework grid in the windows, dangling one in each pane. As she decorates, a cinnamon-scented candle burns on the table.

"One more thing," Jane muses. She digs deep into her tote and pulls out a can of spray-snow, then frosts the corners of some of the panes with sparkling faux drifts. "Perfect."

After scanning her mother's covered bridge painting into the computer, she studies it on the screen. The sunroom's now-festive windows inspire her to add glittering lights along the bridge roofline and to dot silver bells on the harness of a horse emerging from the bridge, pulling a crimson-red sleigh. *This is just a mock-up*, she tells herself. *Just another draft*. If Cobblestone Cards happens to love it, well, she'll have a heart-to-heart talk with her mom. According to Lillian, those dusty paintings are ancient history. Maybe Jane can prove her otherwise. Which she starts to do, her fingers hovering over the keyboard, hesitating. On impulse, she clicks the necessary keys … and off goes the covered bridge design to her boss.

The problem still is, the painting *is* her mother's again; there's no denying that. First the picket fence scene, and now this. And they're so wonderfully charming, she fears that charm can't be matched by her own brushstrokes. Channeling Christmas is one thing, but lately, painting it on the page is another. It might help if those vintage cards would *ever* get here to spark the simple whimsy she seeks in her own work.

But the mail hasn't come yet, which makes her think of Wes and of how uncomfortable her wedding coffee-cheers made him yesterday. So she takes a piece of paper and with watercolor pencils, lightly sketches a gentle white-tailed doe standing straight with wide eyes and alert ears, then adds a note:

Oh deer! I've meddled, I fear.
Coffee truce, tonight? At Whole Latte Life?

Yes or No

P.S. I would need a ride there.

With one look back at her faux snow-covered windows, Jane hums *Dashing through the snow, on a one-horse open sleigh*, all the way through the house, all while setting the umbrella stand in front of the testy door, and all the way down the stone walkway to the mailbox, right until she flips the red flag up.

A fireman reaches from the top rung of a ladder leaning against a maple tree. Perched on one of the low branches covered in golden leaves, a black cat—looking obstinate—

glares down at the fireman's outstretched arms.

Wes shakes his head while driving the mail truck past the scene. Addison's scarecrows get more and more realistic in the fierce competition for the annual scarecrow trophy. Driving along Main Street, a scarecrow teacher stands with straw arms jutting from a blue dress in front of the elementary school; stuffed black garbage bags with squawking yellow beaks become a flock of crows lining a wooden bench at the garden nursery. When he turns onto Brookside, the mailboxes are decorated with hay bales and, of course, miniature scarecrows—burlap hats on their straw heads, denim patches on their overalls. If nothing else, this town throws its heart into the changing seasons.

Apparently Jane March is no exception. A few blocks later, he pulls up to the March house on Old Willow Road. A small cornstalk and tall sunflower are tied to the mailbox post with an olive-plaid ribbon. He taps down the red flag and reads Jane's deer note, seeing the heart she put even into the jotted coffeehouse apology. Really, he doesn't owe her anything more than a polite decline. His truck idles in front of the yellow farmhouse, its own jaunty scarecrow standing at the lamppost, seemingly tipping its head at him much the way Jane does. He scratches his face, puts the truck in gear, then throws it back into park before pulling out his cell phone and calling his father.

"Dad. What's going on tonight?"

His father asks him to hold on while he pulls his own mail truck over to the curb. "Distracted driving's the worst," he finally says. "And I'm busy tonight, getting ready for Twinklin' Pumpkins."

"*What* pumpkins?"

"Twinklin'! On The Green. Selling my deer there this weekend. I'll need you to help me set up on Saturday."

"So another night in the shed later? Whittling?"

"Got two does to finish. It'll be nice and peaceful out there."

"Okay, I'll stop at the grocery store and pick up something easy for dinner on my way home. Need anything?"

A stately oak tree rises beside the March house, its leaves deep yellow. The tree catches his eye as he scribbles items on a scrap-paper grocery list. But his eye doesn't stop there; it continues on to that blue front porch with the paned windows and cushioned porch swing and heavy-temperamental-slamming wooden door.

Then he looks down at the deer with gentle eyes on Jane's invitation, circles *Yes*, folds the paper in half and slides it in her mailbox. He slams on the brakes right as he starts driving, stretches his arm back and flips the red flag up.

seven

SUMMER'S GERANIUMS AND MARIGOLDS HAVE been replaced. Now the barrels on The Green are filled with gold and burgundy mums, and tall wisps of purple fountain grass, with lush vines trailing down the sides. Their colors are deep in the pools of light thrown by the colonial-style lampposts.

"How pretty it all looks," Jane tells him when he parks his pickup nearby.

Wes gets out and opens the passenger door to help her down from the truck. Beneath her fringed poncho, she wears fitted, cuffed jeans and suede ankle boots.

"All those mums have a way of hinting at the holidays, don't you think?" she asks, tipping her head with a wide smile, her long blonde hair falling to the side as she does.

Wes sees it, how everything is game for a greeting card. He takes her elbow and they cross the street toward Whole Latte Life. It seems other couples have the same idea this Thursday evening, many of them out strolling. Some stop to snap silly pictures, leaning into faceless wood cutouts of a black cat and a white ghost propped on the cobblestone walkway. At the coffee shop, silver barn stars are mounted high on the wood-sided, gabled wall; maple-leaf garlands and colorful gourds spill from the café's window boxes; sunflower pinwheels spin on either side of the doorway. He holds the door open for Jane and right when they walk into the crowded shop, a woman hands them each a large white card.

"You're just in time," the flustered hostess says. "I've got one spot left." She leads them to an empty table off to the side. Chatter and laughter fill the room, and Jane looks over her shoulder at Wes as they wind through the crowd. He pulls out a chair for her at their table. With her arm in a cast and sling, he's not sure how much assistance she might need.

"Thanks," she says while settling in her seat.

"What do you suppose this is?" Wes asks Jane when he sits across from her. He flips to first the front, then the back, of his white card. It's filled with a list of numbers and empty boxes. "A new way to order food?"

"I'm not sure." Jane sets down her tote and scrutinizes her own numbered-and-boxed card.

"First round's complimentary," their waitress tells them when she breezes by and leaves a carafe of coffee on their table.

"Free?" Jane tries to ask her, but the waitress has hurried off to other customers. So Jane turns to Wes, who takes the carafe and fills their cups.

"Must be a special going on," he says, setting the carafe off to the side. "And I guess this town loves a sale." He glances around the café while pulling off his hat. Each seat is occupied, making him a little skeptical that this turnout is merely for a pre-holiday coffee sale.

"Welcome all," an announcer says into a microphone at the end of the café's long counter, also lined with people, white cards and coffee carafes. "Are you ready to raise your cups to a season of change?"

Whistles ring out, assorted coffee cups clink high in a toast, someone claps briefly, and Wes wonders what the heck is going on here.

"On this cold, dark night," the announcer continues, "you're about to find the sweetest arms to wrap yourself in tight."

And it's the way he says it, the tone of his voice, that has Wes briefly close his eyes, suspecting what they've blindly walked in on. Or maybe not so blindly. One more look around the room confirms it. Tiny pumpkin lights crisscross the ceiling, and a cornstalk is propped near the doorway. But it's the scarecrow couple that does it—one in wide-stitched denim overalls, the other wearing a red gingham dress, her straw hair in braided pigtails. A scarecrow couple exaggeratedly leaning in and lip-locked in a spicy kiss beside the cornstalk. "Oh no," he says to himself.

"That's right, folks." The announcer clears his throat. "Settle in for a slice of pumpkin pie, maybe with the apple of your eye ... at Whole Latte Life's very first *Fall* in Love Speed-Dating Night!"

"Are you serious?" Wes asks, his voice quiet. "Did you plan this?"

Jane turns back in her seat and faces him with a small laugh. "What? I had no idea, honestly!"

At that moment, a bell rings and the announcer calls out, "Ready? Set? Go!"

Jane gives Wes an imploring look, even though he's *not* looking at her. And he *will* not, under any circumstance. Oh, he's mad; she can see it in the way he shoves those sweater sleeves up, then folds the plaid cuffs of the flannel shirt beneath it. Anything, *anything*, to not meet her eye, as though he won't be able to contain his anger if he does.

And she gets it. She knows he's been, well, there's no easy word for it. He's been … jilted. But sometimes, when all else fails, you just have to go with the flow. Like she's done lately with her card designs, seeking some creative *flow*, regardless of a broken wrist and the possibility of looming layoffs.

Her options are certainly limited here, too, sitting with one unhappy, jilted mailman in the middle of a speed-dating session, so she decides to do it—to go with the flow. After a quick breath, she tucks her hair behind an ear, then leans close across the table.

"First time speed dating?" she asks, lightly touching one of those arms with the shoved-up sweater sleeves.

Wes glares at her and sits back in his chair. "Yes, as a matter of fact. I'm assuming it's not yours?"

"No! You're wrong." She gives a slight shrug. "I was dating someone steady from college. An art major, like me. He's a full-time artist now, but recently moved to Brooklyn."

"Let me guess." Wes crosses his arms in front of him and squints a little. "Skinny tie, black-framed glasses?" Then, yes, he does it. His fingers air-quote the next word. "*Hipster?*"

Jane turns up her hands and nods. "Opening his own store-front gallery."

"Without you?"

"Greeting card art isn't his—" She reciprocates with her own air-quotes. "*Thing.*"

Wes glances over at the couple sitting beside them, chatting easily. If he leans any further back in his chair, arms still crossed, Jane thinks it'll tip.

"Wes," she says, desperately wanting to convince him she didn't set him up. He shifts his gaze to hers as she sips from her coffee. "So what do you like to do?" She asks it in the friendliest tone she can muster, as though, yes, they're just here for that truce, like she'd suggested in her note. No dating, no ties, simply an innocent coffee.

"Travel." He grips his chin, running his hand over a shadow of whiskers there. "Planning a trip to California. You?"

"You mean, besides annoy the mailman?" she asks with a wink, to which he does not respond. Instead he turns sideways in his seat, then looks over at her again. "Your turn," she barely whispers.

"For what?"

"A question."

"All right." He clears his throat. "What can't you do?"

"Can't?"

He nods.

"Cook. You?"

He softens a bit, caught up in the rapid-fire questions, when he distinctly takes a second to think about his answer. "Dance."

"Aw, I'll bet you can." Then, silence. This is harder than she would've thought, coming up with the right questions. "Hmm. Dream job?"

He drags his hand over a scruffy cheek. "Still trying to find it."

"Really? But your pin! Ten years and all. The post office isn't your forever thing?"

He shakes his head, leans forward and drinks his coffee. His dark eyes watch her over the rim as he does. "So, you've *really* never done this before?"

"Speed dating?" she asks. "No, I swear to you this is all a coincidence. But it *is* kind of fun."

"Ever online date?"

"No way. So not my thing, with all that profile matching. I'm more old school. You?"

Just as he starts to respond, the bell rings again, loud and clear, rippling through the room. The man at the table beside theirs stands and nudges Wes.

"What's up?" Wes asks him, leaning away.

The guy hitches his thumb to the side. "Out." He gives Wes' shoulder a light shove. "Come on. New round, new date. Get moving. My turn here." With that, the man actually starts to sit, leaving Wes no choice but to stand and shake his head before taking a seat at the next table. A woman wearing a skirt and sweater sits there, her black hair pulled into a loose bun.

If she's not mistaken, Jane thinks Wes is about to lose it, the way he gives those sweater sleeves another shove up his arms. Like he's about to throw a punch at this guy. But he doesn't. He keeps it together as a new round of questions begins, and this new man pulls in close to Jane.

"Favorite novel?"

Why didn't he think of that question? Women love reading books, then talking about them afterward, getting all book-clubish. He leans to the side, but can't hear what title Jane tells her speed-date. Instead, he sees how the man laughs easily, and even brushes Jane's cast with concern. *Please.*

His date, a pleasant-enough woman with wisps of black hair slipping from her bun, asks how long he's lived in Addison.

"All my life," Wes answers bluntly. "You?"

The long list of places she rattles off gives Wes the opportunity to tune her out and try to hear the questions asked at the table beside them. When Jane catches his eye, he raises an eyebrow at her, then nods to her *date.*

"Favorite food?" Date Number Two asks her, oblivious to

the eye communication going on.

Now that was a good one. His questions were so lame, Jane would never rate him well on the white scorecard. When he rubs his jawline and steals a glance over at her again, she looks his way at the same time. But does she really ever-so-slightly wink?

"I'm sorry?" he says when his current date fires another question at him.

"Night owl or early bird?"

If he could *sleep* at night, he'd be an early bird. But the way he tosses and turns lately, it feels like he's both. So he shrugs uncomfortably.

"Cup half empty, or half full?"

Wait, that's not his question. That's Jane's. She smiles before answering it. He can see that smile in her eyes first; they're all a-sparkle as they dart quickly to him, then over to Date Number Two. "Full," he hears her say, simple as that.

"Favorite month?" his date asks as she touches Wes' hand.

"May," he says, knowing darn well if *Jane* had asked that question, he'd consider the months differently and say, probably, October. Right now, with her. "You?"

Instead of hearing his date's answer, what Wes hears is this: "If you could live anywhere in the world, where would it be?"

Again, it's Date Number Two asking Jane. Damn, his own questions were so pathetic.

"Anyway," Wes begins to his date, turning toward her at the sound of her voice, then tipping his head down and scratching the back of his neck. "To your question, I guess I'd have to say ..." If he only knew what she'd asked. And the stall works—finally something goes his way when the bell rings. So he reaches out to shake the woman's hand and, heck ... Here he is two weeks' single and what's this he's feeling?

Is he honestly *jealous* when another guy—this one wearing, *seriously*, a sweater vest—rushes over and sits with Jane? Envious when she tucks that long blonde hair back so that her gold hoop earrings glimmer? And her smile ... there it is for the new date, filling her brown eyes first with a twinkle, right before her mouth turns up in that fine way that it does.

There's no point in continuing; he's supposed to be home, planning his trip west. So he walks around the table, uncuffs his flannel sleeves and heads straight for the door. Better to wait outside alone than to be subjected to another dating round. To watch as another dapper dude vies for Jane. It reminds him of something his father says every fall when the deer get their antlers, something about the bucks butting heads for a doe.

⁓

"Wes, wait up!" Jane calls moments later, breathless, those suede shoes clipping along the cobblestones, her soft poncho swaying.

He obliges, one black hiking boot crossed over the other as he leans against a nearby storefront, a candy-corn garland draped in its display window.

"Oh, hey! You'll be happy to know ..." Jane brushes through the huge tapestry tote she's brought along. "Look! I have a key, at last!" She holds up a shiny key between them.

"That's great, you're all set then, with picking up your mail. So ..." He shifts his stance against the wall. "Yeah, and thanks for the coffee tonight."

"Did you even get to finish yours?" she asks. "Gosh, it was crazy in there."

He gives a short laugh and pulls on his black beanie. "I did, actually. But you left Mr. Sweater Vest behind?"

52

"Oh Wes, he was a nice guy."

"Come on," Wes says, his hands shoved in his pockets as they begin walking side by side. A chill wind blows a scattering of leaves around their feet. "A sweater vest?"

She tips her head and looks over at him with only a small smile.

"Yeah, well. What a night, Jane." They cross the street toward The Green, the sidewalks empty now. Once beside his parked pickup, they pause for a couple seconds. Either it's that kind of brisk, want-to-linger October evening that has them do it, or it's something else. He finally opens the passenger door and helps her step in.

"So much for my coffee truce," she says, turning to face him when he gets in on the driver's side. "But no harm done?"

"No, we're good." He starts the truck and heads through town, crossing the train tracks on the way to Old Willow Road. Jack-o'-lanterns flicker on front stoops, and the scent of burning woodstoves reaches through his partially open window.

"And you're not mad?" she asks, her voice soft beside him. "Because really, Wes. I honestly had no idea speed dating was happening there tonight."

"I get it. No problem, Jane. It's cool." He adjusts his wool beanie, lifting it slightly as he turns onto Old Willow Road. "Did you at least meet anyone interesting in there, to make it worth your while?"

When she doesn't answer, he glances over and she merely nods at him in the dark. Just a nod, just enough for him to notice. He notices those darn wide-set eyes, too, and the beautiful way they have of giving away her smile.

eight

WHEN JANE TURNS HER BRAND-NEW key in the front door, the house is quiet, with only a few dim lights left on. The wind outside rattles a windowpane in her bedroom and the furnace starts up. In moments, the radiators tick with rising heat. Though it's still early, she figures her mother must be upstairs, maybe reading beneath a down comforter.

Or not. The first hint that her mother is up to something is on Jane's bed. Neatly folded cupcake pajamas sit on her pillow, with a new pair of fluffy slippers on top of them.

The second clue comes with what she hears while holding the flannel jammies to her face and closing her eyes with the softness.

"Operation Pajama Party?"

Her mother stands in the doorway in her own new pajamas, a blue doggie set covered with haughty French poodles and spotted Dalmatians and wagging Scotties. And that plate of brownies balanced in her open hand? Jane just knows they're out-of-the-oven warm; that's the only kind of brownies her mother ever surprises her with.

"Raspberry chocolate-chip ice cream in the freezer. To go with?" Lillian asks, raising the plate a tad.

"Let me get changed into these first," Jane says, grinning from ear to ear. "This will be so much fun, Mom!"

And it truly is, so much so that Jane doesn't know which part is best: the cold, fruity ice cream heaped on top of the gooey chocolate brownies, or the twinkle in her mother's eye when Jane explains how Wes reluctantly revealed his cancelled wedding and she had simply asked him out to apologize for meddling. Maybe it's the way she and her mother browse through each and every one of Lillian's Addison paintings while sitting at the planked kitchen table, the one custom-made out of salvaged wood panels from their old carriage house.

"I want to show you something," Jane says. She takes her mother's hand and leads her to the computer set up in the sunroom. "To try to get my jingle back, I'm creating a Christmas vision board using your work. See?" She pulls up her mother's image of the red covered bridge on the screen. "With my editing software, I added icicle lights to the roofline, and the balsam wreath." She turns toward her mother. "I actually sent this to Cobblestone Cards, just to see if something *like* this would work. And guess what, Mom? They loved *this*. Which was not my intention."

"Did you tell them it isn't yours?" her mother asks.

"Well, not yet. But I plan to," Jane assures her while shutting down the computer and returning to the kitchen, where she pulls another painting from the box. "I find such inspiration in your vision."

"Jane? I couldn't be happier. I'd love to see these paintings go to good use. It's better than collecting dust in a dark closet."

"Look at that one," Jane says around a mouthful of brownie and ice cream.

"I painted it right here." Lillian touches a hand to the watercolor image of a bird feeder set beneath the snowy overhanging branches of a tree. "In our own backyard."

"It's so sweet, the way those red cardinals are gathered in the snow. I've been designing cards for ten years now, and my work doesn't match this charm." Jane slides over a painting of a cat sunning itself on a stone wishing well wrapped in sweeping pine garland. "How do you do it? How do you capture the magic, the heart?"

"I used to tell my high school students, before I retired, that sometimes you have to put the paintbrush down and go out. Live life. Then, well then come to the canvas and paint what you lived. So, I think what you have to do is *not* hole yourself up trying new card designs, searching for your jingle. Get back to your roots, dear." Lillian reaches over and touches a strand of Jane's hair. "You've been working so hard, maybe you've lost touch with them?"

"My roots?" Jane looks from the paintings to her mother's gentle face. "But I'm here, back in my childhood home."

Lillian shakes her head. "No. The roots of *Christmas*. Every canvas of mine was painted straight from my heart." She holds up a snowy sleigh ride scene. "I *lived* each of them, experienced them with Edward, or with you and Chloe. My senses engaged with the actual experience."

"But Cobblestone Cards wants more designs, and fast! How will I ever accomplish it?"

"You'll think of something, I know you will."

Jane leans over and gives her mother a sleepy hug, then stands and starts to collect the paintings into one pile.

"Leave everything, hon, I'll clean up. You need to heal that arm and get some sleep."

"Maybe visions of sugarplums will dance in my head?"

Her mother nods, and so Jane pads easily in her cozy new slippers toward her bedroom, but stops at the sound of Lillian's voice calling out.

"I forgot to tell you, Chloe called. She's coming over with the girls tomorrow so we can decorate their pumpkins." While standing at the farm sink filling the coffeepot, the one she'll surely set for Jane's morning coffee, her mother says over her shoulder, "Twinklin' Pumpkins is this weekend. And Olivia and Josie want you to bring on the glitter!"

⌒∾○

"Greg stopped by tonight."

Wes drops his head back in the club chair and closes his eyes. His father sits beside him in a recliner, and it's all there, in his words. Wes had mentioned earlier that he was going out for a drink *with* Greg, so now his father's on to him. His bluff is blown.

"I thought Sheila might be back in town, and you're trying to work things out privately, maybe?" his father presses. "Because I'm not sure why else you'd use Greg as a cover. Maybe the wedding's on again?"

"No Dad, that's not it. I went out for a coffee, okay? But not with Sheila. She's long gone now. I said I was meeting *Greg* because I didn't want you to get the wrong idea." Wes meets his father's curious look. "I had a coffee with Jane. Jane March."

"Jane?" His father lowers the TV volume and turns his head toward Wes again. "So soon? It's barely been a couple weeks since Sheila ended things. Don't you think—"

"It's *not* what you're thinking. Just coffee, Dad. Really, I was only doing her a favor."

"If you're sure. Because you *are* on the rebound, son, and your decision-making can't be trusted. Shouldn't rush into anything, and risk hurting someone else."

"Don't worry." Though Wes wouldn't call it *rebound*. He'd

call it something like being debt-free. Owes no one anything, and is free to come and go as he pleases now, whether it's going out for coffee or flying to Californ-i-a.

"Good people, the Marches." His father flips his reclined chair upright and stands, turning the lamp between them to dim. "Too bad about Edward passing." He heads toward the staircase. "Goodnight, Wesley."

When his father is nearly to the top of the stairs, Wes calls out after him, "Don't forget to floss. It's not just for your teeth. Good for the heart, too, gets rid of bacteria that can adversely affect it."

⌒∾◯

The thing is, something's got to be good for the heart besides flossing, because his own dejected heart has been keeping him up at night. With each jilted heartbeat, he turns right, left, punches his pillow, tosses the covers.

Nothing settles his heart down.

So it's no surprise that when the moon illuminates his bedroom, Wes gets out of bed and opens the window. He gives it a good shove and leans on the windowsill facing the backyard. The moonlight is so bright, it looks like pale sunlight, even throwing shadows beneath the outstretched, mostly bare, tree limbs. It's hard to tell if it's his thoughts keeping him up, or that baffled heart, or what. He picks up his robe from the end of the bed, puts it on and heads for the kitchen.

Maybe water will help. Maybe he's dehydrated from all that coffee earlier. After downing a glassful, he lies on his bed again, arms folded behind his head, eyes open. In a few minutes, he reaches over and switches on the bedside lamp, opens the nightstand drawer and pulls out a photograph.

But he doesn't look at it right away. Lord knows the image is clearly memorized from the hours he spent studying it, trying to read Sheila's face, to figure out why she simply changed her mind about marriage. So he can just see the photo in his mind: Sheila sitting with him on a bench near the town wishing fountain. She sits sideways on the seat, wearing denim cutoffs, her knees pulled up, sandaled feet on the bench, not quite leaning into him. He remembers how she *refused* to say what she wished right before the picture was taken. So what *did* she secretly hope for when she tossed that penny into the fountain that September afternoon—an easy way out?

Finally, he holds the photo up to see it as he lies there in his tee and flannel pajama pants, his head on the pillow. Yes, the picture is the same as always, except for one thing. He lightly touches Sheila's smiling face. Funny how he never noticed before, and squints closely at it.

There's one way to be sure. With two fingers, he covers her lower face so that only her eyes show. And in his mind, he's picturing Jane. Even under speed-date pressure, her eyes sparkled with laughter when she'd glance over at him.

Now he looks at Sheila's face, her actual smile blocked by his fingers. "How do you like that?" he asks himself, studying her face, particularly her eyes. The truth is plain as day.

No, Sheila's smile never—there's no doubt now—never once reached her eyes.

nine

THE FARMHOUSE SITS ON A slight hill, more like a sloping rise in the New England land. It's enough of an elevation so that the wind gently howls when it gusts outside the windows. Jane pulls her plaid flannel comforter up high around her face while listening to that autumn wind. Winds of change, she thinks, picturing the changing foliage and the changing decorations on neighborhood homes. In mere weeks, those cornstalks and pumpkins and twig wreaths will be changed to pine garland and balsam wreaths, their velvet ribbons fluttering in a cold breeze.

But for now, a chill morning dawns on this sleepy town, a place she's depicted often on her greeting cards. Curls of smoke rise from colonial chimneys, icy frost laces the landscaping, and tree branches lose the last of red and yellow leaves in early morning sunlight. It's *that* image that has her bolt upright in bed, holding the cozy comforter up to her chin. The edges of her window blinds are much too bright with— it can't be—golden *midmorning* sunshine. She grabs the bedside alarm clock.

"What! Jeez Louise." In a flash, she's slipping on the robe her mother customized by significantly widening the left arm to an almost shawl-like proportion. Tying the sash around her waist, she trots out to the kitchen. "Mom?"

Of course, there'll be no answer. Her mother gets up with the sun, then hurries to the community center to teach her early-bird painting class. She says that particular morning class is the largest, filled with retirees pursuing new passions. Still, Jane rushes to the window to check. The car is gone, and her mother is no doubt dabbing a paint-coated brush onto canvas, teaching a lesson in perspective, or depth of color, or light and shadow, at this very moment.

Having slept away half the morning, a working breakfast is in order. Jane scuffs along in her fluffy slippers toward the sunroom to set up paint and paper. After finishing some quick watercolors from her latest sketches first, she'll enhance them with her software later.

"Mom," she whispers at the sight of a note left on her worktable. "What are you up to?" While pressing back her sleep-mussed hair, she begins reading:

Dear Jane,

Good morning! Hope your day is off to a merry start. There's an apple spice muffin on the counter with some fruit. I also set up the coffeemaker just the way you like, and added a sprinkling of cinnamon to the grounds. Now let's get brewing, shall we?

So she stops reading right there and hurries to the kitchen to turn on the already-prepared coffeepot and to butter and warm that waiting muffin. Which she does, leaving her standing in a perfect moment when fresh-brewed coffee aroma fills the room; when the cuckoo clock ticks steadily from the dining room; when the microwave oven beeps with her delicious pastry. Lastly, she nudges up the thermostat to heat the sunroom, then settles in there with breakfast, and with her mother's surprising note at hand. Her eyes carefully read the message while she sips her steaming coffee.

About that box of paintings ... Well, I was certainly surprised to find you tinkering with my dusty images. And I love the idea of seeing those old wintry watercolors on your holiday greeting cards, but there's one thing you must know. No, scratch that. There's one thing <u>I insist</u>*! So long as you're staying under my roof (which I also love, by the way), I insist that you complete the following list.*

Because, dear, you asked me something last night. You asked me how I did it, how I captured that old-fashioned Christmas magic in my art. It's simple, really: You must live it. You must immerse yourself in the season, and our little town of Addison will surely put it on display. When you and Chloe were children, I wanted you both to have beautiful Christmas memories. Remember all the fun things we used to do?

Well, if you've forgotten, get checking on my I Insist List *below. Your cards will be jingling again in no time, you'll see.*

Love,
Mom

Jane notices that her mother moved the box of paintings beside her worktable, then reads the very first item on the Christmas *I Insist List* designed special for her:

Feed the cardinals. The Christmas season will fly to you on red wings. Fill the bird feeder to begin the wonder of the season.

Outside the sunroom windows, their old bird feeder hangs empty from a low branch on the dogwood tree. An abandoned birdbath stands nearby in a small landscaped area covered in brown bark mulch. With a sigh, Jane glares at the arm-in-a-sling that hinders her, then looks back outside. If her eyes squint just right, there's a vague silhouette of her father near the tree, reaching up and filling the very same bird feeder, the sky covered with gray autumn clouds, brown leaves swirling at his feet.

Just as quickly, her sweet memory's gone, evaporated into thin air with a sudden sharp knock at the front door.

Wes turns up his bomber jacket collar against the wind. His thick scarf—non-regulation, too—looped around his neck beneath it, helps keep him warm on these recent cold days. As he's about to give the front door another rap, it sweeps open.

"Wes?"

"Jane." There's no way around it, really. His eyes can't stop checking out the full ensemble she wears: from a plush velour robe coming untied to show pink flannel cupcake pajamas beneath, to brown shearling-fluff slippers, to a tangled mess of blonde hair. He clears his throat and holds up a large padded envelope, all while stepping back and, okay, looking away, then right at her again. "I think this is the order you were waiting for."

"Order?" she asks, taking the envelope while trying to tuck her mussed, unruly hair behind an ear.

"The vintage cards? I didn't want them to get bent in the mailbox."

"Of course! Thank you so much." She moves a little behind the door and glances down at her attire. "Sorry about my, well. Well, I overslept, and then I was going to get ready to buy some birdseed."

"Birdseed?"

"For the cardinals. Out back. But it's too late, my mom's working and I tried my sister—for a ride—and she's at work, too. Oh, shoot. Look at me rambling."

The funny thing is, he's enjoying this longwinded episode. Enjoying watching Jane's distressed expression when she realizes how she looks, and sounds. He tugs his wool beanie down in the back, against that darn wind.

"Anyway. Thank you," Jane says. "For bringing my cards." She holds up the envelope the best she can with her casted wrist—a wide robe sleeve hanging loose around it—while slowly closing the door with her other hand.

Wes nods. "No problem, Jane." He checks his watch, then gives her a quick wave as he turns away. "I'm late, I'll see you around." No matter what, he won't turn back, not to see if she waves, too. Or to see if she watches him go. No, because if he looks again, she'll see the grin on his face that he just can't seem to shake off.

Wes puts on the radio, and after delivering the next few houses' mail, realizes his smile is still there. A good country tune should put a stop to that. And it does, when the next song reminds him that his own heart was recently stomped on and boot-kicked straight out of another woman's life, and so he best stop smiling at thoughts of Jane. It's more important to plot his California escape.

Doesn't matter, because between the dejected lyrics and a suddenly imminent attack on his mail truck, down-and-out rules once again. His pathetic routine is now restored, courtesy of the resident Canadian goose at the far end of winding Old Willow Road. Wes supposes the goose has made itself plenty at home in a patch of woods there, where a murky pond is set further beyond the trees.

Problem is, the goose also has a peculiar attraction to the mail truck; Wes spots it three homes before the turnaround. No one could miss that bird, waddling out of the trees and heading straight to the curb at the historic sea captain house.

"Damn it," Wes says under his breath as he accelerates and beats it to the mailbox. Once idling in front of the old stone colonial, he tosses the mail in the box before the goose can get close enough to snap at his hand. The house has a grand, two-story white-trimmed porch overlooking the distant Connecticut River. Which is exactly where Wes wishes this rogue goose would fly to, permanently.

But this feisty fowl has plans of its own. As Wes cautiously pulls away, the chase begins. The goose runs alongside the truck and lunges at the side of it, wings outspread, neck stretched high. It takes small flying leaps, flounders, then resumes its chase until Wes can safely pick up speed and leave it behind. He shakes his head and watches in the rearview mirror when the goose eventually gives up its chase— probably of the eagle imprinted on the side of the mail truck—and skulks off into the trees.

By the time he turns around, finishes delivering to the other side of the long, curving Old Willow Road and drives to the town center, he's so ready for a break from wayward geese and slow-going student drivers and temperamental mailboxes falling open. He can't get out into the sunshine soon enough for the walking part of his route, and stops first in the hardware store.

"Wes, what's happening?" Derek Cooper calls out from behind a counter.

Wes catches a whiff of popcorn popping right past the registers. "Hey Coop, what's the scoop?" he asks as he wanders over to the vintage, red corn popper and stuffs a paper cone with hot buttered kernels.

"How's things?" Derek looks up from jotting notes on a clipboard. "Wedding plans just about wrapped up now? The big day's getting close, man."

"Yeah, well," Wes says around a mouthful of the popcorn. Reaching into the mail pouch buys him another half minute while Derek waits at the paint counter, baseball cap on his head. Wes finally drops Cooper Hardware's mail there. "Yo, dude," Wes continues. "How can I put this? Well, you probably didn't get the notice yet from Sheila. Ah, hell. The wedding's called off."

"What? You kidding me?" Derek asks, sliding the mail aside. "What happened?"

"Long story, believe me. But Sheila pretty much got cold feet."

"Just like that?"

Wes nods, then tips the paper cone to his mouth and shakes in more of the buttered popcorn. "Came out of left field, that's for sure."

"It's definite?" Derek asks, folding his black-denim shirt cuffs.

"Yup. She already moved back to Indiana."

"That's too bad. Wow, I never thought—well, I guess you never do. Hey, listen. I've got a delivery coming in. Snow shovels, roof rakes, windshield scrapers."

"Already?"

"You bet. This *is* New England. Could snow any day. So how about we go out to Joel's later? Have a brew, drown your sorrows in peanuts."

Wes moves over to a tiered rack of paint-chip color samples. "Nah. But thanks, guy. I'm living home with my dad again, for now. You know, temporary thing."

"Sure, I get it."

The olive and tan paint colors catch Wes' eye this time, so he grabs a few chips. "Got some plans with my father tonight. Have to settle on a paint color for the house." As he says it, he slowly backs away, toward the door.

"Careful," Derek says, pointing beyond him. "Zeus alert."

Wes looks to see the big yellow lab stretched out, sleeping in a circle of warm sunlight on the wood-planked floor. "Coop, by the way," Wes says when he turns back. He checks his watch, calculating just how behind he is on his route now. "You carry any bird food? Something for cardinals?"

"Two rows over. Grab the black-oil sunflower seeds."

"Sunflower seeds."

"Right." Derek heads toward the side door, which leads to a loading dock. "Add a few berries," he calls out when he grabs a cargo jacket off the wall hook. "And apple chunks. Mix it in with the seed. The cardinals love it."

ten

I'LL GET IT, MOM. IT'S okay." Jane reaches up with her right hand and slides the seatbelt over, snapping it locked.

"You sure it's secure?" Lillian asks, standing outside the car's passenger door.

When Jane gives it a tug, her mother rushes around to the driver side holding two coffees to-go from Whole Latte Life. She gets in the car and quickly closes the door. "Brr! It's a cold day for pumpkin festivities. I'm glad we dropped Josie's and Olivia's off early."

Jane looks over at The Green where pumpkins have overtaken Addison's town center this Saturday morning. The wishing fountain water has been turned off for the winter, and now jack-o'-lanterns fill its empty pool; plant barrels are dotted with carved pumpkins; and portable bleacher sections are filled left-to-right, top-to-bottom with smiling and scowling and grinning pumpkins of every size, shape and color. "What a sight. There are simply hundreds!" she says before opening her tapestry tote.

"I know." Lillian lifts Jane's coffee from the carryout tray. "The whole town comes out for this event. And when you see those pumpkins all aglow tonight with candles in them twinkling like fireflies, you'll see why. It's really magical."

Jane digs in her tote and pulls out a wooden ruler buried on the bottom. She lifts her wool poncho and inserts the ruler between the cast and bare skin on her broken wrist, then slides it back and forth. "Oh, sweet relief. This itching is driving me batty."

"Be careful, dear. You can get an infection if you break the skin!"

"I'm very gentle with it." Jane drops the ruler back into her tote. "Okay, that's better. And I'm so craving that cinnamon dolce latte to warm up." She takes the coffee from her mother and peels off the cover for a taste. "Delish," she whispers while holding the sleeved cup close.

Lillian turns the car onto Brookside Road, heading toward the covered bridge. "I think Josie and Olivia might win a prize tonight. When Olivia's ballerina is lit with a flickering candle, it'll look like the pumpkin is dancing."

"And how about Josie's *cat*-o'-lantern, as she calls it. She's so cute, Mom. I have *thee* best nieces." Jane loosens the scarf around her neck and sips her latte. Outside the car window, tall oaks hold on to their golden leaves; a white split-rail fence runs alongside the grounds of a small chapel; mums of red and yellow line the porch steps of nearly every historical house. "Addison could be straight out of a picture postcard," she muses as the car approaches the covered bridge. The tires thump over its wooden floor until they emerge onto Old Willow Road.

"What's that over there?" Lillian asks. She points ahead while driving. "Is that another phone book someone delivered?"

Jane leans forward to see their blue mailbox—with its flag up—and fights a smile. A brown bag is set at its base, and though she has no idea what's in it, she knows exactly *who* left it there. "Drop me off in the driveway. I'll get it."

"What about your arm?"

"I have to be as independent as possible, Mom. You can't be at my side always, you know." Jane unbuckles her seatbelt and pats her mother's arm. "I'll be fine."

"If you say so." Her mother turns the car into their long driveway. "Then I'll bring in the pastry and coffee."

Once out of the car, Jane hurries to the mailbox and pulls out a penciled note. The message is a little curt, which makes it all the more charming. It's obvious Wes is not too comfortable with her. She can see his guard is definitely up, just like that mailbox flag.

Stopped at Cooper Hardware. Sale going on there—discounted birdseed. Hope this works for you. —Wes

Her thumb brushes over a few words, and when she holds the note up to the sunlight, erasure marks are visible as he tried to get the right tone. She smiles and scoops up the sack of sunflower seeds. At least now she can feed the cardinals, and, according to her mother, let the Christmas season begin!

Lillian is waiting at the front door and takes the package from Jane's good arm as soon as she's on the porch. "What is this?"

"Black-oil sunflower seeds."

"For the cardinals? But how did—" She stops and looks out at the mailbox. "Wesley?"

Jane nods and walks past her mother, dropping her tapestry tote on the hall table and lifting off her poncho. In the kitchen, Lillian already set out the Whole Latte Life coffee and pastry on the table.

"His wedding was a big to-do around here. I still can't believe it's cancelled," her mother says while pulling the sack of sunflower seeds from the bag on the kitchen countertop. "But what's he doing getting you birdseed?"

How can she even begin to explain? Jane sips her coffee, thinking of how she looked yesterday when opening the door to Wes: disheveled, her robe crooked over her cast, her hair tangled, her cupcake—*cupcake!*—pajamas clearly visible to this guy on her stoop who happened to be nicely dressed and professional, doing his respectable job as she blathered on and on.

Now her inquisitive mother pulls out the chair across from her. Sunshine streams in the kitchen window over the white farm sink, where a basket of red McIntosh apples sits on the counter beside it.

"Oh, I just mentioned the cardinals to him the other day," Jane quietly says. Then, because there's really nothing else to add, well then she gives her mother a nonchalant shrug as she gets up for her poncho. "So how about it, Mom? Help me with the first item on my *I Insist List?*"

◦◦◦

"Visuals are important to sales." Pete flips open a leaf-patterned tablecloth and lets it float down on top of the long folding table. "It's all part of marketing, getting the customer comfortable with the product."

"That right?" Wes asks. The growing crowd makes him uneasy as people set up their wares at Twinklin' Pumpkins. The Green is filling up fast with jewelry and craft tables alongside food booths. Families are also arriving early with costumed kids, and the last thing he wants is to be bumping into familiar, wedding-querying faces all day.

"Yes, visuals speak to people. Learned it from an online business seminar. Recognize this?" his father asks as he reaches over and presses out a wrinkle in the red-and-gold foliage tablecloth. "It was your mother's. She used it on Thanksgiving, remember?"

"Yup." Wes lifts a pumpkin out of a brown carton.

"Made myself a sign, too." Pete sets a carved block of birch wood on the table. Pieces of white bark curl off the sign. "Business needs a name. Look, what do you think?"

"Near and Deer. That's catchy, Dad." Wes sets his pumpkin on the end of the table. "Very clever."

"What've you got there?"

"Part of your marketing strategy. I made this for you. Help dress up the table." He sets down a jack-o'-lantern of a deer's head, the rack of antlers curving up toward the stem.

"You did this?" His father takes the pumpkin and turns it slowly in his hands.

"Yesterday."

Pete looks over at him. "Yesterday? When? You worked all day."

"Last night, okay? Couldn't sleep, so I carved this for you. In the kitchen."

"This is mighty fine. It's got all the details: the antlers, the tuned-in ears, eyes. You sure you won't consider being my apprentice whittler? I could use the help."

"Nope, not my thing, Dad." Wes nods to the carved pumpkin. "One-time deal there."

"So you're still not sleeping?" his father asks as he sets the deer-pumpkin down.

"Sometimes." Wes reaches back into the box. "Here, wear these," he says while handing over a pair of fingerless gloves, then putting on his own pair. "Keep your hands warm, we don't need you getting arthritis working out in the cold all day."

"Fingerless, huh?" His father carefully pulls them on, then

wiggles his exposed fingers. "Nice, I can still handle the merchandise, no problem."

A line of children forms at the table beside theirs. In no time, there are eight or ten, some cowboys, some ghosts, a panda bear, a ladybug, a couple princesses—none more than three feet tall.

"Really, Dad?" Wes asks. "You had to set up next to the face painting?"

"Better than at the moon bounce. They tend to get out of control there."

Wes spots the inflated yellow castle, its red turrets towering high into the sky, across The Green. As he does, he hears it, his father's voice low beside him.

"Could've been you there at that castle. You're what? Thirty-five, almost thirty-six now? Thought I'd have a grandson maybe, sometime soon at least."

"Are you kidding me?" Wes whips around and glares at his father, who is zipping up his canvas jacket, the one with the brown corduroy collar.

Pete shrugs. "I told you already, I need an apprentice. And since you're not interested, was kind of hoping for a junior whittler one of these days."

"Wes!" a woman calls out, and Wes looks toward the crowd as Sara Beth Riley breaks away from the face-painting line. "You stay right there, Owen," she says to a little dragon no more than four years old. "Just wanted to say hello, Wes. Good to see you out," she tells him with a quick glance at her costumed son. "Get that fresh air …"

Wes waves and nods to her as she rushes back to Puff, or Owen, when he starts whipping his dragon tail around.

"That the lady who owns the antique place near the covered bridge?" Pete asks.

"Circa 1765. Nice shop she's got. She heard about the

wedding when Sheila returned some vases and things." Wes pulls his cell phone out of his plaid jacket pocket and checks the time. "Hey listen, I've got to run, Dad. Call me when this is done and I'll help you pack up, okay?"

"Like hell you're leaving." Pete sets a tin box down on the end of the table, beside a line of whittled deer—some standing straight, some grazing—with a few carved pine trees mixed in for atmosphere. "This is a two-man operation. Why do you think I set up near the face painting? Steady stream of parents with kids, ready for Thanksgiving decorations. I'll be plenty busy supplying them, and need a cashier."

With his hands shoved in his jacket pockets against the cold, Wes walks over to his father. "Jesus, Dad," he whispers harshly so as not to offend the vampires and pirates hovering in the nearby line. "I don't want to see my friends here and have to explain everything."

"Friends? Like who?"

"Look around. This place is mobbed. Lots of people know me. You know how it is … I'm their mailman."

"Excuse me," a woman interrupts, picking up a carved deer. It's one of Pete's best, the deer in leaping position. "These are lovely," she says. "How much for this one?"

Wes waits as his father walks over to his first customer. Then it happens: while his father talks to her, another woman sees the deer and joins them. And Wes knows it; he's trapped. That darn face-painting line is going to waver back and forth with the deer line all afternoon.

"Twenty-four dollars," his father tells the inquiring woman. "Negotiable."

So Wes takes a breath, preparing for a long day as he gets the wool beanie out of his jacket pocket and pulls it on his head, before resuming position at the tin-box register. At least he put on his trail boots this morning, so his feet'll stay warm.

"Do you have anything to wrap it?" the leaping-deer customer asks Wes, who looks over to Pete.

"Dad. Got any paper?"

"Under the table, in the box," Pete tells him.

That's it, nothing else. Not when his father's got two more mothers browsing his whittled fawns and does and bucks. So Wes finds a box of shipping paper beneath the table, folds a piece over the leaping deer and takes the woman's cash in exchange.

"Thank you so much," she tells him. "Your father does great work. This will be pretty on my mantel for the holidays."

All Wes can hope is that most of these women don't live on his mail route. So long as he's not recognized and doesn't have to answer annoying wedding questions, it's busy enough here—between the food booths, the moon bounce, the ongoing scariest, prettiest, most original pumpkin competitions—to quickly pass the hours.

"You want a sausage grinder?" his father asks him later, right after making a two-deer sale.

Wes motions for him to wait as he sorts out a handful of singles he just received. "Here's a suggestion, Dad. You need a *real* cash register so people can pay with credit cards."

"Now how am I going to lug a cash register to these craft shows?"

"There are apps available that let you scan purchases on your phone. Technology can help you."

"Really? Now that's an idea."

"Oh no," Wes says to himself, but of course his father is right there beside him.

"What's the matter?" Pete asks.

"Nothing." With an agitated breath, Wes looks up to the sky.

"Wes?" Jane March asks. She's wearing a rust-colored jacket

with billowing dolman sleeves to accommodate that cast, and has a camera looped around her neck. "Hey there, we meet again!"

"Jane, good to see you." Wes nods as he says it.

She briefly lifts her camera. "Taking pictures for inspiration, for my cards. And what do we have here?" she asks, touching a larger carving of a grazing deer. "Near and Deer?"

"They're my father's. He whittles."

"He makes these by hand?" Jane asks. "They're absolutely a-*deer*-able!"

"You're Lillian's daughter?" Pete steps past Wes and extends his hand to shake hers. "Back in town, then?"

"Why yes, I am! I'm actually recuperating here." Jane lifts that billowing sleeve to show her arm in its cast. "Took a nasty fall."

"You all right, other than the arm?"

"Yes, I'm fine. Mostly bruised my dignity, when it happened."

"And how is Lillian? She still teaching those painting classes at the community center?"

"Sure is, and loving it." Jane points toward a crowded food tent. "She's over at the caramel apples with my sister Chloe and her two girls."

His father scans the crowd for Lillian before annoying Wes with his next question. "How about you?" he asks Jane. "Any little ones of your own?"

"Me? No. No kids. But Josie and Olivia keep me and my mom plenty busy."

"I'm sure they do," Pete says with another glance in Lillian's direction.

"Dad." Wes leans closer to his father. "Customer wants to talk price on the stag."

"Nice to see you, Jane." His father gives her cast a light pat. "Tell your mother I send my regards, and take care of that arm."

"Okay! Definitely," she says with an easy smile before turning to Wes. "And I meant to ask you, Wes. What do I owe you for the birdseed?"

"Nothing." Out of the corner of his eye, Wes can't miss his father looking back with a raised eyebrow at Jane's question. "Don't mention it."

"Well, that's awfully nice," Jane says. "I already saw a cardinal, thanks to you. He was sitting high on a branch, trilling a happy song after filling his belly with that birdseed."

As she says it, the smile on her face is so wide, and so genuine, darn it if Wes can't help nodding and smiling in return. And of course, that's the exact, precise second a reporter for the *Addison Weekly* walks by and snaps a photograph of the deer booth, abuzz with activity. Surely someone is about due to ask him how his wedding plans are going; there are too many familiar faces circling around like vultures, and he's feeling like the helpless prey.

"Glad to hear it," he tells Jane as he tugs down the back of his wool beanie. "Did you add berries to the seed?" Of course, there's no doubt his father is tuned in to every word he says.

"We did, this morning. My mom had some fresh fruit in the fridge, and we filled the old feeder my father hung in the yard years ago. It was so nice."

"Jane? Wesley!" Lillian March comes up behind Jane, her silver hair pulled back in a low twist. "Wonderful to see you here."

"Lillian," Wes says. He sees how the deer keep luring people close. Lillian gives a quick hello before she and Jane admire a wooden doe first, then a sleeping fawn curled in the grass. He moves along behind the table and straightens the carvings people picked up and set down again. Something about keeping them neatly in order feels like it'll help that marketing visual his father mentioned. Order gives a nice, even sampling. Jane and her mother continue browsing the deer when out of nowhere, Wes feels someone come up from behind, put an arm around his shoulder and lean in.

"Hey man, Amy told me about the wedding. And I got the call from Sheila, cancelling the catering," George Carbone says.

Right from the get-go with the wedding plans, Wes had wanted The Main Course to cater the affair. George is the best food man in town.

"Was sorry to hear it," George is saying. "But hey, looks like someone's getting right back in the game?" He nods toward Jane … Jane in her fitted jeans and brown hiking boots, that jacket sweeping down over her tall body, her blonde hair falling forward as she scrutinizes a carved deer with a quick glance at Wes, too. And yes, there it is, the smile—sparkling in her darn brown doe-eyes.

"Game?" Wes steps back. "No. No, it's not like that." He gives George a friendly shove just as Amy approaches with her daughter. "Amy, hey there. You're keeping this guy in line, I hope?"

"Always," Amy says with a light laugh before bending and gently showing the deer to her young daughter, who's wearing fluffy ears and a fluffy collar around her kitty costume.

"Tell her to pick her favorite," George tells Amy as they slowly move along the table. "Any one for Grace."

When Wes turns and looks out at The Green, the late-afternoon sun shines low in the sky, casting soft shadows. Children mill around with tiny pumpkins painted on their cheeks, caramel apples in hand; the aroma of apple fritters and warm sliced pie rises; and there it is—the twinkling's beginning as a crew of volunteers sets candles inside each of the hundreds of jack-o'-lanterns. By sunset, the flickering flames will bring each carved pumpkin magically to life against the night sky.

eleven

WHEN THE SAUSAGE LINKS SIZZLE in the frying pan, Wes carefully turns them. "I bought these yesterday at the store, they're low fat. Thought we'd give them a try. See if they can cure a case of the Mondays, too." Satisfied that the food is browning evenly, he drops two slices of bread into the toaster. "Got this wheat bread there. The fiber's good for your digestion."

"You want mayo on your sandwich?" his father asks from the other counter where deli meats and cheeses are spread out for their brown-bag lunches.

"Just mayo. No mustard." Wes lowers the heat on the scrambled eggs and pours two mugs of coffee.

"I'm tired this morning," his father says while wrapping their sandwiches. "Stayed out in the shed too late. But I finished another doe, working on custom orders from Twinklin' Pumpkins."

"I bought strawberries yesterday, too. Have some with your eggs. Fruit gives you an energy boost to jump-start the day. And hey," Wes says, setting the mugs on the table. "Did you put those new padded inserts in your shoes? The ones I brought home from the drugstore?"

Fighting a small smile, Pete looks back at him with an open roll in his hand.

"What?" Wes asks, hands on hips, wearing his mother's old checked-and-ruffled apron that he tied on before standing in front of spattering sausage links. "I didn't want to get grease on my work pants, okay?"

"Okay, okay. I've done it myself." His father lifts a leather athletic-shoed foot and gives a shake before returning to packing their lunches. "And the insole cushions are in place as we speak." He adds a bottled water and ice pack to each bag, and—Wes sees it—sneaks in wrapped chocolate chip cookies someone gave him on his route. "I heard you up last night," his father says while zipping his lunch bag. "Couldn't sleep again?"

Wes lifts the pans and slides the food onto two plates. "Yeah, you know. I got some agita, I guess. Maybe I should take a walk at night, try some deep breathing outside."

With the packed lunches set near the door, his father first drops a whittling knife in his pants pocket, then sits in one of the straight-back chairs, tucks a napkin over his uniform shirt and picks up a fork. "You're just like the whitetail."

"And I'm sure you're going to tell me why." The aroma of cooking breakfast has got Wes starved. He sets their plates of sausage and eggs on the table, then grabs the hot toast slices and drops one on each dish.

Pete slices his fork through a sausage and spears it. "The whitetail are active at twilight, during the shadowy time of day." He dips the sausage into a piece of egg and tries it. "Coincidentally, son, for the deer? That's the time of day when their vision is the very best," he says around the food, then takes a swallow of hot coffee. "You sorting things out, maybe seeing more clearly at that time, too?"

Wes lifts the apron off over his head and loops it on a wall hook. Before sitting, he slips on his blue zip-up sweatshirt, then reaches over and turns on the countertop TV. "That's about enough of you comparing me to a buck. I want to see the weather, so be quiet." He sits facing his father and adds butter and jam to his toast, then slides the jar across the table. "Homemade locally. The farm stands are filled with this stuff now. Try some." He scoops egg onto the toast and folds it in half before downing it all in a couple bites.

"Bundle up, folks," Leo Sterling concludes his early morning television forecast, "on this cold November Monday. And by golly, be sure to hold on to your hat. The wind'll be blowing—this way and that!"

Everything's on hold lately. Jane paces the house for what must be the third time. She makes her way around the living room, passing the stone fireplace, into the dining room across the soft Oriental rug, through the kitchen, where, if she had a free hand, she'd swipe an apple to munch on. The problem is, one hand's broken and the other's holding the phone pressed to her ear. Finally, still on the line with her orthopedic surgeon's office, she ends up in the sunroom at her computer. The computer on which she *was* editing her latest snowy design until it hit her. Greg had said he'd see her Monday after next.

Monday, not Tuesday. She'd confused the dates with her mother, who is—at this very moment—teaching one of her community center art classes. Gripping the cordless phone, Jane paces into the kitchen again, around the wood-slab table, and into the living room where she sees the white mail truck parked outside at the curb. But no Wes.

So she edges over to the window, and there he is,

straightening their precariously tilted scarecrow. Wes' vest collar is flipped up, his beanie pulled down low, and it looks like he has fingerless gloves on. When he doesn't hear her rap the windowpane, Jane rushes to the front door.

"Wes!" She opens the door and leans on it, her right hand still gripping the phone to her on-hold ear. "Leave it. The wind will just blow it over again."

"No problem," he calls to her. "Won't take me a minute. Got any twine?"

Jane dashes inside to the kitchen pantry and searches the shelves, up and down. "Twine, twine … Aha!" She snags the roll and heads back to the front doorway. "Wes, catch!" With that, she dares to set the phone on the hall table and toss the twine across the yard before snatching up the phone again. "I'm on hold," she shouts. "With the doctor's office."

"Everything okay?"

"Yes, yes." She leans heavily on the door, tucking a loose strand of hair into her bun. "Just a minor fiasco. I mixed up my appointment dates and Mom went to work, so I have to cancel. No ride."

Wes pulls off a length of twine and ties it around both the staked scarecrow and lamppost. After knotting the twine, he fusses with wayward straw at the scarecrow's neck. "Greg's office?" he eventually calls out. "In the medical building?"

"That's the place. Appointment's in an hour. I'll never make it today."

A sudden gust of wind has Wes turn against it and shove his hands in the pockets of his blue insulated vest with reflective trim stripes across the front. "I drive right past it." He hitches his capped head toward the truck at the curb. "Hop in, I'll give you a lift."

"Seriously?"

He turns up his half-gloved hands and glances from the mail truck to Jane. "If you don't mind cramped quarters."

❧

When he raises the rear door of the mail truck, Wes doesn't know why he ever offered. It's like an obstacle course in here, with a freight dolly off to the side, and plastic bins filled with sequentially ordered envelope bundles lining two fold-down shelves on each side wall. Then there's the small toolbox, some loose papers blowing around, and hell, does anyone ever sweep the floor in these things? At least he's not running late with his deliveries. Yet.

"Wes, Wes, how'd you get into this mess?" With that, he rearranges several mail bins to empty off a side shelf, flips the shelf up and out of the way, then hoists himself inside. "What? Now I'm talking to myself in rhyme? Just like a greeting card?" He tosses a few more mail bundles aside and wipes off the corner of the now-empty bench-shelf, directly behind the front seat. After brushing away the dust, he presses on it to test its strength. "That'll do."

But suddenly the space seems too quiet. So he leans through the opening to the driver area and switches on the radio. "Nah," he says when some commercial jabbers on about a local discount car dealership. Right after he switches it off, the sound of Jane's voice has him jump and nearly hit his head on a shelf.

"Knock, knock?" she says, standing at the open window of the driver's door. "Wow, is there room for me in here?"

"Go around back, I'll help you in." He gives the overloaded space one more scan as she does. And like that, Jane's standing at the rear of the truck, her hair pulled into a loose bun. She wears a cable-knit poncho with black leggings, a pair of slouchy boots over them. "Here, give me your good arm," Wes says, reaching down and lifting beneath her arm and shoulder as she steps up.

"Thanks, this is so unexpected!" Jane straightens her poncho and looks around. "And definitely nice of you. But are you sure it's okay?"

"Well." He shrugs. "Come on, I'll get you settled. Watch your head." They walk slightly bent over as he leads her to the cleared-off side bench near the driver area. "My father's a mailman, too, and we have lunch together. At the cove. When it's really cold, or raining, we do this sometimes. Clean off a shelf for him to sit on. Which is totally against regulations, and a little illegal for driving a passenger." He motions to the mail bins now crammed to the other side of the cargo area and clears his throat at the same time. "Keep it under wraps?"

"Oh, of course." Jane squeezes onto the corner of the bench shelf and clutches her tapestry tote beside her. Mail bins filled with stacks of envelopes and catalogs and packages surround her. "I've never been in a mail truck before."

"You all set?" Wes asks. "Comfortable enough?"

"Sure, this works! I'm good."

Wes heads out the rear door and closes it before walking around to the front of the truck. On the way, he pulls off his beanie, runs his hand through his hair and tugs the cap back on, clearing his throat again, too.

"This really isn't out of your way?" Jane asks after he gets in again and starts the engine. She's leaning into the space between the back cargo area and his driver's seat.

"Not at all. Let me finish up a few houses with the mail I've got here." He motions to the large tray beside him, stacked with mail bundles. As the truck moves along Old Willow Road toward Brookside, he makes decent time, quickly opening, tossing in and snapping each mailbox closed. There's got to be a good country-western tune to accompany that snappy mailbox rhythm, if he'd only left the radio on. Now he wonders if he should've. "I'll finish the rest after I drop you off."

"I don't want you to risk losing your job. Are you sure about this?" she asks.

He glances in the rearview mirror to where she sits, and of course, at that precise moment, she meets his look in the reflection. So he nods slightly, hits his blinker and carefully maneuvers the curves and turns while driving the mail truck through town to the medical center.

"I saw another cardinal," Jane tells him. "At the bird feeder."

"So they like the food I picked?"

"They do, and it's so inspiring seeing them. Those cheery red birds show up in my paintings now."

That quiet comes again, with Wes concentrating for the next several blocks on not making any jarring moves that'll shift Jane off her bench seat. When she eventually says something, it startles him.

"I can call my mom to get me when her class is over."

Wes pulls into the medical center's parking lot. "I'm meeting my father for lunch in a few minutes, then I'll swing by and pick you up afterward." He parks alongside the curb near the main entranceway. "I know it's cramped back there, but it's no problem. Really, Jane."

"Okay, if you're sure. I don't want you to get in trouble, or to delay your route. Believe me, I know how people wait for their mail."

So does he; he sees them standing at their front windows, holding aside a curtain, watching. Wes opens his door and walks around the truck, unsnapping the vest over his

86

sweatshirt. When he lifts the back door, Jane is standing close on the other side, bent a little so as not to hit her head.

And there it is, that smile twinkling in her eyes.

twelve

THERE'S NO WORSE SOUND. SO Jane tries to keep it to a minimum as she sits herself on the examining room table, that dreaded paper crinkling beneath her. Thankfully she wore her zip poncho, easy on, easy off. She sets it beside her on the papered table. Labeled skeletal diagrams are framed and mounted on the wall because here, bone is boss. That's what Greg told her during her last exam. Boss. Well, the long tank top she wears over her leggings allows her arm bones to be easily examined.

Someone lifts the clipboard from the other side of the closed door, then gives a brief knock as the door slowly opens and a familiar, tall man walks in.

"Hey now, there's a ray of sunshine in my day, chasing away the Monday blues," her doctor says.

"Hi, Greg. How's it going?"

"I should be asking you that question." Greg Davis draws a finger along the clipboard before setting it down and leaning against a counter, crossing his arms in front of him. "Any changes since our last check?"

"Not really. Every now and then a little aching. Otherwise, as good as can be, I suppose."

"Well, let's take a peek." He steps closer and gently raises her left arm, checking for swelling, tenderness and range of motion. "Any pain?"

Jane shakes her head and he carefully releases her arm.

"I checked your X-rays, they look fine. The healing is progressing typically for a distal radius fracture." He motions to her casted arm. "It's a really common break, I see them all the time."

Common or not, Jane's not used to having broken bones. So when Greg pulls a pen from his lab coat pocket and jots a note on the clipboard, a worried alarm goes off in her thoughts. "Nothing serious you're keeping from me?" She sits up straight and tries to peer over the clipboard first, then to read his blue eyes for concern. "I don't need surgery or anything like that?"

"No, not at all. Strictly routine notes," he assures her. "But a few more weeks, at least, till the cast comes off."

"That long? Even if I favor it? Maybe do some physical therapy?"

Greg steps back, his hand to his jaw, considering her and her poor arm. Finally, he points to a framed painting of a buck with full antlers, the deer emerging from a wooded thicket. "See that picture? My father gave it to me when I started practicing medicine. I like to remind my patients that those antlers on its head? They are the fastest growing bone tissue on the planet Earth."

"Seriously?"

Greg nods and smiles over at her. "Unfortunately, human bones do not grow at that pace, even bones as healthy and lovely as yours."

"Swell. A few more weeks in a cast. What about this itching that drives me batty?"

"First, whatever you do, Jane, don't stick anything under

that cast. It can cause a skin abrasion, an infection, and lead to more problems. I've had to actually remove casts to get out pencils, hair clips."

"Is there *any* solution?"

"Yes, some things help." He motions his arm like he's drying his light brown hair. "Try using a blow-dryer set on cool, and blow the air between the cast and your skin. You can also wrap an ice pack around the cast to relieve the itch area."

"All right, I hope they work." When she makes a move to get off the table, the doctor steps forward and helps her. "Thanks, Greg." She turns to gather her poncho, swinging it over her left shoulder.

"Hey, I've got an idea," he says then. "You're my last appointment before lunch. Can I treat you?"

"Oh." Jane's back is to him at the moment, and she takes a second to think this through. "It's just that my ride …" She turns and smiles lightly, feeling a gosh-darn blush rising on her face. "I'm afraid I'll be keeping someone waiting."

"It'd be a quick bite to eat, no worries." He lifts her poncho over her other shoulder, then straightens it with a light pat. "I've got a full roster this afternoon."

"Well."

"Is it your mom? She can come, too. We'll walk over to Sycamore Square. The Main Course has great sandwiches and we can all catch up over ketchup?"

If only. Jane squints at this Greg Davis asking her to have a harmless sandwich with him. "No, it's not my mom," she explains. It happens when she hesitates. He gets her to change her mind when he turns his hands up, tips his head and looks as innocent as can be in his shirt and tie beneath a white lab jacket, which she's sure will be replaced by a sport coat of some sort. "I'll tell you what. If I can first make a call, a sandwich sounds really good."

"Sure. Need a phone?"

She knows without checking that in her rush to ride here with Greg's very own brother, her phone was long forgotten and left behind. But she gives an obligatory brush through her tote, regardless. "Yes, actually. I can't seem to find mine."

Greg hands her his personal cell phone. "Be my guest."

"Oh, there's one more thing."

He turns back from the examining room door he was starting to open.

"Do you have your brother's phone number?"

⁓

Wes figures he'll be grilled on being late as soon as he peels into the Addison Cove parking lot and stops his mail truck precisely beside his father's, window-to-window. When he opens *his* window, it begins: the questions asking what happened, who slowed him down. And they still come when Wes unhitches his seatbelt and sets up a small tray.

"Just had a delivery I was waiting on, Dad," he says. "Don't worry." And it's true; delivering Jane ate up a few minutes of his schedule. He pulls his lunch bag from the duffel on the floor. "Meant to tell you, I bought new lanterns for your shed. Battery operated, so they're safe. To replace those oil lanterns."

"That right?" Pete asks, fussing with his sandwich in his own truck.

"They were on clearance," Wes continues. "End-of-season sale at the mall." As he fills his father in, Wes unwraps the foil from his sandwich and flattens it on his tray. "You'll like them. They're a good size, painted black."

In the truck beside him, his father opens the twist-top of a bottled water. "Your mother always said it's so easy to make things nice. She was right, you know," Pete says from his window. "She was a smart woman that way."

Even though she's been gone for a decade now, there's a wistfulness in his father's voice, all from missing her. Sometimes people have a knack for making life, well, making it nice like his mother did, with her little touches. Wes bites into his sandwich, the cove spread out in front of him. It changes color with the seasons, just like the foliage. Now, the water looks gray beneath the November sky.

When his cell phone rings, Wes grabs it off the dashboard and checks the caller ID. "It's Greg," he tells his father.

"Hope he's not cancelling our weekly supper. Was planning on a pizza night."

"Scrubs," Wes says into the phone. "What's up?"

"Um … Wes?" a woman's voice answers. "It's Jane."

"Hang on." Wes sets the phone down, moves his lunch aside and slides open the driver door. After squeezing out between the two trucks, he reaches back in for his cell phone on the dash. "What's going on? Everything okay?" he asks once out of his father's earshot. At the water's edge, a chill breeze blows, so he tugs at his sweatshirt to lift its hood around his neck. One of the resident mallard ducks paddles close to shore, parallel to his walking.

And his heart drops—yes, *drops*, he can't believe it—as Jane's words come through, straight from his brother's cell phone. He bends into the call as he walks along the shore, followed by that lone duck, its green neck shimmering. All the while, Jane apologizes. She mentions his tight mail delivery schedule, and his brother just buying her a sandwich, after which he'll drop her off at home. When Wes glances further out to where Addison Cove meets the Connecticut River, her soft voice finishes the call.

"I hope you don't mind." The words come with reluctance,

as though she somehow suspects that he might.

"*Women*," he says under his breath when he tosses his phone on the mail tray in his truck a few minutes later. Tosses it a little too hard.

"Sheila?" Pete asks from his neat-as-a-pin driver's seat. "I thought it was Greg."

Wes settles back in his own seat and is surprised to see that same pesky duck—its webbed feet waddling along to keep up with him—walking near the truck now. "Scram!" he calls out the window and it flaps off with a squawk.

"What did Sheila want?" his father persists through *his* open window.

"It wasn't Sheila. I told you already, she's long gone." Wes takes a bite of his sandwich, then downs half his water. "Greg seeing anyone?" he asks while pulling his California airline ticket out of his duffel and setting it on the dashboard.

"Greg? Greg's seeing *everybody*. Someone even bid for a date with him at the historical society fundraising thing. Why? What was that all about?"

"Are you kidding me? They auctioned off a date with him?"

"Guess so. Him being Addison's Bachelor of the Year and all. Hear they got a pretty good bid, too."

Wes almost asks who would *bid* for his brother, but Pete's concentration is directed at the new deer he's begun whittling. Wood shavings cover a napkin beneath his hands. "You really done eating already?" Wes asks. "Do you know how bad it is for digestion to eat that fast?" He takes another bite of his own sandwich, then sets it down on the piece of foil. California can't get here soon enough. He picks up the airline ticket and reads the Christmas Eve departure date, quietly calculating the weeks till then. "Shit, I'm not even hungry."

"Cut me a piece, I'm starved," his father says right as Wes starts to rewrap his lunch.

He does; he cuts his father a sandwich half from the untouched side and passes it out the window to him.

And he supposes there's a certain apology in order, too, so he gets out of the truck. At the water's edge, a small flock of ducks paddles in place, waiting for a piece of bread. The duck way over on the right, with the bright green neck, looks like the one he shooed off.

"Here," he says, tossing the remaining hunk of his sandwich in its direction. "Sorry about before."

thirteen

BY MIDWEEK, WES IS ABOUT ready to board that jet airliner a month and a half ahead of schedule and hightail it out of Addison. Isn't it enough that he had to see the image all day yesterday? Tuesday was *Addison Weekly* day, and he delivered the local newspaper to every single mailbox on his route, over and over again. Open box, shove in mail, close box. Squeak, whoosh, slam.

When he gets home with more paint samples on Wednesday, he's sure every fine citizen of the town has had a good look at him. And yup, he's nicely reminded by the *Addison Weekly* his father left on the kitchen table, front and center. Just like the photograph that the newspaper placed in the center of its front page: he and Jane at the Near and Deer table at Twinklin' Pumpkins. The two seconds his face was— wait, it couldn't have been that glowing; yes it was—aglow with a smile, that was the moment the camera flashed.

He picks up the paper and studies the photo. There he stands, smile wide, eyes twinklin' like those goddamn pumpkins, wearing his plaid jacket, the wool beanie on his head with his dark hair curling from the bottom, a shadow of whiskers on his face. Smiling at beautiful Jane with the broken arm.

The thing is, it wasn't supposed to be Jane. The only pictures of him smiling with another woman were supposed to be of him and his bride, Sheila. Him in a black tuxedo, clean shaven, standing with Sheila, a white veil wafting around her face. Especially pictures in the town newspaper delivered to every mailbox.

If he just gets busy, time will pass and everyone will move on—to page two, anyway. So he brings his paint samples out the back door and around the side of the house to an old wooden sawhorse. It's surprising his father hasn't carved *that* into a leaping buck yet. But with a couple hours of daylight left, Wes can at least add some new colors to the mossy greens and historical browns and trim golds he's already brushed across the wood siding.

Since the paint shows better over raw wood, he heads to his father's shed for sandpaper and a putty knife. The door creaks when he opens it. Inside, three different carvings-in-progress wait on the rough-hewn worktable: one chipmunk and two squirrels. In November's long shadows, it feels like the wooden figures are silently watching him poke through his father's things. Wes turns on one of the new battery-operated lanterns, and its flickering, artificial flame throws a soft glow on the semi-carved woodland animals. Several knives of varying sizes line the table. His thumb runs over the blade of one knife, testing its sharpness.

The real test, though, is on the wood. So Wes picks up the whittled chipmunk eating a nut, and, holding the knife in his right hand, pushes the blade with his left thumb along its curved back, angling the blade up and shaving off thin slices to smooth the surface. Curls of wood fall on the table at the same time a vague pine scent rises. It's like a tonic—the aroma, the wood texture—that washes away his worries. Finally he holds the chipmunk at arm's length, brushes a bit of wood dust off it and sets it down with the squirrels.

Okay, enough putzing around. He heads to the back supply shelf, the one under which two large carved deer stand. Two deer he doesn't want to see. They're beautifully crafted, a buck with a full rack of antlers, its head turned and looking to the side; and a doe standing beside it, her ears straight, her eyes gentle. Those life-sized deer are the reason Wes doesn't like coming out to the whittling shed these days. His father spent the past year carving the pair, all for Wes' boathouse wedding reception. The deer were to stand at either end of the head table, and are now relegated to beneath-the-shelf status.

"You and me both," he says to them as he grabs the putty knife from the shelf and gets back to his painting project outside. Three sample paint jars are lined up on the sawhorse in his order of preference. After doing some scraping, he dips sponge brushes in the paint and dabs assorted stripes on the wood siding. These shades seem well suited to the Victorian, and one in particular seems suited to his father: Fawn Brown. It's a nice shade, similar to the tawny flank of a very young deer. Squinting closely in the late-afternoon light, Wes steps aside and scrutinizes the dozen paint shades now covering the side of the house. He pulls off his beanie and resettles it on his head as he does.

"I like that brown one." His father's voice comes up behind him.

"I thought you might." Wes glances back at his father, wearing a casual jacket and hat. "Missed you at lunch today," he says. "Ended up stopping at the hardware store for more paint."

"I really, really like that one, there." His father steps closer to the Fawn Brown swatch.

"What'd you do on your day off, Dad? Finish those deer for Coveside Cornucopia?"

"No, I had some other things to do."

Wes dips a brush into a pale cream paint, a perfect color to accompany the fawn. "The fair's this weekend, though. Your inventory will be kind of sparse, no?"

"I'll get on it." Pete stands a step behind him while Wes slathers the cream sample on the house. For a few seconds, there's only the sound of the wet paint being dabbed on. "Listen," Pete says then. "I don't know how to tell you this, but there's someone here to see you."

Wes stops painting, pausing the brush midair. "Here? In the house?"

"No. Over by the birch tree."

When he turns quickly, Wes spots a lone black dog sitting at attention.

"He won't move until you give the command to come. Well trained, yes he is."

"A dog? We don't need a dog, Dad."

"Not *we*. You. That's Comet, and he's all yours."

fourteen

THE LAST PERSON JANE EXPECTS to hear on the phone is her boss. Especially since it's been a mere ten minutes since she emailed Cobblestone Cards her latest watercolor card samples. Her plan was to only scan and edit them with her design software. But after adding just the right amount of sparkle, and a lacy snowflake border on one, it felt like she might be on to something. This set depicts busy cardinals snacking at a wooden bird feeder hanging from a snow-weighed branch beside a farmhouse porch. The snow glistens, and on one watercolor painting, a cap of fresh white flakes covers the red cardinal's crested head.

So that's who it is on the phone: her boss, loud and clear and excited.

"Jane!"

"Rocco?"

"How is my favorite designer today?" he asks. "Is that arm healing nicely?"

"Exactly the way you like things, Rocco. Right on schedule, according to my doctor."

"Great news. Because we've missed you, Jane. It's not the same around here without your smile brightening our days.

Been keeping the intern hopped up on caffeine to get the work done in your absence. You managing okay, recuperating and designing at the same time?"

"I'm doing fine. My mom takes good care of me. It's nice being home, actually."

"Well don't get too comfortable, Jane March of newfound Christmas card fame."

"Pardon me?"

"Can you send more?" Rocco asks.

"More? When?"

"Yesterday! These cardinal designs are perfect. New England settings are the heart of our work, and just last week we signed a deal expanding our distribution west. People can't get enough of that whimsical New England charm."

Jane stands up, phone to ear, and paces the farmhouse sunroom. Her view out the windows has changed, seemingly right before her eyes. Two short weeks ago, the distant trees were ablaze in red, yellow and orange. Now? There's nothing but bare tree branches, and sweeping wild grasses topped with feathery plumes of seed.

"So what are you working on there, back in idyllic Addison?"

It was all she could do to come up with the red cardinal series, thanks to the birds visiting her feeder now. And thanks to a recent notice in the classifieds, yes indeed. Cobblestone's ad seeking a temporary card designer for the holiday season— with potential for more work in the coming months—did *not* escape her attention. Sadly, she suspects the new designer may be intended to replace her.

In a panic now, Jane snatches up her mother's *I Insist List*, with visions of a pink slip dancing in her head if she doesn't make up something, and fast. "Well, I'm working on a few very classic images, very wintry New England."

"Okay, let's hear details."

Jane studies her list. "Well, I had an idea. It's a new *concept*, I guess you'd call it. How about a series of cards that builds an entire town? You know the bit: the whole white-steepled church, general store, carolers, Christmas trees tied on top of cars. It'll be … it'll be a snowy New England village set up on the card racks. I'm designing them so when they're lined up, shoppers will see, um, quintessential Main Street Americana right before their eyes. I'll contrast the images with a snappy verse to keep them modern."

"Brilliant! Love the visual arrangement of an *entire* snowy village. Now you've got to Rocco and roll, Jane. Shoppers will buy the whole town of cards."

That's all it takes for the fear to set in—she doesn't even have one new design completed. When Jane ends the call with her boss, her thinking shifts into high gear. "Inspiration, inspiration." The scene outside the sunroom's back window is too November to inspire; too Thanksgiving. Where is there a Christmas sight, right now? Her eyes fly down her mother's *I Insist List*, stopping on number two:

Spend some time in the old barn at the cove. It's ever and always Christmas in this special treasure trove.

It begins immediately. Jane realizes it as she walks along the winding sidewalks of Old Willow Road, her wool poncho zipped up, a chunky scarf looped around her neck. Maybe it's good her mother's at work and couldn't drive her. Walking in the late-autumn sunshine, the pedestrian view transports her. Imposing sea captains' homes are set back on deep lots, tall oaks rising beside them, beyond which are distant glimpses of the glistening Connecticut River. Pumpkins linger on farmhouse front porches, and brown leaves scatter across lawns of saltbox colonials and shingled Cape Cods. Walking across the red covered bridge in her shearling-lined suede boots, it feels like she could very well be in the nineteenth century when a horse and buggy might clip-clop through the planked overpass.

Once she turns onto Olde Addison's Main Street, her mind is in full card-designing mode, picturing flickering white candles in the paned windows along the way, and maybe a small skating rink on the town green, the ice skaters leaning forward and swooshing across the ice, with a dusting of snow sprinkled everywhere.

All of Addison—the vintage bridal boutique, the local nursery lot filled with garden statues, the cozy coffee café— it'll all be a part of the winter village in her thought-of-on-the-spot Christmas card line. Even the calico kitten on the sidewalk ahead of her, rolling in the autumn leaves, will find a place on a card.

At last, Jane can barely contain her Christmas excitement once she sees it: the old barn at the cove. A distressed-silver slab of barnwood hangs over the door, the words engraved in midnight blue: *Snowflakes and Coffee Cakes ~ A Christmas Shoppe and Bakery.* Three glimmering gold snowflakes are painted around the words.

"Vera?" Jane calls out when she opens the red entrance door.

"Jane? Is that really you? I heard you were back in town." Vera Sterling, the shop proprietor, rushes over and gives her a warm hug, careful with Jane's cast between them. "I heard about your arm, too. I'm so sorry about your fall."

"Thanks, but you know something? It is so good to be back and seeing my friends," Jane says, stepping into the large barn, completely mesmerized. The *I Insist List* is right. Gold sparkling snowflakes dangle from the rafters; a model train scoots around a track surrounding—of all things—a miniature village; candy cane displays and wreaths and trees and ornaments abound. How wonderful to be able to open a simple barn door and step straight into Christmas.

"We've got a selection of your gorgeous cards, over here." Vera leads her to a card rack beside the front counter. "You being our local, honored artist."

"That is so nice of you." Jane lifts out a card she designed a couple years ago. The painting of red and gold ornaments nestled in sprigs of green pine is lovely, but it doesn't capture what she just told her boss. Or what her mother's *I Insist List* is insisting she find. "Do you mind if I browse? Take some pictures?"

"No, not at all." Vera turns to the door when a woman walks in with her young son.

"My mother told me you reopened the old Christmas Barn," Jane says. "But seriously, Vera? I had no idea it was this wonderland. It's simply breathtaking."

Vera leans in and gives Jane's good hand a squeeze. "Listen, I've got customers. But hey, a few of us are going out for pizza later. Come with us?"

⁣⟞⟝⟞

"The days are getting shorter," Pete says when he walks into the kitchen and flips on the light at dinnertime.

Wes glances to the window from where he's standing in front of the open refrigerator. "We should have a salad, to go with the pizza. But I don't even have time to cook with this dog now."

"Really, Wes?" His father sets three cloth place mats on the kitchen table.

"Yes. Between taking him out, and having him follow me around the house. And buying him food and supplies. That dog's taking up all my free time." He pulls the vegetable drawer open and lifts out a half-head of lettuce and one tomato. "Shoot. This'll never do."

"What time's Greg getting here?" his father asks while lining up knives and forks on their napkins.

Wes checks his watch. "I told him I'd pick him up when I went for the pizza. I better hit the road, it's getting late." He tugs on his wool beanie and snags a blue hooded cargo jacket from the back of one of the kitchen chairs. "We won't be long."

It's something new, but Wes hears it: that clicking noise of the German shepherd's paws following him through the house. Anytime Wes moves, a clicking shadow is behind him. While opening the back door to the driveway, he pulls his keys from his pocket with a jangle.

"Hey!" he calls when Comet rushes past him and through the doorway. "Get inside." He stands there with the door open but the black dog is heading straight to his pickup truck. Wes squints out into the dusky evening, then follows after him. Leaves crunch beneath his boots, and his father must have switched on the back porch light because suddenly the driveway is illuminated.

"Everything okay?" Pete calls out.

If he could turn this stubborn canine around, it would be. Wes tugs at Comet's collar. "Let's go, pal. In the house now." When the dog doesn't budge, Wes yells over to his father. "Dad. Call the dog!"

A clear whistle sounds, but nothing. "Comet!" his father orders from the porch. "Comet, come!"

But instead of moving, the dog lets out a sharp bark at the sound of Wes' cell phone dinging with a text message. So Wes opens the truck door to get in and read it, never thinking his new four-legged friend would one-up him and slip in first.

"Hey! Hey!" Wes reaches in after the dog.

A *determined* dog—purebred German shepherd, no less—with its own ideas. Comet finagles his way into the rear seat of the pickup and promptly lies down, muzzle on paws, brown eyes peering up directly at Wes. So now there's a wayward dog on one side of him, a text message from his brother on the other side, and his father standing on the porch, watching it all go down. Is this really what his life's come to?

"Fine." Wes gets in, closes his door and texts Greg in return, telling him to order a large pizza from Luigi's. Afterward, he backs the truck out of the driveway, giving the horn a quick toot to his father. "And I don't want to hear a peep out of you," he says to the reflection in the rearview mirror of two tall, furry ears tuned to his every syllable.

It's a good test, at the very least. His father told him the dog was well trained, so this will prove it, or not. And wouldn't you know it? Comet stays silent during the entire drive through town, and still is when the pickup idles in front of his brother's condominium.

"You okay there?" Wes finally asks, turning to see that the dog hasn't even moved, as though he's so thankful just to be riding along and doesn't want to press his luck. Only those brown eyes look up at him in a soulful gaze.

Until the passenger door swings open and Greg slides in. "Hey, bro."

But it's what happens next that makes the whole canine fiasco worthwhile. Greg nearly jumps out of the truck when Comet stands, leans into the front seat and plants a sloppy lick across his brother's face.

"What the hell is *that*?" Greg spins around in his seat as

the dog sits in the back, looking pleased as punch, panting and holding up a paw for a shake.

"Scrubs, meet Comet. My dog."

"Your *what*?"

"Dog."

"What is it? A German shepherd?"

"That's right."

"He's kind of small."

"He is, must've been the runt. All black, too, with a white streak on his shoulder, like a comet. And I guess Dad was right."

"Dad? What are you talking about?"

Wes pulls out of the condo complex onto the main drag. Traffic's busy, and they stop at the railroad crossing when the gates drop down, lights flashing. "Dad's got someone from the police force on his route." A freight train passes in front of them, clanging and chugging over the tracks. "You've heard him mention that sergeant. Arthur, right?" Wes asks, taking off his cap and tossing it on the dashboard.

"Sure."

"According to Arthur, the department was trying to find a home for our friend here. Part of their K-9 unit. Come to find out, they had a dog that wouldn't bite a soul. Ever."

"Don't they test them, before they're accepted?"

"They do. Comet made it through the selection process, but once the formal instruction began with his trainer, the problem showed itself. He's a willing and interested canine, but interested in being everyone's *friend*, it seems."

"How do you like that," Greg says with a glance back at the dog.

"Even with remedial training, it didn't work out." Wes drives over the railroad tracks when the crossing gates rise, then heads into downtown Addison. "Not a mean bone in that dog's body."

Greg wipes off his cheek. "I guess not."

"When he didn't make the cut after all that training, Dad volunteered to take him."

"So he's a police academy dropout?"

"You got it. Dad says I need something to fret over after being stood up by Sheila."

"Are you kidding me?"

"Nope. Guess he got tired of me telling him how to eat, when to exercise, how to keep house, so this is how he quieted me down."

"A dog." Greg says it under his breath, looking back at Comet.

"For a while, anyway."

"You're not keeping him?"

"I got plans, Scrubs. Headed to the West Coast next month, and who knows what'll develop there. Either way, I'm eventually moving out. What the hell am I going to do with a dog?"

"Oh." Greg reaches over and scratches the dog's head. "Too bad. He is kind of cute."

fifteen

IT'S HAPPENING ALREADY. WES HAS been noticing it
all over town, but when he and Greg walk into Luigi's Pizza,
it's apparent Christmas cheer is now bubbling over in
Addison. Swags of gold tinsel garland drape across the ceiling,
with red glitter bells angled in each curve. Strings of colored
twinkle lights outline framed paintings of Italian garden cafés
and villages, of still-life images of Tuscan tables set with wine
bottles, cheese and grapes. But it's the buzz in the air that
clinches it. Coats and scarves hang over the backs of chairs at
tables alive with easy chatter and laughter.

And that's the problem, because Wes has seen it before,
the way happy faces drop when people spot him. In the
middle of their holiday merriment, his cancelled wedding is a
reminder that gloom is among them; he's the definition of
coal in the stocking. So he's perfectly content to pick up pizza
for takeout, instead of staying and ruining the holiday hoots
and smiles.

"Hey, there's the mailman!" a voice calls across the room,
and Wes' heart sinks. In this darn town, there's no escaping
familiarity. He and Greg both turn to see Derek Cooper
waving them over to a crowded table. It couldn't be *just*

Derek, or Derek and just a friend. No, it's a large booth with a button-tufted seat on one side, ladder-back chairs lining the other, most of the seats full.

When Wes feels Greg's elbow jab his arm, he heads over, pulling off his wool beanie and shoving it in his jacket pocket. He runs a hand through his hat-mussed hair as they're invited to *Grab a seat* and *Join the party*. It's practically a high school reunion, with so many recognizable faces watching him.

"What's going on?" Greg asks the friends seated at the wooden table. "Ah, Vera," he adds with a slight nod. "Always a pleasure to run into you."

"We're having a casting party," Vera pipes in, air-quoting the word *casting*. She leans into Derek beside her on the booth seat. "Get it? Sign your name and leave a message on Jane's *cast*."

The thing is, until now, Wes didn't realize that Jane March was seated with them. But there she is, wearing a pink-and-purple plaid shirt, her blonde hair falling in waves as she watches Vera's sister, Brooke, write on her cast. Jane looks up from her broken left arm at that very second.

"Hey, guys," she says, motioning Wes and Greg closer with her good hand. "Would love to have your autographs!"

Greg doesn't waste any time. He's by her side in a flash, picking up a permanent marker from the colorful array spread out on the table. Wes can't hear him, but he sees Greg saying something to Jane as his one hand holds her arm steady, and his other jots a message on the cast.

"Sorry about the wedding, man," Brooke's husband, Brett, says as Greg is still writing.

"Yeah, well." Wes turns up his hands. "It is what it is, just wasn't meant to be."

"Too bad." Brett raises his glass of beer in a sympathy toast, to which Wes nods.

"Hey, stick around and ring in the season." Derek slides over an appetizer tray of overstuffed mushrooms topped with Parmesan cheese. "The more the merrier."

"Definitely," Brooke tells them. "Kick-start the holidays with us."

When Greg is done writing, and—okay, Wes sees it—done giving Jane's arm a friendly, little-too-long clasp, he straightens and announces Wes' personal business to the festive table. "Really can't stay. My brother's got a dog to tend to. It's waiting in the truck."

"What?" Jane asks, tipping her head with that wide smile. "A dog?"

"I'm taking care of it temporarily," Wes tells the gang watching him. "Until I find it a home."

"No shit," Derek says. "It'll keep you busy anyway, you know …"

A quiet second follows that everyone surely is filling in with sad thoughts finishing the sentence—thoughts of lonely, jilted Wes needing to occupy his time. Finally, Greg turns to him and hands him the marker. "Have a go at it."

Wes takes the pen and drops the cap as he pulls it off.

"Smooth," Greg tells him as Wes bends to pick it up from the floor.

"Wait, Greg! What's this you wrote next to your name? A secret message?" Jane calls out, looking up from reading his signature on her cast. "Rx?"

Greg grabs a chair at the far end of the table, spins it backward and sits, holding his leather gloves in his hands. "Sure," he answers with a grin over the stuffed mushrooms and drinks and cheese nachos. "If you need anything from the doctor—a long walk, a movie, maybe—I've got the Rx. You just let me know."

Does Wes then see what he really thinks he does, across

the table? Does his perennially single brother throw a wink into his words? Wes slides over a chair and sits beside Jane. He scans the well-wishes scribbled across the cast, thinking of his own message. First, still uncertain if he'll do it, he just signs his full name. But after pausing and feeling Jane watching, he continues with the marker. Actually, he's never done this before, never drawn a picture of a mailbox on its post. Until now. Never outlined the latch on the lid, never sketched streaks of wood grain on that post. He adds diagonal lines to shade it, and jots in blades of grass at the base.

"That's cute," Jane says quietly.

He shifts in his chair to face her. "And if you need anything from *me*, well …" There it is, that smile of hers. Though it's not on her lips, as though she's keeping a personal secret between them; it's all in her eyes. He also notices the brushed-gold ball earrings, and a hint of blush on her cheeks, until he realizes he's noticing too much. So he reaches in front of her and picks up the red marker. "Well, you know what to do." After a brief hesitation, he carefully finishes his cast drawing, adding a prominent flipped-up red flag to his mailbox sketch. "Just flag me. Okay?"

Jane nods, her eyes still doing that smiling thing.

Wes pats her cast and stands up, motioning over to Greg. "Come on." He hitches his head to the take-out counter. "Food's ready, Scrubs. Let's go."

"You sure you can't stay?" Jane asks them.

"Another time, definitely," Greg answers while pulling on his gloves.

Wes waves them off as he and Greg return to the counter. He puts on his black beanie while Greg pays, before heading to the truck, pizza box in hand.

His father wouldn't let up tonight at dinner, over the pizza. He's more worried about Wes than he lets on. *You need to get out, get your mind off things. Especially this weekend, of all weekends. So you'll help me at Coveside Cornucopia, it'll be good to be distracted there, lots of hustle and bustle.*

To escape his father's voice in his head, Wes gets out of bed hours later, wraps his green terry robe over his flannel pajamas, steps into his moccasin slippers and shuffles to the kitchen. First stop? The wall calendar. "One, two, three," he whispers, his finger moving forward one week with each counted number. "Four, five, six." In a little over six weeks, he'll be high in the sky, Wes headed west.

Comet's tail wags against the floor when Wes walks past him. "At least someone's glad to see me," he says while opening the dog's crate. "Let's take a walk, Comet. You and me, bud." Before going out the back door, he stops and tightens his robe sash, then snags a beer from the refrigerator and a dog biscuit from the box on the counter.

Of course, Greg and his father know full well what was *supposed* to be happening tonight. Wes walks with the black German shepherd toward the whittling shed. It's a clear night, and moonlight casts a pale glow on the lawn ahead. His good suede slippers get damp from the dew, but heck—he has no wife to nag him about it now. Once in the shed, Wes hits the light switch, snaps open his beer can and walks straight to the carved deer beneath the high wall shelf. It's eerie, how real they appear, standing there in shadow. If things were different, the two life-sized deer would have been moved to the Addison Boathouse today. They'd have been carefully wrapped, wheeled in on a hand truck and set on either end of an elegant table draped in white linens and topped with fine china for the next day's wedding. He stands in front of the large deer now and takes a long swig of his beer, the dog sitting behind him.

"That's right," he says over his shoulder to Comet. "And my rehearsal dinner was supposed to be tonight. Mine and Sheila's." He turns the buck a little for a better look before taking another swallow of his beer. "It would've been a good time, just like at Luigi's. Lots of laughs, a few drinks, some reminiscing, some fine dining." He runs a hand over the carved doe's head and down along her face. What is Sheila doing right now? Is she walking circles around her bedroom in the dark of night? Does she look at photographs of him, or even think about him anymore?

He turns toward the open shed door, which is letting in that November wind. There's a change in the air. Feels like snow, if he had to name it. He and Sheila planned on setting the carved deer in artificial, sparkling snow at the wedding reception, to set a rustic atmosphere.

"Well, it's just you and me tonight," he says to Comet. Wes raises his can in a toast and gives the dog the biscuit. "Cheers."

sixteen

WES COULD EASILY IMAGINE BOATS with billowing sails arriving and docking here. Because hundreds of years ago, Addison Cove was a small shipping port and destination for sea trade from the West Indies and British colonies. It's the reason many of the cove's surrounding colonial homes have widows' walks. The stately houses belonged to ship captains, and their wives kept a lookout for their husbands' return from sea.

It's still an active port, Wes thinks late Saturday morning. Beneath crystal-blue skies and beside the calm water, people are still trading goods. The difference is they're *driving* past those old colonials with paned windows and center brick chimneys to get here, arriving in cars instead of tall ships. And rather than trading grains, sugar, red onions and molasses, they're buying and selling handmade birdhouses and locally jarred jams and twig wreaths and watercolor paintings. And whittled deer.

Standing at their modest tent, Wes glances at the inventory lined up on the table. "A little slow today, Dad," he says, whittling a thin branch with one of his father's knives.

Pete tries rearranging the carved wood pumpkins on either

end of their table in an attempt to perfect that visual marketing he likes to talk about. "Got to draw the customer in," he says.

Wes already sliced the bark off the stick he holds so that it's nearly white, and now makes shaved cuts along the length of it. Each piece curls like the boughs of a pine tree. When he's done, he picks up a thick chunk of bark, notches it and stands his tree in the hole.

"Not bad." Pete sets the white whittled tree beside one of his smaller does. "Got any more?"

"More? I was just killing time. Don't think you'll sell much today."

His father rushes off to the wooded area nearby and returns in minutes with a few straight branches. "Make me more of those trees." He pulls a folding knife from his pocket. "I'll help. It'll look like a forest if we spruce things up."

"I don't know." Wes puts on a pair of fingerless gloves and picks up the pocketknife. "It's cold this morning. Maybe people will start buying after lunch, when it gets warmer."

But the weather doesn't really seem to be the problem. People dressed in sweaters and jackets and wool scarves mill around the other booths. It's obvious they're drawn to the home décor, wanting to dress up their walls and rooms for the holidays. Even Greg is strolling around with a shopping bag, having purchased some amber pitcher filled with a bunch of wheat stalks tied with a wide brown bow. With his busy surgeon schedule calling him away so often, his brother always treats that little condo as his personal haven.

Still, Wes has to admit he doesn't mind that the Near and Deer tent is quiet. It means no prying questions and forced smiles will be directed at him. Today of all days, he doesn't need any of that. "It's just a slow day, Dad. They're walking right by your whittled deer."

"It's no wonder. No one's going to approach us with that scowl on your face."

As if anything else would be on his face today. After showering this morning, he didn't even shave. Shaving would've conjured too many images he didn't want to see looking back at him in the mirror. He did dress in black, though: a black crew sweater beneath his black corduroy vest, black hat and gloves, all with jeans and black trail boots. All to mourn the black tux he *isn't* wearing on what should have been his wedding day.

"You know, you're probably right," Wes admits while peeling more curls of wood on another stick. He sets it down with the knife. "My sorry mug isn't doing you any favors. So I'm going home. Make a sandwich, check on the dog."

"Like hell you are," Pete says as he pushes the stick and knife closer to Wes. "You checked the dog an hour ago, and you can eat here. Makes no sense to go home alone and stew in your own juices thinking of wedding vows and brides and all that."

Wes glares at him and snatches up the knife and stick, directing his energy to whittling mini pine trees, making each row of branches slightly longer than the preceding. A collection of wood chips gathers on the table, beneath his hands.

Pete picks up a stick, too, and begins peeling off the bark. "Besides, I need you here to cover for my bathroom breaks, and so I can take a walk and move my arthritic legs a bit."

"You don't have arthritis."

"But I will, if I don't move around in this cold. You've said so yourself."

Wes' focus doesn't waver from his whittled tree as they go at it. "Greg's here. He can cover for you."

After a quiet moment that gets Wes to look up at his

father, Pete tells him, "Greg's here for *you* today. So stick around." He sets down his whittling. "I'm going to get us some lunch."

"Forget it, Dad," Wes calls after him, but it's no use. His father keeps going, patting Greg's shoulder at the booth beside theirs, one selling patchwork quilts. His brother looks back at Wes, but Wes ignores him and gets on with his whittling, feeling more at ease with each contemplative slice of the knife. As he steadies another mini pine tree in a chunk of bark, only seconds pass before his peace and quiet ends.

"Nice seeing so many folks out," Greg says. "Once the snow falls, they'll all stay home."

"Yup." Wes stands his newly whittled tree next to the first.

"What's going on with you and Dad?"

"Hey there, Greg," a woman's sing-song voice rings out. "Good to see you!"

Two women stroll past holding their coffee close, right as his brother waves a gloved hand at them. Greg won't get any prying questions from them. No. No sad smiles are directed at Greg in his dark jacket and fleece earmuffs. Just sparkling greetings and happy small talk.

As soon as Wes picks up another stick, his father returns overloaded with two paper-wrapped grinders. Wes takes one and spreads the paper out on the very end of the table. "What about his?" he asks, nodding to Greg.

"I'm good." Greg checks his watch. "I grabbed a bite already. After running the Cornucopia 2K this morning, man was I starved."

"A 2K did you in? Are you serious?"

"You bet. Stopped at The Main Course tent. George makes the best sausage and peppers."

Wes lifts the top of the roll. "What is this, anyway? Definitely no sausage here."

"Zucchini sub," his father says. "With mushrooms, onions and cheese."

"No meat?"

"Keeping it healthy, Wes. Just like you've been telling me. That's even a whole-wheat roll you've got."

Wes tastes the surprisingly delicious sandwich dripping in melted cheese and apparently some secret sauce that carries a mighty zing. He dabs his mouth with a paper napkin, then takes another bite.

"Hey, is that Jane?" Greg asks. "We had lunch the other day and she promised me a hay bale dance."

That healthy food has a way of lodging right in his throat then, gagging Wes. He grabs a sip of the soda his father also bought.

"You okay?" his brother asks.

A quick, urgent nod keeps Greg back, stopping him from doing some physical maneuver to save Wes from choking. Because really, that's precisely what he doesn't need: his brother's fisted hands compressing his torso right here in front of everyone. "Went down the wrong pipe," Wes assures him hoarsely.

"You sure?" Greg still stands close, observing him cough.

"Yeah." Wes sets down his grinder and glances at the crowd, trying to pick out a tall blonde with her arm slung in a cast.

"All right, then. I'm going to go cash in on a hay bale dance. Do a little do-si-do with a pretty doe." Greg slips off his earmuffs and leaves them on the table. "You don't mind, do you, Wes?"

Wes picks up his dripping zucchini grinder and takes another bite. "Why would I mind?" he asks around a mouthful. "Suit yourself."

Greg studies him for a second longer than necessary, then

turns and walks over to a booth that looks to be Lillian March's. Framed watercolor paintings hang on its tent walls. Wes watches him go, but the problem is, he doesn't stop watching. He watches Greg escort Jane to the makeshift dance area set up near a country-western band. And he watches Jane step lively in her taupe cape-coat with a red tartan scarf gathered around her neck, her black jeans tucked into equestrian boots. In no time, Greg gets her tapping and swinging around the hay bales, broken arm and all. So here's his hot-shot younger brother, in his thirties just like Wes, dancing and looking fine at a bustling town fair. Is it so much to have wanted the same?

Wes keeps a close eye on them, trying to figure what Greg has that he doesn't. But he can't figure for long, not when a middle-aged couple wanders over to the carved deer, blocking his view, asking him price questions, admiring the freshly whittled trees.

"I can even smell the pine scent!" the woman exclaims. "I'll buy the two trees and one deer." She points to a grazing doe. "That one, there."

All Wes can manage is one more dance-area glance before setting down his lunch and wiping his hands on a paper napkin, right as the fiddle-and-guitar combo segues into a slow song. He nicely wraps the trees and deer in tissue paper, but leans to the side hoping Greg and Jane ended their dance. Not hoping to see what he does: Greg taking Jane in his arms, holding her close and gently moving with her on the straw dance floor, swaying to lyrics of love, and driving in a truck, and country roads and endless nights.

There's no getting around one thought. That should have been him, slow dancing today. Him in a black tux, holding his wife in her white lace gown, moving beneath a spotlight in their first married dance. Over the summer, they'd even snuck in ballroom dance lessons to surprise their guests with a perfect waltz. Wes, who'd never danced a step in his life, had perfected placing his hand on just the right spot on Sheila's back; perfected raising his other arm to lightly hold his bride's delicate hand. As he sets the customer's deer and trees in a shopping bag, he discreetly moves his left foot forward, moves his right foot alongside it, then pulls his left foot in close to it.

Today was his day to waltz.

❦

"Dad." His father looks up from talking with another customer. "I'll be back in a few minutes."

His father will never argue because it might risk a possible second-deer sale, so he just nods. Argue or not, Wes simply can't stand there any longer, tormenting himself with wedding thoughts of dancing and food and merriment that never came to pass, no matter how hard he'd tried.

Working his way through the crowd, he stops at the water's edge and scoops up flat skimming stones. After joggling them in his open palm, he carefully picks one, turns and gives a sidearm throw out over the water. The stone plunks straight in with a small splash, so he tries again. Nothing. Nothing except the realization that he's really off his game lately, in practically everything he does.

Eventually, a stone skims three skips over the calm cove water—a stone that Wes *didn't* throw. He looks over his shoulder at Greg approaching behind him, a little flush from his hay bale dance, but with no Jane in sight.

"She tire of you already?" Wes asks.

"I'd give it right back to you, but under the circumstances ..." Greg skims another stone. "She's helping her mom."

Wes glances toward the March tent, then watches two ducks paddle close by.

"Perfect day for a wedding," Greg says. "Figures the day you were supposed to get married has to be the most beautiful day of the year. Like rubbing salt in a wound."

"No shit."

His brother pulls out his cell phone. "At least in Indiana," he says, holding out the phone so that Wes can see the weather app on the screen, "your ex-bride is in the middle of a gullywhumper. Rain's coming down in buckets there."

"Today can't be done soon enough. It wasn't a pretty breakup." Wes leans down to grab another flat stone. "After tonight, it'll finally be behind me."

"Heck, might as well put it behind you now. Because what else are you going to do? Go on all day with your pity party?"

The water barely has a ripple in it, just begging for another stone-skip. Wes throws his and it skims flawlessly, merely brushing the surface. "Shut up, Scrubs. At least I *almost* got married, which is more than you can say."

"Fair enough." The two of them start slowly walking toward the far, wooded side of the cove banks. "Listen," Greg says. "You good here, you and Dad? I can leave?"

"Yeah. Between Dad and the dog, my day's wonderfully booked. Why? Where you headed?"

"Thought I'd ask Jane to a movie, maybe stop afterward at Cedar Ridge Tavern."

Wes squints over at him, then hesitates at the water's edge. He flips up his vest collar and throws another stone.

"You know," Greg continues beside him, "they've got that nice fireplace going on there, kind of romantic. Me and Jane have had a couple talks, maybe I can get somewhere with her."

"Seriously?" Wes starts walking again. "That's how you

talk about her? You're such an ass, being her *doctor* especially."

"So?"

"So why don't you back off?"

"I knew it."

"Knew what?"

"Admit it. Why don't you just admit it?"

"Admit *what?*"

"Listen, Wes. I'm not seeing Jane. I'm going to *work* tonight. And I would never talk about Jane, or *any* woman, like that. All I was doing was giving you the bait."

And he fell for it, simple as that. Wes stops walking and shoves up his sweater sleeves, folding the flannel shirt cuffs beneath them. He watches his brother silently as he does.

Greg steps beside him and tosses a stone far out over the cove, waiting for it to splash. "So what's really eating you today?" he asks while still watching only the water. "Sheila?" Then, and only then, he faces Wes. "Or Jane?"

∾

Jane can pick out Wes and Greg from a distance. So much about them appears the same: their stance, their height, the casualness in their clothes. There's no missing that they're brothers.

"Hey guys," she calls out from behind them, a little breathless. They both turn at the exact moment. "Hi!" she says as she nears, her cape flapping in a light breeze. "Don't mean to interrupt."

"Jane," Wes says. "What's going on?"

"I was talking to your father." She motions toward Pete standing alone at his deer table. "We were discussing his sales, and trying some things to boost them. I told him an idea … well, it's the designer in me. Sometimes I just can't turn it off.

And since I had a tube of glitter," she says while holding up her tapestry tote, "I made a couple of his deer very festive, sprinkling silver sparkles on them. And the way it looks like snow, it worked! He sold the deer right away. So I wonder if one of you could do me a favor."

"What do you need?" Greg asks.

"A ride," she explains. "My mom's busy at her booth, and Chloe's over at Plymouth Dock watching the kids." Jane points to the dock area at the other end of the cove where her two nieces are dressed as Pilgrims.

"I *thought* that was Bob Hough's boat." Greg shields the sun from his eyes and looks toward the pier.

"Sure is." She smiles at the sight of Chloe's husband, Bob, in his buckled black hat, and her nieces wearing long aproned dresses and white bonnets. They stand on her brother-in-law's boat, waving to shore where families with children are lined up behind plywood Pilgrims and Indians with cut-out faces. Everyone wants a Thanksgiving picture taken at Plymouth Dock. "Wait," Jane says, turning slowly back to Wes and Greg. "Are you sure I didn't interrupt something here?"

"No, just a semi-extreme skimming competition going on," Greg says. "It's a brother rivalry thing."

She looks from one face to the other: Greg clean-shaven, Wes scruffy and a little tired around the eyes. "Well, any chance one of you brothers can give me a ride home? I promised your dad I'd get some deer decorating supplies. Glitter, glue, cotton, that sort of thing."

"Why don't we skim for it?" Greg asks. "Wes, it was supposed to be your big day. You go first."

"It's your birthday?" Jane asks. "Happy birthday!" She moves to give him a friendly hug but he backs up a step to stop her.

"No, no it's not that. Thanks anyway, but it's not my birthday."

He says nothing else, just stands there, joggling a stone in his hand.

"Oh," she says, with a sad smile and shrug. "Well, let the best man win?"

"Okay." Wes looks at her a second longer, then turns and sidearms his stone over the water.

"That's decent," Greg tells him. "Three skips." He bends and picks a stone. "Nice flat one, should do the trick."

Jane senses some tight-wire tension strung between them. It's wordless, but obvious. Greg moves to loosen up his arm, shaking it, then blowing his fist. He doesn't stop there, though. Next he stretches his arm out straight, and then, yes, he actually cracks his knuckles, which gets Jane to laugh. But something's going down between these two brothers, something left unsaid.

"Okay, here we go." Greg positions his feet and skims the stone, which plunks deep into the water after only one skip. "You beat me, Wes," he says under his breath, with a slight nod as he pats his back. "I guess the best man won."

seventeen

"DO YOU MIND IF I make a pit stop at home?" Wes asks as they leave the cove parking lot, driving beneath the *Cornucopia Ye Olde 2K* banner strung across the entrance. "I've got this dog I need to check on."

"I'd love to meet it!" Jane says. Her casted arm leans on the cushioned armrest between them. "I used to have a cat ..."

Wes glances at her with a quick nod. And for the first time, his new pickup truck's fancy interior options don't seem all that great. Because with Jane sitting beside him, the thick padding and insulated glass painfully exaggerate the quietness in the cab.

"Everything okay?" he finally hears.

Jane's voice is soft, her head tipped in that concerned way she has, her straight hair tucked behind an ear. From her caring words, to her gentle look, it all gets him to let out a long breath he hadn't realized he'd been holding in. "Just a little tired. Haven't been sleeping too well."

"Really?"

"Yeah, being back home, and in a new bed, I've been up some at night." As he says it, he turns the truck into his driveway, stopping beside the front porch. "Hang on," he tells her while unbuckling his seatbelt. "Let me help you, with your arm and all."

As soon as he gets out, he stops beside the truck and takes another long breath. Just one. Still, by the time he circles around to the passenger side, Jane's seatbelt is unhitched and her tote slung over a shoulder. "Easy," he says while holding her arm as she steps down. "There you go."

"Okay!" she whispers when her feet hit the ground and he steadies her balance. She looks over toward the painted Victorian, her eyes scanning the decorative trim, the detailed shingles. "I always admired this gingerbread house, Wes. I really don't mind waiting on that pretty porch."

There it is again, that quiet between them as they both take in the sight of the old house. But even with the faded, peeling paint, and the overgrown hydrangea bushes pressing against the siding, its charm has a way of showing through. The dried hydrangea flowers are a pale tan with a tinge of blush, and he thinks that color combo might actually look good painted on the house. "Sure, I'll just be a minute."

Walking around the house to the rear entrance, now Wes wonders why he left so many paint samples on the siding. To the uninformed eye, it might look like a sloppy, eccentric mess. He opens the back door to find Comet standing in his crate, tail wagging into the cage sides with a steady thump. Wes lets him out, then grabs a drink of cold water, the German shepherd following him to the sink. "Come on, two minutes," he tells the dog. "You can stretch your legs in the yard."

As usual, though, Comet has his own ideas. He scoots through the doorway, hangs a sharp right and hightails it straight to the front as though he knows exactly who is waiting there. By the time Wes catches up, Jane is sitting in a rickety rocker … and Comet stands beside her with his muzzle resting on her leg.

"Aren't you a handsome one?" she says while scratching his long nose. The dog's tail never stops swishing back and forth.

Wes climbs the steps to the porch and leans against the railing. "I should have leashed him, but he's been crated all day. Hope he didn't spook you, running up like that."

"No way. He's too cute." Jane strokes the dog's head and moves her hand along his fluffy neck. "What's his name?"

"Comet." Wes steps closer. "Sit, Comet." The dog immediately sits, perfectly straight. "What a show-off, look at that posture. And you'll notice that white patch on his shoulder, there." Wes strokes the dog's side.

"How do you like that!" Jane leans over to see. "So striking." She looks up at Wes standing beside the dog. "Like the tail of a comet?"

Wes nods and pulls his keys from his vest pocket. That's all it takes for the dog to fly down the steps toward his parked pickup truck. "Oh, damn."

"What's the matter?"

There are so many ways he could answer that loaded question. *Do you mean, besides that I should have been wearing a black tuxedo instead of jeans right now? That two words—I do—should have been forming on my lips? That I should've been slipping a gold band on a woman's ring finger today? That my airline ticket to a tropical paradise has been changed to LAX?*

Wes sits on the top step of the porch, his elbows on his knees, watching the jet-black dog frozen at his truck. "Comet's a former police dog," he says, instead of everything else. "His handler must have trained him to get to the squad car at the sound of jangling keys. Once Comet hears them," Wes hitches his head toward the dog, "there's no getting him back. He thinks it's time to get to work, patrolling with his master. He lives to patrol." After another second, Wes looks again at Jane. "So we'll probably have some company in the truck now."

"Why is he a *former* police dog? Is he injured?"

"No. His issue is that he doesn't have a mean bone in his body. He somehow made it through the selection process, and enjoyed engaging with his handler. Problem is, he wouldn't bite a soul. Loves everyone, as you've just found out. So they had to let him go."

"You know what?" Jane stands and hikes her tote over her shoulder. "I bet Comet would like to ride along on your mail route. He'd think he's patrolling, and wouldn't people like seeing him on duty, all alert and keeping a friendly eye on things."

"I'm sure it's against postal regulations, but the dog would definitely *love* it."

They walk down the porch steps and alongside the house toward his pickup. When Wes gives his keys another jangle, Comet whines and paces closer to the truck. "Mind your manners," he quietly orders the dog. "Ladies first."

"We're back!" Jane calls around the people milling about, some in full reenactment Pilgrim dress: men in waistcoats and breeches, women in aproned dresses and cloaks. She makes her way through, sets her heavy tote on the end of Pete's table, and pulls out cans of spray glue and tubes of glitter.

"What've you got there?" Pete asks as she continues to unpack her tote. "Let me help. I don't want you to overdo it, with that broken arm of yours."

"I'm fine!" Jane says. "Now let's make this booth a winter

wonderland." She presses tufts of cotton around the whittled pine trees. "You're okay with me adding glitter to the deer?"

"Absolutely. I'm not sure why sales are slow; I did so well at Twinklin' Pumpkins." He motions to the passing crowd of young couples, of parents with children, of friends browsing together, pseudo-Pilgrims included.

"Well, there's a lot of competition for everyone's attention here." Jane points to a roped-off area. "I mean, look at the line to get into the petting zoo. Who would've thought people are so fascinated by the livestock of early Plymouth?"

As if on cue, a goat bleats there, which prompts a sheep to run circles around the makeshift corral.

"You've got a good foundation, Pete, but when you're putting it out on display, Near and Deer needs to *shine*," Jane explains. "Because I can assure you that on the card racks, shoppers pick the cards with sparkle, especially at holiday time." Silver flecks flutter from her fingers onto the cottony snow. "So this should help."

Wes sets down a stack of cups and two large tan boxes with a bright white spout on each. "This might help, too."

"What's that?" Pete asks.

"Cocoa-To-Go. It's all the rage," Jane says while spraying glue on one of the smaller does. "We picked them up at the coffee shop."

"Whole Latte Life?" Pete asks.

"Just a quick stop. Twelve ready-made servings of hot cocoa in each box, Dad." Wes lines up the insulated cartons side by side. "All you have to do is open the spout and fill a cup. It's for your paying customers; they can have a free cup of cheer." He glances over to Derek's popcorn-popping tent. "And after the popcorn-eating contest in honor of Indian corn, folks will be wanting something to drink."

"I don't know." Pete reaches for the paper cups and neatly

stacks them. "You think this'll work?"

"Trust me." Jane dusts silver glitter on a buck, adding flecks to the antlers, too, before eyeing the freshly sprinkled deer. "What you've got now is a little snow deer and cocoa cheer … at this magical time of year!" She turns to Wes and sees it on his face, that slight side smile of his. "Aha! See? It works. And wait, that's a greeting card jingle if I ever heard one." Favoring her casted arm, she digs deep into her tote for a notepad and jots it down, whispering *Snow deer and cocoa cheer!*

All the while, Pete's been pacing, watching the wintry transformation of his Near and Deer tent. He touches the white cotton around his whittled trees and tucks some by the sparkling deer. "I have to hand it to you, Jane," he tells her. "It does look like snow on the deer. Christmas snow."

"Or fresh-fallen snow, don't you think?" Jane asks. "And did you know that snow doesn't melt on a deer's back? So your snow deer are authentic to the real thing. A deer's fur is so thick, its body heat can't get through to melt it."

"Now where'd you learn that?" Pete asks while adding spray glue to the pine trees in his display.

Jane slides over a tube of glitter. "My dad told me. We always see deer out behind the carriage house, near the river. He used to tell me things like that."

"Smart man." Pete shakes a dash of glitter on the boughs of his whittled trees. "Your mother stopped by when you and Wes were gone. I'm glad to see Lillian's keeping herself busy. When your father was alive, I remember bridge night at your house. So it'll be good to be there again, on Thanksgiving."

"What are you talking about, Dad?" As soon as Wes says it, a young couple stops and peruses the snow deer.

"For turkey dinner," Pete explains, arranging two shimmering trees.

"What do you mean?" Jane asks while sprinkling more glitter on a pair of does.

"I guess your sister's going out of town for Thanksgiving? Your mother and I were talking and she said it'll be awful quiet, especially since it's been almost a year since Edward passed. So she invited me and the boys."

"Oh, how wonderful!" Jane turns to Wes, surprised to see him pulling on his fingerless gloves and getting his keys from his pocket. "It'll be a nice—"

"Comet's in the truck." Wes tugs his wool cap a bit lower.

"Okaaay," Jane says with an uncertain smile. "But—"

"How much is this one?" a woman interrupts as she lifts a now-snowy stag and holds it to the sunlight, watching it glimmer.

"Don't know," Wes tells her as he starts to walk past the people lining up along Near and Deer's display table. "I'll see you, Jane," he says then, almost as an afterthought, looking back at her and hesitating, before turning and shouldering himself through the growing crowd of deer browsers, young and old, scarved and gloved and reaching for cups of hot cocoa, too.

When Pete's done setting the stag in a gift box for his customer, and Jane finishes pouring cocoa for another, she walks over to him. "Does Wes feel okay? He seems a little, I don't know, cranky today."

Pete looks out past the crowd, as though trying to get a glimpse of his son—maybe to stop him and give him a piece of his mind, from the expression on his face. "Jane," he finally says, kindly patting her hand. "I'm sure it meant the world to Wes that you're here and took some time to help me like this. Though he'll never admit it, that's for darn sure."

The way Pete shakes his head when he catches sight of Wes' black pickup pulling out of the parking lot, Jane glances that way, too, then back at Pete.

"It's just that, well …" Pete sighs. "Today was actually supposed to be Wesley's wedding day."

eighteen

"WE HAVEN'T REALLY FELT *CHRISTMAS* in the air yet," Leo Sterling is saying early Tuesday morning on the kitchen countertop TV. While Jane sips her coffee, the meteorologist points to a weather map of the country. "But folks, don't you fret." A pale blue streak approaches New England on that map. "Snow's on its way these November days, as indicated by this blue."

"Yes!" Jane whispers, cupping her steaming mug.

"Yet there's no need to worry, it'll be little more than a flurry."

Even a dusting will be lovely; sometimes less gives the perfect amount of sparkle. So Jane brings her coffee to the sunroom to begin a snow-inspired painting session. A lone cardinal pecks at the nearly empty bird feeder outside the paned window.

"Hello, my friend," Jane says while setting her coffee on the sill. "With snow coming, you definitely need to fatten up." After pulling on a puffy down vest over her cast and wrapping a turquoise plaid scarf around her neck, she treks out the back door, carefully grabbing the sack of bird food on the way. The cold air has her bristle into her thick scarf as she sets the sack on the ground at the feeder. Working with only one good arm has definitely slowed her, but no way will it stop her. So with her right hand, she opens the top of the feeder, then fills a scoop with sunflower seeds and slowly pours it in. Afterward, she searches for any flittering red waiting to be fed. But the only reds in sight are clusters of bright berries nestled in green leaves, on a nearby holly shrub.

If anything, a decade of researching Christmas facts and folklore for her card designs has made Jane an expert on all things Christmas, including the festive holly berries. Seeing them reminds her of Wes telling her about his sleepless nights, though he was loath to admit that jilted anxieties might be the culprit. Now she's got the perfect cure.

Back inside the sunroom, she sets down several sprigs of holly snapped from the branches. Heat ticks in the radiators, warming the room. "Holly, holly," she says while folding one of her recent cardinal sketches to turn it into a notecard. Her eyes scour the cluttered worktable for a red pencil, which she uses to add a holly accent to the corners of the sketch.

Still standing with her vest and scarf on, Jane finally sits and opens the paper, carefully crafting her note:

Wes, I saw these in my yard and thought of you, and your recent sleepless nights. By golly, what you need is a sprig of holly! Ancient folklore claims that if you tie a sprig of holly to your bedpost, it will keep away bad dreams. —Jane

Sometimes believing is all it takes. So after tying a ribbon around the holly sprigs and placing them in a bag, Jane lifts her new key from the hall table and walks outside along the stone path to the mailbox. It makes a creaking sound when she opens it, so she waggles the stiff lid to loosen it up. Then she places her note and holly gift bag inside, closes the mailbox and glances down the long street. Before returning to her latest designing frenzy in the house, she does one last thing: flips the red flag up.

⌒◯

"You want how many?" Pete asks into the phone.

Wes sits at the kitchen table where a library book is propped open near his plate of pancakes.

"I'll do my best, Vera. Thanks." Pete hangs up the phone and jots something on a piece of scrap paper.

"You talking to Vera Sterling?" Wes asks, turning a page of his book.

"Sure was. She wants to carry my snow deer in Snowflakes and Coffee Cakes. Says local crafts sell really well there." Pete pulls out a chair and sits across from Wes. "She placed a large order after Jane put in a good word for me. I'm going to be busy."

Wes slices his fork through three stacked pancakes dripping in maple syrup.

"Flapjacks?" Pete scrutinizes his plate of pancakes before dropping a hunk of butter on them. "You made these? Not too many health benefits, no?"

If a look could, well, not kill, but be annoyed, Wes is sure his does. "They're whole-wheat buttermilk pancakes. Lots of fiber in there. And it's getting late, so eat hearty."

Pete tucks a napkin beneath his uniform shirt collar and drizzles maple syrup on his stack. "What do you have there?" he asks, waving a forkful of dripping pancake in the book's direction.

Since he's mid-chew of a mouthful, Wes closes the book to show the cover. A German shepherd stands at full attention on a rocky ledge. "Got it at the library." He opens to his page again and swigs his coffee. "Says here that German shepherds like to work. Originally bred as a herding dog." He turns in his seat to Comet, who is sitting in his crate with the door open. "We have to find something for you to do."

"Seems he was accustomed to going to work with his officer partner, the way he likes to get in the pickup with you."

"Can't be pulling that stunt all the time, though," Wes says as he carries his dish to the sink and rinses it. Yet he's uncertain what to do with the dog, who is still sitting in the crate and watching his every move.

"We meeting at the cove for lunch today?" Pete asks when he brings his empty plate to the sink and starts packing their wrapped sandwiches in lunch bags.

"Sounds good."

"Same time?"

"Twelve-thirty."

After a moment, Pete walks closer and motions to Wes' face. "Hey, you shave today?"

Wes reaches up and scratches his own chin. "No, thinking of growing a beard, maybe."

"Looking a little messy, so I don't know if that's a good idea. And what happened there?" his father asks, pointing to Wes' hand.

"Where?"

"Your thumb. Got a good nick on it."

Wes turns his hand and gives it a shake. "Whittling those pine trees is what happened to it. I carved a few more last night."

"You still not sleeping?" Pete walks over to the wall hook and lifts off his jacket, zipping it up tight, then pulls on his blue cap, regulation.

Wes shrugs and tosses him his lunch bag. "Sometimes."

"Not good, son. You need your rest."

136

"Got a lot on my mind, one of which is Thanksgiving, by the way. For your information, I am *not* sitting over there at the March house. Bad enough being grilled by family about my breakup, don't need any sympathy from the March clan, too."

"It's just a simple dinner, for crying out loud," his father says from the back door. "Better work things out and handle it. I'll see you at lunch, we'll talk there. Window to window." The door he'd been holding open to argue slams shut now.

And suddenly, quiet. There's no noise in the house except the swish of dishwater. Wes puts the rinsed griddle in the dish rack, dries his hands and grabs his leather bomber and brown scarf, both non-regulation. His work duffel sits on the floor near the back door, with gloves and hat and clipboard inside. He unzips it and adds his lunch bag and a bottle of water. But when he pulls his keys from his pocket and opens the door, a blur of black flies out ahead of him.

"Hey! Get over here." After a moment—and a long, exhaled breath—he checks his watch, then steps outside and locks the door behind him. "Fine, get in," he tells Comet when he opens the truck door. "And *only* because I'm late. Not that it matters," he adds while adjusting his jacket and scarf. "Just got written up for wearing non-regulation shoes. I'll probably get fired anyway." He scratches the dog's head once it settles in the seat behind him. "Or get put on probation, at the very least."

By the time Wes pulls into the post office, any vacant employee parking spaces are in the rear lot, which suits him just fine. "You stay," he tells Comet as he grabs his work duffel, but leaves his bomber and scarf in the pickup because the last thing he needs is to get written up again. After a quick glance around to be sure no one sees the dog, he continues, "I'll be back in a few minutes. Be quiet now, you hear me?"

Everyone's enmeshed in their work routines when Wes rushes inside the building. With no time for small talk, he readies his mail truck at the loading dock, moving methodically and stacking the packages and bins in the cargo area, filling the front-seat mail tray, then hopping in and turning left toward the rear employee parking lot, instead of right, to the street.

"What's going on?" a voice calls out, and Wes suddenly sees his father pulling up beside him, ready to start his route.

"Forgot my coat, Dad," Wes lies while waving him off. "Meet you at the cove later."

Once his father toots the horn and leaves, it's time—and Wes' window of opportunity is mighty slim. He blocks the view by angling the white mail truck sideways, in front of his pickup. Only then does he jump out, open the pickup door and have Comet dash from one vehicle to the other.

"Get down, get down! Hurry!" he orders the dog when it jumps in the mail truck. Comet seems to know the routine—thank you very much, Addison Police Department—and squeezes behind the front seat to the cargo area, then lies on a tiny empty space on the floor.

Funny thing is, the German shepherd thrives on the tension. At least better than Wes does as he pulls off his wool cap and wipes a bead of perspiration from his forehead, then tosses aside the jacket and scarf he grabbed from his pickup. "Hell, you're going to get me screwed. You know that, don't you?"

Hearing the dog's tail thump the floor, he kind of senses the attachment K-9 unit officers have with their dogs. So after driving several blocks of his route, he feels a little sorry about the way he shushed and ordered around the poor thing. In the rearview mirror, he can see Comet watching him with his brown dog eyes. "Okay, okay, you can sit. But just sit. Don't move around."

A block later, they approach a red Cape Cod with a low stone wall around the front yard. "That's the Hobson place," Wes says as he slips on his bomber now. "Nice enough family. But they keep their Christmas lights up all year. Those icicle-type." He points to the house roofline. "See them? I can assure you they'll still be hanging there in April."

A few mailboxes later, right before turning onto Old Willow Road, they stop in front of a gray saltbox colonial. "Here's the Grinstead house," Wes tells Comet, glancing back at the dog, who—wonder of wonders—is stretching forward to see out the window. "Margaret Grinstead retired from town hall last year. Ran the show at Parks and Rec. She makes nice brownies, sometimes leaves me a couple in the mailbox."

It's taken this long to completely calm down, so when he turns onto Old Willow Road, Wes relaxes enough to tune the radio to a country song about driving in the rain and feeling a lonely pain. He flips a few mailboxes closed in beat to the song, tapping his hand on the steering wheel at the same time.

"March house is coming up, around the bend. You met Jane the other day."

And that's all he says. Because when his mail truck rounds the curve, the first thing he sees is that red flag flipped up. He slowly pulls alongside the Marches' slate-blue mailbox, opens it and reaches in for a package. After scanning Jane's note, he sets it all aside, puts their mail in the box, flips the flag down and drives away.

"Yoo-hoo! Lunch is served."

Jane looks up from the antique-trunk coffee table she's wiping off in the carriage house. "Chloe, at last! I'm famished," she says while tossing down the dust cloth.

Chloe walks in through the barn-door entranceway, holding a restaurant take-out bag. "Wow, it's rustic. Loving the exposed beams."

"Come on over here, we'll eat and look outside." Jane motions to a white-painted table in the back, beside a bay window. "There's a nice view down to the river."

Chloe pulls out two sandwiches and bags of chips, then hangs her tweed blazer on a chair. "I got us grilled cheese, your favorite."

"Perfect."

"I also brought a bag of rock salt and left it on the back stoop. They're saying snow on Thursday."

"So I heard," Jane says, taking a bite of the gooey, warm sandwich. "I filled the bird feeder this morning so the cardinals don't go hungry. And you remember that holly shrub? It's bursting with berries, and I cut some sprigs while I was out there."

"That's good, giving that arm a little range of motion? But I don't want you or Mom clearing the walkways, it'll be slippery. Bob will come by with his pickup and clean away any snow, okay? Oh, and I ordered this for you online." She pulls a snowflake-patterned sling out of her large purse. "For the holidays! You can dress up your cast."

It's not surprising that her big sister thinks of Jane that way. Chloe's always been the mother-hen type, tending her chicks. Even as a busy mom of two young girls, she's forever planning ahead, making things special for everyone. "Thank you, it's really pretty," Jane tells her.

"And so is this space! Mom found a great contractor to

rebuild after the old carriage house burned down."

"No kidding." Sunshine streams in through the back windows, and the dark hardwood floors gleam. "It's like a little chalet in here, with the arched ceiling and open floor plan."

"Bob and I should've hired out more of our reno. I thought I could handle it, but the travel agency's swamped with reservations for cruise season. And with Olivia's and Josie's after-school activities? Oh, what a mess things are."

"If your house isn't ready, you don't have to host Christmas," Jane insists. "We can have it here. Josie and Olivia can sleep over, maybe even in the carriage house! My cast will be off by then, so I'll help Mom. I'm sure she won't mind."

"Oh, no. It's my turn. If Bob and I can ever agree on granite colors for the kitchen island." Chloe bites into a hunk of her sandwich. "Wait," she says, holding up a finger while she chews. "Shouldn't you be working? What are you even doing out here?"

"Just dusting. Mom wants to run an ad in the *Addison Weekly* for a boarder, I guess, to help pay her expenses."

"But isn't your boss waiting on new designs? I thought you said they were urgent."

"They are, believe me." Jane snags a potato chip and holds it aloft for a second. "Especially after I saw Cobblestone's report on repeat performances."

"Which is?"

"It's when the best-selling cards from last year's line are picked up for the next year. Thus *repeat* performances."

"Uh-oh."

Jane nods while wiping her fingers on a napkin. "Very few of mine made the cut."

"Ouch. What are you going to do?"

"The only thing I can: tap into my creative freedom. I

mean, my design parameters stay the same with card sizes, but my vision has *no* bounds." Jane tucks a loose strand of hair into her messy bun. "So I have to kick things up a notch, because I got the feeling when I talked to Rocco that it's now or never."

"Really? After all your years there?"

"Yup. Rocco didn't actually say it, but he did hint that the new temp he hired could step in for me if I'm feeling the crunch."

"Now *that* would worry me. She steps in and you're stepping out."

"Right. But I *also* see that Mom hates rattling around that big old house alone. I guess it'll be good for her to have someone here after I leave. So I took one little hour to help get the place ready."

Her mother also asked her to write the ad, to give it that Jane March spin. Of course, there's probably some ulterior motive to her asking, to get Jane back into her jingle mode. She imagines now, as she looks around, just what she'd write: *For Rent. Cozy carriage house, 1BR, 1BA, kitchenette, LR w/FP.* Then she adds the selling points, details that would draw even herself to move in: *River views; long, private driveway; country cupola room to watch the stars and every changing season.* Through the paned windows on the front wall, beside the sliding barn-door entrance, she glimpses the main farmhouse. *Wonderful family memories of barbecues, and leaf raking, and garden planting, and bird feeding; home-cooked meals; spontaneous pajama parties; loving chats; bliss.*

⌒∼◌

Okay. It's hard to tell how many minutes have passed. But when Wes finds himself standing in front of the open refrigerator later that night, not remembering what he even wanted, he slams the door shut. Maybe he needs a drink, so he fills a glass with tap water, sips it and brings it to his bedroom. "Sleep tight," he says to Comet when he passes the crate in the dark.

In his room, he lies on the bed, flat on his back, robe on. His hand reaches to the bedside table and grabs the airline ticket there. Even though he can't see the fine print, squinting at it helps. Anything beats staring at that ceiling. But a sound gets his attention, so he sits up and turns his head, listening.

After another sip of water, he walks to his dresser and lifts his watch, pulls out the pin to stop the slight tick-ticking, then sets it down. When he does, a shadow catches his eye: Jane's holly sprigs, right where he tossed them earlier, beside his keys.

Maybe there's something to be said about folklore. Jane's note seemed pretty enthusiastic about the holly's potency as a sleep aid. It could be worth a shot. He stands there—robe untied, feeling a wreck—and joggles the ribboned holly sprigs in his open hand. Just for a minute.

Just until he walks straight to his bed, and in the dark of night, ties the red-berried sprigs to his bedpost.

nineteen

IN LATE-AFTERNOON TWILIGHT, TALL TREES rise behind the carriage house, framing it with leafless branches reaching skyward. The cupola's frosted windows glow golden against the graying sky; a balsam wreath hangs on the carriage house's planked door; swags of twinkling pine garland loop across a picket fence where a red cardinal perches on one of the posts. And snow ... snow begins to fall, sweeping across the image like a mist, the silvery flakes dusting the ground.

The moment Jane hits Send to deliver her modified Christmas card to Cobblestone, she sits back—until a motion outside has her spin in her seat.

"It *is* snowing!" she exclaims, doing a double take from the computer screen to the sunroom window. She'd been so immersed in the finishing touches of her snowy carriage house card, it felt as though she was right there, hanging the wreath on its door. And now, to see this *real* first snow of the season, well it has her pause with a thought. She lifts a few sketches to find her mother's *I Insist List* and drags her finger down the items to number three.

At the season's first snow, visit Brookside Road. Set your sights on an old New England Christmas.

"Oh boy," she mutters at her cluttered worktable. "The first snow." Her newly purchased whittled deer stands beside the computer screen, its gentle head angled to watch her work. And beside the table, a corkboard propped on one of her mother's painting easels is covered with recently completed Christmas card designs—a wooden gazebo outlined in colored lights on a town green; a lone deer gazing toward an illuminated farmhouse on a snowy night; a florist's shop window brimming with red poinsettias.

But the *I Insist List* draws her eye.

Sometimes, she knows, you only get one chance. Like right now. There will never be another *first* snow this season.

And the flakes are coming down even harder, blowing past the window, the ice crystals tapping at the glass. She has to get to Brookside Road.

Minutes later, after finagling the toggle buttons on her wool cape and tugging on her shearling-lined boots, all it takes for her to rethink *walking* to Brookside is this: one close-call near-fall on the snow-glazed walkway outside, her good arm flailing to keep her balance.

"Gosh-darn wrist!" she says once inside again and slamming the fickle front door behind her. Her mother's teaching her Thursday class at the community center, so transportation options are nil. Until something catches Jane's eye as she hangs her cape in the coat closet, something as close as her arm cast. She runs her fingers over the mailbox Wes drew there, its red flag prominently flipped up. *If you need anything, just flag me*, he'd said that pizza night at Luigi's.

If she ever needed anything, this is it. Keeping her job hinges on finding the right inspiration. And the first snow is part of it. Back at her worktable in the sunroom with so many paned windows looking out on the yard, the snowfall she can't get to mocks her. She turns away and grabs a blank notecard, quickly sketches those insistent snowflakes on it, then jots her request:

Urgent! Can I please hitch a ride to Brookside? —Jane

After venturing outside again—one cautious, slow, itty-bitty step at a time on the slippery walkway—she places her notecard inside the blue mailbox, peers down the street for any sign of Wes' truck driving through the snow, then flips the red flag up.

"I've got to find you a home," Wes says to Comet. Every time the mail truck swerves on a snowy patch, the dog inches closer. "This isn't a police car. You *can't* be patrolling my route, you know. I'll lose my job." He leans to the windshield and squints through the fast-falling snowflakes. "Then I'll really be a nobody."

There's a motion up ahead: a blur of bounding red coat and black pants tucked into floppy snow boots, a beckoning arm, a worried face calling out. "Typically, you'll see this type of patron when they've forgotten to mail something," he says to the canine muzzle nearly beside his head now. "Neglected some friend's anniversary, or forgot someone on their holiday mailing list." He slows the truck as he approaches the next mailbox, the same one the panicked woman is also now standing at, waving a large envelope like a flag, as though he might not see her. "The more desperate their posture, the more guilty they are for forgetting."

The woman, in her mid-forties, bounces on her toes, still envelope-waving.

"Get back now," Wes tells Comet. "And lie down." When the dog plants a sloppy lick on his face, he whips around and orders it again. "Down."

"Hello!" he hears the woman's anxious voice as he pulls up alongside the mailbox, which is dented and should've been replaced last summer. "I'm so glad I caught you," she says, breathless, her brown hair matted beneath wet snowflakes.

Wes opens his window and takes the envelope. "No problem." He looks down at the address. "Regular delivery?"

She nods, standing there, still bouncing on her toes, shoulders hunched against the sudden snow, blowing into her closed fists for warmth. "Can you check it?"

"Check it?"

"Is it addressed okay, with enough postage?"

It never ceases to amaze him how people who've used the postal service their entire lives become riddled with crippling doubt when they're actually in the midst of a postal transaction. As though some mysterious, secret code is necessary to transport a package from one address to another. He skims the address and lightly shakes the envelope. "All's good," he says, leaning over and dropping it in a plastic bin on the far end of the truck floor.

"Hey! Look at you!"

The enthusiasm in her voice has Wes lurch up and turn. "Damn," he whispers under his breath as Comet stretches across the driver's seat, squeezing behind him to greet the woman.

"I didn't know the post office uses dogs for mail delivery."

"Comet!" Wes quietly commands the dog. "Down."

The German shepherd retreats into the cramped rear cargo area of the truck and lies back down. "Sorry about that,"

Wes tells the woman. "It's just a one-time thing, helping someone ... well, never mind."

"Aw, too bad. Looks like he wanted to deliver an envelope or something." She steps back then, shielding her eyes from the falling snow. "Bye-bye, doggie," she calls as Wes closes his window and pulls away.

"That's it, you're all done," he warns Comet. "Distracting me like that. Don't you know I'm on a strict schedule? These folks want their mail on time." He glares in the rearview mirror for a glimpse of the dog's reflection as it scoots over and squeezes beneath a side shelf. "Supervisors go on the road and monitor the routes, you know. Every day, I'm expected at the same time, no delays," he insists. "People report seeing you in here, and I'm a goner. Not that it matters," he adds while turning onto Old Willow Road. "Might even be doing me a favor getting me fired."

With that, he reaches for the radio—even under the snowy conditions when he should focus only on the road. But before he can find just the right country-western cowboy warbling some forlorn words about the status of his lonely life, one wayward Canadian goose distracts him.

"Not you again." Wes shuts off the radio. "You're a little far from home, aren't you?" While slowing his truck, the goose waddles along the curb, wings partially spread, neck extended. "He must like taking snow walks," Wes tells Comet, who obviously senses the troublemaking fowl and is now standing guard, the fur on his white-streaked shoulder raised in bristles. "Our feathered friend, and I use the word *friend* generously, lives way at the other end of the street. Near the pond."

When Wes stops at the first mailbox, he hears two honks as he quickly opens his window and tosses in the envelopes before the goose can nip his hand. At least he has on his heavy gloves today, should the persistent bird hit its mark.

"Get ready, Comet. It's going to be an interesting ride." He puts the truck in gear and inches forward, careful to avoid the big fowl waddling curbside and keeping pace in the snow. Another goose honk agitates Comet, who begins whining as he stretches his head well into the driving area to see outside.

It's a good thing, too. Because when that goose takes a flying leap up at the side of the truck, pecking hard at Wes' window, Comet lets out three sharp, successive barks. Which practically gives Wes a heart attack, but that's okay. The sight in the truck's side mirror makes it worthwhile, heart palpitations and racing pulse and all: The startled Canadian goose jumps back onto the sidewalk and nearly falls over, catching itself on one of its outstretched wings. It rights its balance, fluffs its feathers, then spreads those mighty wings and takes flight, straight toward the distant pond. Sky-bound, far, far away from any barking German shepherds.

"Way to go, Comet! If I had a biscuit, I'd give you one." Wes lifts his gloved hand and rubs the scruff of the dog's neck. "Smooth sailing ahead," he says, giving the truck gas and whooping when the back end fishtails. "We're cruising now, pal."

When he rounds the curve ahead, his eyes go to where they always go—straight to the March mailbox, today with the flag up. He figures that, okay, it's that kind of day, one with unexpected things happening. He stops and reads Jane's snowflake note while Comet sits patiently in the cargo area, quietly watching out through the windshield, clearly patrolling the street for any lingering, unruly geese.

Wes reads the few lines again, looks at the farmhouse, clears his throat, puts the truck in park, flips up his jacket collar and tells Comet, "Stay." After a glance in the rearview mirror that has him question why the heck he didn't shave *again* as he runs his gloved hand over his shadowed face, he cautiously jogs the snowy front path toward the house. When he looks up, Jane is already opening the door.

⌒∾○

Jane tugs the obstinate wooden door closed just as Wes is taking the porch stairs two at a time.

"Jane?" he calls from behind her. "You need a ride? Everything okay?"

"Oh, yes. Yes, I'm fine." She turns her key in the lock while asking over her shoulder, "Do you mind? Because I hate to impose."

"It's all right." He takes her arm from beneath her toggle-buttoned cape and holds her steady while walking down the stairs. "Careful, it's slippery."

"Okay," Jane says, concentrating on her footing on the snowy walkway. The last thing she needs is another broken arm.

"I got your note. What's happening on Brookside?"

"It's kind of hard to explain." She winces against tiny snowflakes hitting her face as she focuses on her footsteps. "Long story, I'll tell you while you're driving."

They walk around to the back of the truck. "You know the routine." Wes unlocks the door, then turns to her before opening it.

"Something wrong?" Jane asks. "If you really shouldn't do this, I understand."

With some hesitation, Wes brushes snow off her cheek with his gloved hand. "No, it's not that. Just so you're aware, you'll have some company today." When he lifts the rear door, his black German shepherd stands right there, front and center, tail wagging.

150

"Comet!"

Wes steps in, clears a shelf and flips it up against the side wall, moves two full mail bins off the bench and onto the floor, then takes Jane's arm and helps her up into the truck. "Comet, sit now," he tells the dog at their heels.

The dog does, but as if he knows, he sits right beside Jane's corner-of-the-side-bench makeshift seat, within easy petting reach of her mittened hand.

"I'm headed in the direction of Brookside anyway," Wes tells her after he closes the rear door and returns to the driver's seat. "So I'll finish delivering to the houses along the way. If that's okay."

"That's fine. As long as it's snowing, I'm good."

"What? You *need* it to be snowing?"

Jane nods, and when Wes shrugs and puts the truck in gear, she explains her mother's *I Insist List*, and how she must experience every item on it to get her jingle back. "Hopefully, that'll inspire new designs for my job, which *is* kind of on the line. And guess what? The list works! I can feel my jingle coming back with each item I complete. Feeding the cardinals was first. So wouldn't you know it? One of my latest designs was cardinal-inspired with the little red birds at the feeder, all sprightly in the snow, and my boss *loved* it. Now I'm trying to work my way through everything on that list."

"I guess Lillian's on to something, then."

"She is. It's all about putting myself right into holiday settings and special Addison scenes. Like I'm doing today."

Wes stops beside a picket fence. He reaches to his mail tray and sorts the envelopes before putting a handful in a mailbox attached right to one of the fence posts.

"That's pretty, set up like that on the fence."

"I've seen it all, believe me. From top-of-the-line mailboxes, to, well, I guess you'd call it country chic, or something like that." He closes his window against the blowing snow and slowly moves on. "Listen, Jane. There's Mrs. Crenshaw up ahead. She's a real nervous Nellie; always thinks I'm putting her mail in the neighbor's box. If you could lie low so she doesn't see you. It'll get her shook up, otherwise."

"Will do," she assures him, glimpsing out at an elderly woman with a kerchief over her head, approaching the mailbox. Jane leans back, pressing herself as flat as she can, so as not to be seen.

"Mrs. Crenshaw," Wes says while opening the window. "What are you doing out in this snow? You could slip and fall."

"I'm very careful, Wesley. I've got ice grippers on my boots."

Jane sneaks a peek from her bench seat, seeing Mrs. Crenshaw standing and peering into the truck.

"Do you have my electric bill in there, by any chance? It might be late, and I hope you didn't leave it at the Gallo house. They're funny about things like that, and I think they throw out any of my mail they get."

Wes thumbs through a stack in the tray. "No bills today." He hands her a magazine folded around a few envelopes.

"Are you sure?" she asks, looking further into the truck.

In a comical sort of way, Jane sees the scene unfolding one second before it happens; one second before Comet fears Mrs. Crenshaw is encroaching on his master's space, and so he lunges forward and lets out one sudden bark in defense. It's all Jane can do to not laugh as she slaps her mittened hand over her mouth, watching the woman and Wes jump at the same time.

"Wesley Davis! Is that a *dog*?" Mrs. Crenshaw takes a step closer, craning her neck to see inside just as a gust of spinning snowflakes blows in, too. "I don't believe postal regulations allow dogs in the trucks, do they?"

"No. Well, you see …"

Jane notices that he stops then—completely stops talking. And why bother continuing, with the way Mrs. Crenshaw is reaching her hand through the open window and petting Comet's muzzle.

"Aren't you a cutie? You remind me of my Pepper. So hang on a second, I'll get you a treat." She turns and heads up her walkway, motioning for Wes to wait.

"I'm running late, Mrs. Crenshaw," he calls out the window he's slowly closing against the blowing snow. "Have to go."

"Hold your horses, buster. I'll be right back."

As soon as she's out of earshot, Jane can't resist. She laughs, quietly though, but laughs just the same while watching Wes' reflection in the rearview mirror. "Did you see her face when poor Comet barked?"

Wes catches her eye in the mirror. "Hers? What about mine? That bark scared the daylights out of me." He looks toward the snow-covered sidewalk. "Okay, here she comes."

Comet seems to know he's found another friend while mail-patrolling, and when Wes opens his window again, the dog steps right on his lap to reach past him and plant a friendly lick across Mrs. Crenshaw's cheek.

"Oh, you are too sweet!" She gives him a large dog biscuit. "Come and see me again, pup. I'll be waiting."

"Okay," Wes says as he pulls away from the mailbox. "Saved by the dog. Now go lie down, Comet. And behave yourself, for crying out loud."

The rest of the trip to Brookside is slow-going in poor driving conditions. But something unexpected happens on the ride. Wes is busy sorting and delivering; Comet is busy gnawing on his biscuit; and Jane is busy seeing each colonial and Tudor looking cozy and inviting. Peaked roofs rise behind the blowing flakes; snow nestles on branches of evergreen shrubs; country lampposts wear a cap of glistening white. Her New England Village card line is coming to life, right before her eyes.

"Where to, Jane?" Wes finally asks when he turns onto Brookside Road.

"I'm not sure." She watches out the front window as he slowly drives along the street. "Mom's list didn't specify. She only said Brookside Road." They pass houses set back on lightly wooded yards, one with a garden wishing well. "Oh my gosh!"

"What?" Wes hits the brakes and the mail truck skids to a stop right before the red covered bridge ahead.

The snow is falling the same way Jane remembers, the red wood planks just as vivid beneath the bridge's snowcapped roof. "It's my mother's painting."

twenty

ME AND MY BROTHER USED to come here when we did our paper route." Wes leans on the sill of one of the bridge windows looking out at the brook below. The water babbles along, tumbling around large rocks. "We'd stop and have a snack our mother packed. Maybe toss a stone, or a snowball, down into the water." Something about the crossbeams and exposed timber inside the covered bridge cocoons them. He and Greg told secrets in this very spot decades ago, and that's what it feels like he's doing again today: telling Jane secrets.

Wes looks over toward the far entranceway where he parked his mail truck alongside the road. Snowflakes fall steady just outside the bridge. "We'd race," he says. "After our snack. Sometimes on foot, sometimes on our bikes, to see who could make it across first. I can still hear the sound of our sneakers hitting the planks of the floor."

"That's nice," Jane says beside him while tugging off her mittens. "It's such an old-fashioned memory, especially when you tell it in here. You must miss your mom when you remember those days."

"I've got good memories, though."

After a moment, she pulls her camera from her tapestry

155

tote, steadies her casted arm on the sill and frames pictures of the snowy scene beyond. "My mother did a painting of this bridge, years ago," Jane says as she turns her lens on the view of the rough-hewn interior, dark and shadowy in contrast to the snowy scene outside. "I scanned her painting, and with my editing software, added white twinkling lights on the roofline, and silver jingle bells on a horse and buggy. Now it'll be the lead card in my new Christmas series, thankfully with her blessing."

"So you're *living* the cards you're designing? Is that the plan?"

Jane snaps a few more pictures. "That might have been my mother's intent." She looks over at Wes, her eyes sparkling with that hidden smile as she immerses herself in her work.

Wes turns back to the window ledge, pushing up his fleece jacket sleeve to check his watch, and hoping a supervisor isn't out monitoring the routes today, of all days. A wind gusts through the bridge and the cold goes right through the fabric of his regulation uniform trousers. "I'm sorry about the other day, at the cove," he quietly says. "It was my wedding day, actually." Jane steps beside him so that they're both gazing out the window at the peace beyond. "I wasn't having an easy time with things."

Her hand reaches over and gives his gloved hand a brief squeeze. He doesn't look at her, doesn't say anything. In a minute, he whistles for Comet at the other end of the bridge. The dog hightails it straight to them.

"You ready, Jane?" he asks. "Unfortunately, I'm running a little late. The mail calls."

"Oh, by all means! I'm good." She pulls her mittens on as they walk side by side through the length of the timber bridge. "I saw exactly what I needed to see."

While maneuvering the snowy streets back to her house, Wes listens to Jane talking from her makeshift mail-truck seat. Her voice is like a greeting card itself: soothing, gentle, sharing snippets of stories sounding like the verses she might write. Little phrases tell whole tales about her job and her mother's paintings, and her own lost jingle, all in between his mailbox stops, where he opens and closes the boxes while passing the hushed old homes. Even the dog is eased by her voice, and lies quietly at Jane's feet.

When he pulls the mail truck up to the March house, he turns into the driveway so she won't have far to walk. "You stay," he tells Comet after lifting the rear door to help Jane off.

"Goodbye, Comet," Jane says, standing slightly bent over and patting his head. "We had fun, didn't we?"

"Ready?" Wes takes off his damp gloves and tosses them in the truck before putting his hands around Jane's waist as she steps down. "Careful, now."

He leaves the rear door open, with Comet sitting still as a statue. His father really was right—Wes sees that more and more each day—because the dog won't budge under the *stay* command. He's well trained.

"I'm so glad I thought of you this morning," Jane says as they walk amidst falling snowflakes toward the front porch. "It was beautiful there on the bridge, with the first snow. To think I would've missed it otherwise."

"Anytime. You just put up that flag if you need something."

On the porch, she sets her tote on the antique milk can and digs out her key ring. "Thanks, Wes. I truly appreciate it." Looping her right arm around his shoulder, she leans close with a startling quick kiss on his lips.

When she does, though, it's completely natural the way he

raises his snow-dusted arm and hugs her back. The way his hand reaches around behind her blonde hair as he kisses her a moment longer. It doesn't escape him, the way she steps closer, close enough to lean into the kiss, her face raised to his, the slightest surprised sigh escaping from her.

That's when he raises his other hand so that he's holding her flushed face, kissing her deeper, before forcing himself to back away. But his hands stay there, gently on either side of her face, his thumb brushing away a snowflake as he asks, "You all set?"

She nods, just enough for him to see, those brown eyes of hers sparkling. It makes him feel awkward, or forward now, so he looks down at his watch and steps away. "Okay then, I'll see you around. You take care."

At his truck, he orders Comet to move further in, closes the rear door and gives a half wave to Jane, who is standing with that unpredictable front door held open as she reaches for her tote and waves back.

So now he has that, too. How much can add up in one ordinary Thursday? A wayward Canadian goose *finally* put in its place; mail route folks charmed by his police-academy-dropout dog; and a snow kiss.

Did Jane really mean it? Or was her gentle touch on that farmhouse front porch as fleeting as one of those spinning, melting snowflakes?

twenty-one

DO YOU KNOW HOW LONG it's been since I bought one of these?" Saturday morning, Jane slides several hangers to the left and considers a sweater. It's bright red, with two antlered white deer facing each other nose-to-nose, the entire sweater edged in snowflakes.

Chloe lifts two sweaters from the rack, the hangers clicking together. "Wow, it's really busy here. If you see something you like, grab it."

That deer sweater caught her eye, so Jane *does* grab it while continuing to browse beside her sister. Everywhere around them, wreaths hang; swags of green garland loop; lights sparkle; shiny ornaments and icicles drip from Christmas trees. From where they shop, they can easily see out the store's doorway to the mall's center court. A line of children wraps around the roped-off Santa's Workshop, where Santa Claus sits in a large green velvet chair, a tot in his lap.

"It's so mobbed out there today. Thank goodness Mom's home with Olivia and Josie."

"I know," Chloe says, tucking back a wisp of brown hair. "I can get so much shopping done this way. Mom got them a Christmas jigsaw puzzle, then they're eating in the carriage house. She said it'll be a picnic lunch for the girls."

"Too bad they can't see Santa, though." Jane eyes a blue sweater adorned with a Christmas tree decorated with tinsel pom-poms.

"It's okay, because Santa *will* be at the Fire Department Christmas Party. Santa played by the fire marshal."

"Isn't that Bob?"

"Yes! It's his favorite part of *being* the fire marshal. And it's why I'm glad you're coming with me. He'll be busy with the kids for the whole party."

"Which is at the community center, right?"

"It is. And wait till you see the ugly sweater contest. It's hilarious. Last year, Derek and Vera came with us, and Derek actually won first place," Chloe says, sliding over a few more sweaters. "So he has the honor of giving the trophy to this year's winner. When I think of some of the sweaters there, oy!"

"Can I ask you a question?" Jane holds a candy-cane turtleneck to her shoulders. "Do you think it's okay if I bring, like, a guest maybe?"

"Well, you're coming with me! It's not like you'll be there alone."

"No, I know. But I was thinking …"

"Wait." Chloe hooks a hanger on the rack and waggles a finger at Jane. "Do you have a secret boyfriend I don't know about?"

"Not a boyfriend." Jane holds up another sweater, this one red with a smiling penguin. "Just a friend. Wes."

"You mean Greg."

"No. It's Wesley."

"Are you serious? You're seeing him?"

"No, nothing like that. Well." She gives Chloe a quick smile. "We did kiss. Once."

"*What?*" Chloe drapes her pile of Christmas sweaters over her bent arm. "Wasn't he engaged to someone? Shannon? Sherry?"

Jane nods. "Sheila."

"I thought so. And when did this kiss happen?"

"After he gave me a ride in his mail truck."

"His what?" Chloe swats her with a sweater sleeve. "For real?"

"Long story."

"I'll bet. But Wes? The mailman? What about Greg?" Chloe lifts the sweaters hooked over her arm and hangs some back on the rack. "*Doctor* Gregory Davis?"

"He's really nice, too, but there's no spark there. He's just my doctor." Jane shrugs and holds up an elf sweater. "So, do you think it would be okay? Wes is a friend of Bob's, right? I think he delivers mail to the firehouse."

"He does. And he is, like, the cutest mailman I've ever seen. Who wouldn't want to go out with him?"

"Well, I don't even know if Wes *would* go with me. But he is really nice. That Sheila walked out on a good thing, I'll tell you."

"You *should* invite him. The more the merrier is what I think."

It's funny how, now that Chloe semi-approves, Jane's heart does a little flip-flop.

"I like that other one you picked." Chloe motions to Jane's sweaters. "With the two deer. But you'll have to cut off the arm for your cast, won't you?"

"Yup. Then I can use your snowflake sling, to dress it up."

Chloe brushes through her remaining sweaters and picks one for herself that says *Meowy Christmas* beneath a whimsical cat, before returning the others to the rack. "Here, put your deer sweater with mine. My treat, Jane."

"Listen, now don't go telling Mom about the kiss. With Wes," Jane says as they wait in line to pay. "It all might have been something in the moment, it's hard to tell. I probably misread the whole thing. And I don't need Mom getting any romantic notions for Thanksgiving."

"Too bad I'll be at my in-laws' and miss the turkey dinner at Mom's house." Chloe sets their two sweaters down at the register. "Because *that's* going to be one interesting holiday table."

○○○

Wes drives his mail truck close to the cove water and parks beside his father's. He inches the vehicle forward so the two drivers' windows are perfectly aligned. A motion catches his eye—his father is waving for him to open his window.

"What?" Wes asks, obliging.

"Just saying hello."

"It's awfully cold out. Why don't you eat over here?" Wes points to the back of his truck. "I'm leaving the motor running and cranking the heat. You can sit on the bench where it's warm."

His father holds up a sandwich he's already unwrapped and started eating.

"You sure?" Wes asks through the open windows. He reaches for his duffel and pulls out his own lunch bag. But not before stopping to take a deep breath of the cold November air, all while looking at the blue sky over the cove. White clouds blowing past are reflected in the gray, rippling water.

"I've got the heat cranking, too," his father tells him. "So I'm good here."

"Suit yourself." Wes pulls off his fingerless gloves, opens

162

a bag of chips and unwraps a roast beef grinder, lifting the roll top and checking it out.

"It's there, don't worry." His father is watching him from his truck. "Thought I forgot the horseradish when I packed the lunches, didn't you?"

Wes waves him off and bites into the sandwich. "The meat's nice and rare, just right," he says around a mouthful.

"I added a shake of salt. Roast beef can use it."

"Not too much, I hope. Sodium's not good for your blood pressure, Dad."

"You still on me about that stuff?"

Wes wipes his face with a napkin, then takes a long swig of his water without answering. Instead, he quietly observes his father unwrap a fresh cupcake from a piece of tissue paper. "Did you get me one?" he asks after stuffing the last of his sandwich into his mouth.

Pete tosses him a pastry bag from Snowflakes and Coffee Cakes. "Here, catch."

"Thanks." Wes pulls out a chocolate-frosted cupcake. "But don't go making a habit of this. Extra calories will kill you."

"I thought sodium would. And this is exactly why I got you a dog, so you'd quit worrying about me. Where is Comet anyway?"

"Home. Where he should be. And you're the fourth person to ask me that today. Some even had a biscuit waiting for him. Sheesh, he's charming everybody." Wes eats half the cupcake in one bite. "The only good thing to come out of my breakup, that dog is."

Pete pulls his cell phone from his pocket. "Listen," he says while checking for messages. "Speaking of your cancelled wedding, I'm bringing those two big wedding deer I carved over to the community center next week. They're not doing anyone any good in the shed, and Lil says she can use them at her student art exhibit in December." He scrolls through emails on his phone.

"Those deer are bad juju, Dad."

"No, they're not."

"Yes, they are," Wes insists through his open window. "That wedding was jinxed, and those two deer were supposed to be a part of it."

"Right. *Supposed* to be. But I *carved* that doe and her buck, and they never made it to the wedding, so their good juju is very much intact. You're still seeing things too negative, after practically being left at the altar."

"Negative? You're saying I'm being negative?"

"Maybe. I saw something on the news about how working with your hands can help with depression. You know I've always got an extra whittling knife and wood block for you, even today."

"What, now you think I'm depressed?"

"No. Just not seeing things clearly yet. So don't blame your cancelled wedding on those two deer I carved. Those deer are *love* deer, and Lil will put them to good use."

"Love deer," Wes says under his breath.

"Hey, you got any plans tomorrow?"

"Sunday? No, why?"

"Jane told me to add the snow deer to my website, which I did." Pete waves his phone. "And a couple orders came in that you can help package up for shipping."

"No kidding." Wes crumples his napkin and shoves it in his lunch bag. "Fine, I'll help. And maybe you can let Lil or Jane know I'm not going to make it over there on Thanksgiving. Since you seem to be talking to them all the time now."

"But I told Lillian we'd be there, and I'm not about to go alone. Greg's working."

"I have to get ready for my trip." With that, Wes pulls his airline ticket out of an inner pocket in his duffel and holds it up at the open window. "Got a lot to do before heading west." He studies the ticket itinerary, calculating the weeks left. "Besides, I'm not comfortable sitting at their table. It's too soon, freshly broken up with my fiancée."

"Comfortable?" His father reaches for a partially whittled deer from his truck's mail tray and pulls a two-blade knife from his jacket pocket. He holds the wooden deer over his lap, where a napkin is spread to catch any shavings, and slides the blade along the deer's back. "The Marches are old friends. You kids went to school together. What's to be uncomfortable about?" His knife makes another steady sweep over the deer before he turns in his seat and stares at Wes directly. "Unless there's something you're not telling me."

"Yeah, well." Wes looks down at his airline ticket and runs a finger over the printed details. "Something happened the other day with Jane."

"Are you *blushing*?" his father asks.

"What? No. Jesus. Guess I've got it like an oven in here, it's so hot." He drops the airline ticket back in its secure duffel pocket, then adjusts his heater. Finally, he shuts the truck engine off completely.

All the while, his father turns his attention to the whittling again, fussing with the deer's legs now. "Wait a minute," he suddenly says, spinning in his seat to face Wes in the window beside him. "You *like* her."

"Of course I do." Wes shoves his lunch things in the duffel on the floor. "Everyone likes Jane. She's got that way about her."

Pete resumes whittling the deer, shaving a piece here, rounding a bit of the belly, shaping the antlers. "I know that Sheila's got you on the run; you're just like the whitetail running from danger. You don't want to stick around and be attacked by family questions, or explain things to the Marches over turkey dinner. I get that. So you're trying to run west, across the country." He stops talking while making a delicate V-cut on the wooden deer's face to form its mouth. "But when deer run from danger, they don't go somewhere *new*, Wesley."

Wes zips his jacket against the cold air blowing in through the open window, then looks out the windshield at the crystal cove water. A few Canadian geese paddle there, probably stopping for a rest on their way to some cornfield to scavenge for kernels.

"No, a frightened deer runs down trails that are so well worn and familiar, there'll be *no* surprises in their escape. Staying on *familiar* terrain is how they stay safe." His father looks over at him while closing his window against the wind. "You think about that," he calls out, "before you decide on leaving for California. There's something to be said about sticking close to home, where you know it's safe."

twenty-two

THE COMMUNITY CENTER IS QUIET on a Tuesday afternoon. A group of ladies finished their lunch-hour yoga class in time to return to work or pick up kids from school; Lillian's art class is in full swing; a book club intently dissects the latest bestseller over afternoon coffee and pastry.

So at a long table in the back room, beside large windows where rays of sunshine stream in, Jane carefully dips green paint on her brush and sweeps the color onto cutout pine trees. Once the paint dries, she'll dab pinecones and snow on the boughs. She might even be able to string twinkly lights on the cutouts, too.

For now, varying shades of green give dimension to the flat plywood trees. She moves slowly, and holds an extra brush in her left hand, trying to maintain coordination and strength while the cast is on. The only sound in the cavernous space is the swish of paint bristles on the wooden shapes.

Until a loud rumbling fills the room, the sound echoing off the side walls where folding chairs are stacked.

"Jane!" Pete Davis calls out as he wheels in a bulky item. "Good to see you." He rolls his hand truck to her painting area at the window. "Those for the winter art exhibit?"

167

She nods. "My mom asked me to paint them. What do you think?"

"Very nice, and they'll go perfectly with this." He pulls a packing blanket off the hand truck to reveal a very large carved deer.

"Oh my, that is gorgeous," Jane tells him as he shifts the doe onto the floor.

Pete steps back, keeping a proprietary hand on the wooden statue. "I've got the accompanying buck outside. They're a matched set I actually carved for Wes' wedding."

"You made this? That is so sweet." Jane looks more closely at the doe. The deer's alert ears stand straight, her head tipped up as though she's watching something.

"Took me over a year to complete the pair. They're my love deer, meant for Wesley's boathouse wedding reception. One deer for either end of the head table."

"How wonderful they'll still be put to good use. Perfect for the exhibit, especially on opening night. We can keep it understated, with your deer standing in this pine forest I'm working on."

"You've got that imaginative eye." Pete folds up the packing blanket and tucks it on the cart. When he wheels in the buck, he sets it beside the doe while asking Jane if she had a nice weekend. "Must have a handsome fella you're seeing."

"No," she says simply, awed by the buck, his head turned to the side, full antlers reaching tall. "I'm kind of married to my designing right now."

"I get that. Folks around here call me Mr. Whittle. You know, with the different deer I make. My wife, the boys' mother, she adored deer. Had the sweetest eyes, just like a gentle doe."

"She would've loved seeing these statues, Pete."

Pete wheels the hand truck over to the door, preparing to

leave. "Quick question, Jane. You suggested some marketing tips at the Cornucopia thing at the cove, and I did get sales."

"That's great!"

"I added descriptions to my website, with those keywords you mentioned. But I forgot a few. Would you mind jotting them down? Today's my day off, so I'll add them when I get home."

Jane reaches for her tapestry tote on the table. "It would help if I could *see* your website to customize the phrases. Cobblestone Cards has an online shop that does pretty well selling eCards."

"Everything's on my computer at home, even new pictures I'd like to upload. Just not sure which ones to use."

Pete's enthusiasm for his deer figurines is contagious, so Jane checks the wall clock. "I'm really about done here. Wrapping it up for the day so this paint can dry. Is now a good time to take a look?"

∽○

"I've still got to find something for you to do. The books all say German shepherds like to be busy, and you've been having it too easy lounging in my mail truck." Wes grabbed more paint samples from Cooper Hardware, and now parks his pickup in the driveway at home. He eyes the Victorian, its two tones of gray seriously fading, the burgundy window trim noticeably peeling. And that sunburst gable? Definitely losing its luster. "Don't suppose you can swing a paint brush now, can you?" he asks Comet, who stands on the rear seat behind him.

Once in the house, Wes fills a bowl with fresh water and changes out of his uniform. "Been cold all day," he says to the black dog lying in the hallway chewing a squeak toy. Wes buttons his worn chambray shirt and adds a pullover sweater. "Damn wind blowing in the window at each mailbox."

After putting on jeans and hiking boots, he heads back to the kitchen and thumbs through the mail on the table. Among the envelopes is a wedding card from someone who didn't realize the event had been cancelled. The name is vaguely familiar, an old friend of the family. He reads the card's sentiment about dreams fulfilled and everlasting love, then tosses it aside and shoves up his sweater sleeve to check his watch. "Dad?" he calls out, before heading to the staircase and stopping at the banister. "You up there?"

With no answer, he returns to the kitchen window and notices the light on in the whittling shed. "Let's go," he tells the dog already at his heels. They walk through the yard at dusk, the shadows long, his boots crunching over the lingering first snow from last week.

"It's your turn to make dinner, Dad," he says while opening the creaking shed door, then stopping still. "Oh. Jane."

"Hey, Wes. And Comet!" The dog hurries to her, and she scratches the scruff of his neck before wheeling back her chair at his father's computer. Near and Deer's website is visible on the screen. "Your dad's actually outside. He's taking pictures of a whittled deer in the snow, right next to a black lantern. Thought it would be atmospheric at this time of day."

Wes looks out to the yard, then closes the shed door behind him. "Surprised finding you in here."

Jane spins the chair to the computer again, her hand on the mouse. "I saw Pete at the community center, and he mentioned needing help with his online shop." She switches screens to his product page. "I'm showing him how to write descriptions, crop photos, that sort of thing." She glances over her shoulder at him, but is drawn right back to Near and

Deer. "That's why your dad is staging a photo shoot out in the snow, taking pictures with his phone. So we can add snow deer to his new holiday gift guide." She motions with her good hand. "Look what we've done!"

There's a second when he hesitates. Or maybe he's not hesitating; maybe he's simply noticing her gray-and-pink floral tunic sweater over jeans, waves of blonde hair falling on her back. When she turns again, urging him with a "Come see," he catches a glimpse of pearl stud earrings beneath that hair, then moves closer as she clicks various website pages.

"Here you go," Pete says from behind them, waving his phone as he walks into the shed. "Oh, Wesley. Didn't see you come in."

Wes steps aside as his father shows Jane the images on his phone. Okay, so he steals a look, too. His father took one of his black shed lanterns, the flame glowing, and set it in the snow near an evergreen bush they'd wrapped in white lights. Then he stood a little whittled buck beside it. The lantern light casts sparkles on the white snow, and a sprig of red berries gives a finishing touch.

"Beautiful!" Jane says. "This should go on your home page. Just add some keywords to help your SEO."

"Search Engine Optimization," Pete says while petting the dog sitting at his feet. "Learned that in the class I took."

"That's right! Certain words draw more shoppers. Things like, let's see …"

"Wood carving," Pete says. "Rustic."

"How about … handcrafted," Jane adds.

Wes considers the wintry image again. "Nostalgia?"

And that one word does something. The vibe changes in the room.

"Well," Jane begins as she stands and reaches for her fringed poncho. "You get the idea, Pete. And it is kind of late."

"Do I owe you anything for your time?" Pete asks.

"Gosh no! Just get new orders. You're all set, then?"

Pete sits in the chair Jane left and looks at the screen before turning to her. Then—oh yes—Wes sees it, the way his father's look shifts to him. "I really want to finish this. Wes, can you give Jane a lift home?"

"No, really," Jane insists. "I don't want to inconvenience you. I can call my mom to pick me up."

As she tangles her arm in the sweater poncho, Wes reaches over to help, lifting it gently over her head and dropping it into place on her shoulders. "It's no problem, Jane. I have to get something for dinner anyway." With that, he glares past her at his father.

His father, who just barely glances up from his SEO keywords. "Jane, you let Wes know what time your mother's expecting us for Thanksgiving."

"Dad," Wes begins. About that—"

"Oh, thanks for reminding me. By the way, Jane. Wesley makes a terrific green bean casserole. He'll be glad to bring enough for everyone."

Wes drops his head and lifts his hand to the back of his neck until he hears his father mention something about cutting his hair for the holidays; it's looking unkempt. "Speaking of unkempt, Dad, have you noticed the paint on the front porch?" He takes Jane's arm, shaking his head with a small smile. "Let's go, Jane." At the door, he calls back, "I'll stop and get some takeout, because I don't suppose you'll be cooking dinner when I'm gone."

"Cedar Ridge Tavern is on your way," his father says without looking over, apparently unable to tear himself from his website. "Grab me one of their chicken cutlet burgers, would you?"

twenty-three

WHITE TWINKLY LIGHTS ARE STRUNG tastefully through swags of green garland in Cedar Ridge Tavern's entranceway. Wes holds the door open, and Jane walks in ahead of him before stepping aside so he can talk to the hostess.

"Table for two?" she asks from a wooden podium, pencil in hand to skim the seating chart.

"No." Wes pulls off his beanie. "I just need to place a take-out order," he tells the hostess. "Unless," he says, looking over at Jane. "Well, what do you think? You game for a table for two? Have some dinner?"

"Sure. That sounds good, actually."

Their hostess leads them past the dark walnut bar. Amber pendant lights hang over it, and tabletop Christmas trees sit on either end, also strung with white lights. Assorted red and gold ornaments hang from long ribbons in front of the bar's mirror. Wes runs a hand through his—okay, unkempt—hair as they walk beside a half-wall to a tiny table near a stone fireplace. First he helps Jane lift her poncho over her broken arm, then hangs his own leather bomber on the back of his chair while she picks up her menu.

"Okay! This is so nice," Jane says as she leans forward in her seat, talking above the lively conversation and clinking silverware and glasses in the dimly lit room.

Wes nods, looking first at his menu, then at all the filled tables. "Lots of festive dinners going on." Just the type he'd hoped to avoid is left unsaid. Thankfully, he sees no familiar faces that might bring up his wedding-that-never-was.

Jane shifts in her seat while studying the meal options, and her knees bump Wes' knees beneath the tiny table. "Oh, sorry!"

"Not too much leg room," he says, turning sideways in his chair before opening the menu.

The fire crackles close by, the flames dancing and sparking. "Great fireplace," Jane tells him, nodding toward it. "Makes the room cozy."

He agrees. But at the same time, Wes scans the room for their waitress, because it's obvious by their awkwardness that they need a distraction. See what happens when you get involved? One unexpected kiss on her porch, and now they can't talk.

"So." Jane smiles briefly, closing her menu. "So I guess you're going to California soon, right?"

"Booked a red-eye for Christmas Eve."

"Do you have friends there? Or is it a travel tour?"

"Friend from college." Wes reaches around to his jacket and pulls his cell phone from an inside pocket. "We'll catch up, he might have a job opportunity for me."

"That sounds exciting. You'd make that move?"

"Depends." He turns his phone to her and sets it on the table, shifting closer to talk. "Downloaded a countdown app, checking off the days before the trip."

"How do you like that?" Jane says, taking the phone from his, their fingers touching in the process. "Wait. Is that

Comet's picture in the background?"

"It is. You can add any photo to customize the app, so, you know ... I tried it out." He lifts the phone and hits a few buttons. "A little over five weeks before I take to the sky." As he twists to return the phone to his jacket, he asks, "You ever been out west?"

"Not me. I'm an East Coast girl, through and through." She looks up as the waitress arrives for their orders. After they decide on meals and a glass of wine, Jane leans close again, talking over the other nearby voices. "So, here it is one week before Thanksgiving. You'll be getting busy delivering Christmas cards!"

"No kidding. I could use an assistant this time of year. The driving part is okay, but the walking route slows me down. That mail pouch can get heavy." He sips his water. "By the end of the day, my shoulder feels it, carrying all those cards folks are mailing. There are more and more each day, it's pretty crazy."

"Hmm," Jane says with a downturned expression. "You're sounding like a bah-humbug mailman, delivering holiday cheer with no cheer."

"No, no it's not that." He clears his throat and sips his water again. "I like the holiday and all. People are always glad to see me with their cards, it's really not bad." He presses the back of his hand to his forehead. "It's just that, Jane, well I haven't been out like this for a long time. Feeling a little rusty, sitting with you here."

"Really?" She reaches over and gives his hand a quick squeeze. "How about we take a cue from speed-dating night? Remember?"

And there it is, that smile in her eyes, twinkling like the endless white lights strung around the room. "Okay, I'm game. Ladies first." He motions for her to begin.

She considers him closely, squinting a bit. "Favorite vacation spot?"

"Stony Point, down the shore. Season?"

"Oh, hard to pick … I'd say winter, with lots of snowed-in design time! Funniest experience delivering the mail?"

"Okay, let's see. I guess it involves a temperamental Canadian goose who has a thing for the eagle emblem on the side of the mail truck."

"What on earth?"

"Exactly. That's what I say—and more—whenever he starts chasing the truck. My turn, now. Favorite greeting card theme?"

"Easy peasy. Father's Day. When I'm designing cards inspired by my dad and the wonderful things we did together, the life lessons he taught me, well … it feels like he lives on in the cards, in a way."

"That's nice. You were close." When she tears up and nods, he asks another question. "Hidden hobby?"

"Another easy one. I took ballroom dancing way back in high school. Your brother was my partner in the high school club."

"Greg?"

She nods. "That's why we went to prom together. I like ballroom, but there's not much old-style dancing around these days. How about you?"

His heart drops with her words. It doesn't feel like the right time to talk about secret dance lessons, and a wedding reception that never happened.

"Any hobbies?" she continues.

"Not really," he answers. "Comet keeps me pretty busy these days. That, and getting ready for my trip."

"You mean, you don't whittle?"

He shakes his head. "Whittling's my father's thing, though

he does bug me to be his apprentice. Everything he loves about Addison—the deer, the trees—it all shows in his carvings."

She looks at him for a long second with those brown eyes. Eyes that will not look away from his with her next question. "Think your dad kind of arranged this? Here?" She motions her fingers back and forth between them.

Wes shifts in his chair. "Now that you say it …" He picks up his water and takes a long swallow. In the quiet, Jane glances out into the restaurant, as though wondering what's keeping the waitress with their food. He *could* comment about how busy the place is, and that they must be backlogged in the kitchen—but he doesn't. Instead he clears his throat, and she sets that brown-eyed gaze on him again, her long hair tucked behind an ear, a pearl stud earring shining in the dim light.

"First-snow kiss?" she asks, then pauses. "Real? Or just a moment?"

He looks away with a slight smile he *cannot* hold back. Because, damn, he's wondered the same thing so many times since last Thursday. Might as well add a countdown app to his phone, keeping track of how many times he's thought about that kiss before facing the question, head-on. Right now.

"Well, let's find out," he says while leaning across their tiny table. He takes her face in his hands and gently kisses her, barely touching her lips. Her blonde hair falls over his hands, that lovely pearl earring brushes his fingers, and he wonders how you judge what's real. But he wonders for only a second, in the shadowy room sparkling with holiday lighting, warm with a roaring fire, alive with voices and dining.

Because none of *that* makes the kiss real. It's the feel that does it, behind his closed eyes, of Jane's fingers suddenly skimming his face, brushing over his unshaven cheek and reaching behind his neck, running through his needs-a-cut hair, her touch delicate. It's a touch that has him deepen the kiss, his hands pulling her closer. When he reluctantly pulls away, he has to lean in and steal one more, kissing her lips again lightly, then her cheek, too, all while hearing her whisper his name.

"Real," she says softly, taking his hand on the table between them. "Very real."

twenty-four

BY THE NEXT MORNING, RAIN falls so steady it nearly washes away what's left of the first snow. But it doesn't wash away Wes' memory of dinner with Jane. One drink, one delicious meal, one sweet kiss. It was an evening he never saw coming. Now, he squints through the downpour and slapping windshield wipers, the rainwater swishing off the window in flying droplets.

The thing is, he had love before, and not too long ago, either. Look what it amounted to: a big nothing. He ended up losing his rustic apartment and moving in with his father. Okay, and illicitly babysitting a large canine on the job. Comet leans into the front-seat area and sniffs at his face.

"I don't know," Wes tells the dog. "Maybe we're better off, you and me, just being two strays. Footloose and fancy-free. No ties, no broken hearts." He slows the mail truck when brake lights flicker on the car ahead of him. When they flicker again, that's when he notices the yellow plate warning it's a student driver. "Swell." At the next mailbox, after depositing a bunch of envelopes, Wes reaches into his black duffel and pulls out his airline ticket. He sets it on the mail tray to the left, propped in front of a plastic crate filled sequentially with rubber-banded bundles of mail. Sure, happiness is being sent in some of these envelopes, in early Christmas cards. But maybe for him, happiness will be found in another zip code.

"Step on it," he mutters when the brake lights ahead of him flash repeatedly, blurring beyond the rain and crazy flapping wipers. "Student drivers are the worst," he says to Comet, who proceeds to plant a lick across his face. "Hey! Enough of that, you're going to blow our cover." He swipes his arm across his cheek to dry the dog-kiss. "Bad enough sneaking you in here again. If I get written up because of you, we're both unemployed. So no more small talk. Go lie down."

With that, Wes glances at his airline ticket and turns on the radio. When a woman—probably dressed in tight jeans and scuffed cowboy boots—sings about drop-kicking some dude out of her life like a football through the goalposts, he shuts it off because, really, what's one fireside kiss mean after all?

"Two kisses, actually," he tells the dog, then gives a warning toot as he swerves past the hesitant student driver and leaves him behind in a spray of road water. "Two kisses, too quick," he says to Comet, who has returned to his patrolling position at the edge of the cargo space, leaning into the driver area and watching out the windshield. "I'm on the rebound, don't forget."

But if he *was* rebounding, would his eyes go straight to the March mailbox down the street when he rounds the next curve? And for crying out loud, why does his heart sink at the flag *not* being flipped up? "No messages today, Comet." He finally stops at Jane's mailbox and reaches to the tray for the March mail. One envelope is heavily padded, and the address suggests it's another shipment of those vintage Christmas cards she's been waiting for.

Problem is, if rain could come down in buckets, well, that's exactly what it's doing right now. So if this mailbox leaks at all, those cards will get soaked. But the last thing he wants to do is knock on that darn, testy door. Is to have Jane swing it open, her brown twinkling eyes reminding him of their dinner at a tiny, two-seater table. Because that would mean that his life went and changed, again. Nope. He's headed west, and that's it; no one's stopping him.

When the farmhouse door suddenly opens and Jane comes out on the stoop with an umbrella, he motions for her to wait there. Oh sure, he can put on his big regulation rain hat and look like he's on a safari as he personally delivers her vintage cards, or … or Comet can do it.

"If I *ever* get caught sneaking you to work, I can at least say you're helping. Time for you to earn your keep." Wes pulls an extra grocery store plastic bag from his duffel, one he keeps on hand for lunch things, and shoves the March mail in it, then wraps the plastic tight around it. He slides open the door, twists sideways in his seat and tells Comet, "Out."

The dog bounds out of the truck, stops and turns to him for instruction. Wes leans down and waves the bag of mail in front of him. "Come on," he says, and the dog steps close and takes the wrapped parcel in his jaw. "Run it," Wes orders, pointing to the house.

At the same time, Jane must've figured out what he's doing, and so calls the dog. "Comet! Come here, sweetie!" she says with her good arm outstretched.

The German shepherd takes the walkway in a few long strides, flies up the porch steps and drops the package at her feet. She bends and gives his head a thank-you pat, then picks up the plastic bag. When Wes whistles sharply, the dog runs back to him, gives a good wet shake sending water droplets flying, then leaps into the truck and returns to his designated patrolling spot, squeezing into the open doorway to the cargo area and standing mighty proud. Wes waves to

Jane, nods, puts the truck in gear and moves on to the next mailbox. The dog is awfully still, his wet muzzle beside Wes' face.

Finally, Wes throws Comet a look—and darn if the dog doesn't seem to be patiently waiting for him to talk. "Shoot. I just didn't have the nerve, to see what she'd say to me today. Just couldn't get out there and talk to her, face-to-face."

⌒⌄○

The house is quiet the following day, with her mother at a planning meeting for the student art exhibit. So Jane works away the Thursday morning uninterrupted and finishes up a new card for her New England Village series. This latest design, another of the red covered bridge, needed only a little digital editing. A sprinkling of sparkle added to the snow, a vignette border giving it an old-fashioned feel ... and it's complete. One last scrutiny of her screen brings a smile at the two boys she painted, both pulling a heavy sled out from the covered bridge, a sled stacked high with newspapers to deliver, the boys wearing galoshes and winter caps.

But one thing that hasn't stopped all morning is the itching. After emailing the image to Cobblestone Cards, she grabs a ruler to poke beneath her cast, but stops before inflicting any damage. Then she hurries to the bathroom, switches the hair dryer to a low setting and sends a wind of cool air beneath the itching cast, leaning it on the vanity top as she feels the sweet relief. At the same time, seeing Wes' mailbox sketch on the cast has her think of Comet personally delivering her mail yesterday.

"Oh, shoot! I hope I'm not too late." She runs to the kitchen, makes up a very special bag, folds the top, slaps a sticky bow on it and brings it outside to the mailbox. After a glance down the street for Wes' truck, she flips the red flag up.

∽

"Are you kidding me?" Wes asks. From the mail tray, he lifts a small carton wrapped in white paper and tries to manipulate it into a mailbox. No amount of twisting and finagling gets the oddly shaped, apparent gift from Wisconsin—probably from some aunt or long-lost cousin—to fit. That's when he considers his postal patrol dog that snuck out again at home to come to work. "I think I have one more bag, let me check." He pulls another plastic bag from his duffel, shoves the box in it and tells the dog, "Out."

When Wes turns in his seat, Comet scoots past to the sidewalk, looks back and stops. Wes leans down and gets him to take the plastic bag handles in his teeth. "Careful, you hear me? Now *run it*. Quick, so no one sees you and gets me fired!"

Holding his head up high to keep the bag from dragging on the ground, the dog lopes over the front lawn and up the three stoop stairs, leaving the package right at the door. Afterward, one sharp whistle from Wes gets him hightailing it right back to the truck.

"Comet, I think I've found you a job."

Oh, the possibilities seem endless now, as Wes weighs them all. That is, until he rounds the curve on Old Willow Road and, yup, the first thing he sees several houses down is the March mailbox, with its red flag flipped up. "All right, Jane. What's going on today?" While reaching over to his tray for the bundles of mail at each stop prior, that red flag constantly catches his eye. At last, his truck idles at Jane's blue mailbox. He finds a bowed bag inside it, looks up at the farmhouse, then opens the bag and pulls out a jumbo dog biscuit.

"It's for you," he says as he gives Comet the treat and—yes, he shamelessly does it—rummages through the empty bag for anything else. "You're one lucky dog."

If he's not mistaken, when his eyes steal a glimpse of the house, that swag curtain in the living room window drops ever so slightly as he drives off.

By Friday morning, Jane's completed two more New England Village designs and emailed them off to Cobblestone. Epic card design sessions, holiday menu planning with her mom, and, okay, consideration of one certain kiss over a too-tiny restaurant table—they've all distracted her from the calendar. How can Thanksgiving be less than a week away?

But it's that one particular kiss that has her find any excuse to walk through the living room. Like right now, telling herself to check the front closet for more of her mother's paintings. And getting there via crossing the living room, walking past the window that looks out on the street. Crossing her fingers right before stealing a peek at the mailbox. Well, at its red flag, anyway.

And it works! After grabbing her shiny new key from the hallway table, she walks outside to the curb, drops down the red flag and opens Wes' note, skimming a message about his father needing some help. Apparently the Near and Deer orders don't stop coming in since Pete updated his website, and his deer inventory is very low.

In serious need of a whittling walk to gather raw wood.

Sunday morning trail hike?

Yes or No

Jane pulls a pencil from behind her ear and quickly circles *Yes*. After folding the note, she unfolds it again and adds, *Pick me up at 11?* With a squint down the street at the diminishing mail truck, she puts the note back in the box, feeling that smile still on her face as she flips the red flag up.

twenty-five

THE RED WAGON'S WHEELS MAKE a low rumbling sound as Wes pulls it along the rutted trail. A fresh dusting of snow covers the dirt path, and the ground is frozen beneath his boots.

"You okay walking here?" he asks Jane beside him. She's wearing her black wool poncho with fluffy pom-poms edging the hem.

"Yes, it's really pretty. Look how you can see the ancient stone walls, with all the foliage gone for the winter." She points into the woods where a crumbling rock wall zigzags through the distant trees. "In all my years living in Addison, I've never been to this hidden lake. Addison Cove, and the beach in Stony Point? So many times. But never here."

"I think this trail stops a lot of people from coming; they don't want to maneuver it. Even to get here by car, there's only a one-lane road, on the other side of the lake." When Jane takes in the woodland view as they cross a rickety footbridge over a gurgling stream, Wes imagines a greeting card design is taking shape already.

"Wait here." He lifts a small axe from the wagon. "There's a birch limb my father could use." At the trail's edge, he hacks a fallen branch into shorter pieces and lays them in the wagon.

They continue down the quiet trail then, the air so cold, vapor comes with their breaths. Wes occasionally veers into the woods and adds sticks and branches to his whittling wood stockpile. "Look," he says, beckoning Jane to where he stands, scarcely off-trail. "Deer tracks." Footprints dot the light snow beside him.

"How do you know they're deer?"

"Whitetail. Their hooves make heart-shaped prints."

"Imagine that." Jane turns toward the direction of the deer path.

"They're actually perfect walkers," Wes adds. "Their back hooves land right in the prints of the front. It's all about survival—whether walking a wooded trail or running to escape danger, a deer knows its rear steps will land just as safely as the front."

As they move on, the wagon wheels bump along behind them, and even the birdsong has stopped in the cold. When they get closer to the final bend in the trail, though, Wes' heart beats faster. And seriously? He swipes a gloved hand across his forehead, hoping Jane doesn't notice, but is he *sweating*?

Jane gives him an expectant smile. "Say something?"

Wes shakes his head. "Just cleared my throat."

The trail turns, and he motions for her to go first. It gives him a chance to yank off his beanie and run his hand through his hair before resetting the cap on his head again, all while Jane slows her step, then stops still. He comes up behind her and looks over her shoulder toward a stone bench beside the lake. It's such a small lake, most people call it a pond. A black lantern, its flame flickering, sits on the end of the bench, with a gray-and-white knit blanket folded beside it. When he pulled the blanket from the cedar chest at home, that's when he found the fur muff, perfect for slipping over Jane's hands, cast included. The muff is weighted down on the bench with a basket of pinecones, and a thermos stands beside two coffee mugs.

"After you," he says, his face nearly touching the blonde hair beneath her earmuffs.

"Did you do this?" Jane turns to him, tipping her head.

"Well." He drags a knuckle along his jaw. "Yeah, so we could sit for a while, maybe."

She turns back and starts walking to the bench. "I love sitting by the water! What a treasure this place is."

He waits for her to sit on the edge of the bench, then lifts the soft blanket, opens it and drops it over her lap. "Good? Are you comfortable?"

She only nods, that smile of hers sparkling in her eyes, and so he studies the water for a moment. "Looks like it's starting to freeze over."

"I'll bet folks skate on it all winter."

A half-dozen wood cabins, some A-frames, surround the secluded lake. They're seasonal homes nestled among the trees, little getaways from the hustle and bustle of everyday life. Here, all's quiet except for the whisper of a breeze through the tall pines. Smoke curls out of a few of the chimneys; an old sled leans against the front porch railing of one cabin; a pair of ice skates hangs by its laces on the wooden door of another.

Wes sits beside her and drops his head for a second. "Jane," he finally says, looking at her closely.

She reaches over and straightens the wool scarf he'd wrapped beneath his fleece jacket. "This is such a nice surprise," Jane tells him.

"Oh, wait. Let me pour you a coffee." He unscrews the cap on the thermos he swiped from the whittling shed, fills a mug with steaming coffee and hands it to her. "I already added cream. You take cream, right?"

"Yes."

"Okay, good." After he pours his own mug, he cups it close to his face. When Jane sips hers, he sips from his mug at the same time. "Jane," he begins again. "It's just that there's something I wanted to say. And if this doesn't work out … Well, I can't take any more public humiliation, so I thought I'd ask you here."

She has another sip of her coffee, then sets it on the bench. "Ask me what?"

He's feeling pretty lame—or *afraid*, truth be told—and uses any distraction to delay asking Jane his question. Like when he sets *his* coffee down, too, and lifts the fur muff. "Here, it's cold. Let's get this on you." He holds it up as she slips her mittened hands into each side and snuggles into it. "Better?" he asks, leaning over to see her eyes.

"Yes."

"So, what I'm trying to say," Wes explains, "is that I'd like to see you. To go out with you." Beyond them, the still water is covered with a thin ice, forming like lace on the surface. Across the lake, a man in a red plaid jacket stacks firewood alongside his cabin. "And I wasn't sure if you felt the same. I mean … What I'm wondering is, do you mind if we start seeing each other?"

"Wes."

"I know." He raises his hand to stop her thought. "You think I'm on the rebound after the whole Sheila thing. Believe me, I've heard a *lot* about that. Don't worry. And I *get* it, I do."

"It's common, though. And to be expected."

"But Jane, this isn't a rebound thing." He pauses while watching a mallard duck fly in for a landing on the icy water. "Because honestly? I don't want to lose what's starting with *us*, too."

What happens next surprises Wes. There's a hesitation that

he isn't sure how to read. Jane starts to say something, then stops with a quick breath. The last thing he wants to do is to put her on the spot. Maybe her life is too busy, and she's not interested in a relationship right now. She'd mentioned her job is on the line and that she's working hard to save it. Maybe it's time for her to leave Addison and return to her place in Eastfield; her cast surely won't be on that much longer.

"Wes—"

"No, Jane." He tugs her mittened hand out from the muff and gives it a squeeze. "Just think about it, okay? That's all."

Jane nods, but her eyes say something else. Something that will keep him awake tonight as he struggles to interpret the look, a look that will line-dance in his thoughts tomorrow with any country-western tune he finds on his mail truck radio. Because there's something there, *something* she wanted to say, that he just prevented—out of pure fear. He raises his gloved hand to her neck, leans over and kisses her cheek. It's the only way she can't see his eyes close with defeat, after everything he went and arranged here, hoping she'd be interested in him … Yeah, right.

"Either way," he says when he pulls back and brushes a wisp of hair from her rosy cheek. "It's okay. No pressure."

"Wes, I—" she starts to whisper.

"Just put the red flag up when you decide."

twenty-six

THAT NIGHT, WES REACHES OVER in the dark to be sure the holly sprigs are still tied to his bedpost. When his fingers touch the berries, he sits up in bed, puts on his slippers and runs both hands through his unkempt hair. So maybe he rushed things with Jane. But they had dinner the other night, and that kiss, well, he thought it meant something. He gets out of bed, opens the laptop computer on his old school-days desk and puts on his terry robe. There's a new email waiting, which he scans. His California friend is checking in, wanting to confirm the flight now that the trip is only weeks away.

Wes gets his airline ticket from the dresser top, starts to reply to the email, then deletes his words, logs off and snaps the laptop closed. Something's cooking, or burning. He smells the air and realizes it's woodsmoke, which gets him to the window to see the whittling shed windows all lit up. "Really, Dad?" he mutters. "At this hour?"

When he goes into the kitchen, even Comet is gone. So Wes puts on the flame beneath the kettle and makes a cup of green tea. Before heading out to the shed with it, he lifts his down vest from the hook near the door and puts it on over his robe, then pulls his beanie on, too. Walking across the yard, his slippers slide on the lawn, which is covered by a snowy dew.

"I thought I'd find you here," he says when he walks into the toasty-warm shed. The woodstove is snapping and popping with a good fire, and Comet is stretched out beside it. "Here." He sets the hot tea down on his father's worktable, where Pete is bent over a partially formed wooden stag, his thumb pushing a knife over the deer's flank.

In silence, Pete stops whittling to grab a quick sip of the tea, then gets right back to his knife and deer.

"Wrap it up, Dad. It's late and you've got work tomorrow."

"Can't. Too much to get done. I could seriously use some help, Wes. Because that Jane, she's got a way about her. Everything she touches, sparkles. The orders keep coming." He takes another long sip of his tea while sitting there in his chair. Though he's looking at the deer project in front of him, his words are directed at Wes. "Speaking of which, don't suppose you went on that trail walk alone today, with my thermos and lantern brought along."

Wes looks away, then back at his father. "Come on, hurry up. You need your rest. Work tomorrow."

"I took the day off."

"Again? How much free time do you get?"

"That's what happens after working thirty years for Uncle Sam. It's nice. Could be the same for you, if you don't bail out and head cross-country."

"I'm not getting into this now. It's late and you still need to rest. Get tired and you'll cut your hand. Then what good are you? Drink up, and let's go."

His father sips his hot tea, closing his eyes with the warmth. "I really need an apprentice. You've watched me go at it your whole life."

Wes quietly lifts a carved doe off the shelf, running his hand over the deer's back.

"And you've whittled some yourself, I've seen it," his father adds between tea sips.

"Not in a long time, I haven't. And I don't need to be *exactly* like you." Wes returns the doe to her place beside a wooden fawn. "We live in the same house, have the same job, watch the same TV shows, eat the same food. Isn't that enough? Because if the right opportunity comes along, I just might take it, the way my life's been going."

His father sets the teacup down and hangs his knife with others he's arranged on a pegboard above his worktable. "What I think is that you're getting a little *too* bent out of shape over whittling, son."

When Wes holds the door open, Comet rouses himself from his warm nap and runs out ahead of him. "I'll take care of the stove here, you get going inside. Time to get some sleep, Dad."

⌒◯

Monday morning, Wes finally has a good excuse for not shaving: He's too damn nervous. It's not possible to drag that razor over his skin while thinking of what's about to happen, not without nicking his face. Then he'll have to dab tissue on the nicks to stem the bleeding, and it's all too much.

Because when his mail truck eventually rounds that bend on Old Willow Road and his eyes go where they always do now, he knows just what they'll see. Jane is not the type to keep him waiting, and so that red flag will definitely be flipped up. And he's sure she'll put him out of his nervous misery with a polite no. With a *Thank you, but I'm leaving Addison soon. My career calls.* Whatever.

193

Several blocks into his route, he pulls his sunglasses from his duffel and puts them on, then eyes his sweating palms. Which gets him to turn the heat off, even though the temperature outside is only in the thirties. His wool beanie is next: off, then on again after swiping his now-cooled hand through his needing-a-trim hair. The heat can go back on now, too. Behind him, Comet's paws click on the cargo-area floor as he stands whenever Wes makes a move, then squeezes himself into his small space and sits quietly again, albeit leaning more and more into the front of the truck.

"You want to get me fired? Settle down before someone reports me for sneaking you in here."

When the mail truck idles at a decorated mailbox with a faux turkey tail attached to the back, and the turkey's head—neck wattle included—attached to the top, Comet stands and gives a yip beside him. Wes looks over at his dog on high-goose alert. "It's okay. Just a harmless turkey. Sit now." But when Wes reaches to the mail tray for the banded envelopes to slip into the turkey-box, the elastic band around them breaks and snaps sharply against his fingers. "Shit!" he says, giving his hand a shake right as Comet barks again, protecting him from all sorts of attack. Even rubber-banded ones.

But it's the next curve that has Wes clearing his throat and taking a swig of his bottled water as he drives. It's exactly as he'd imagined: The Marches' red flag stands straight up. But does he really want to know what's inside that mailbox? Because seriously, it's just a matter of weeks before he's boarding a red-eye—Wes heading west—seeing what the Pacific Coast zip code has to offer.

He pulls up to the curb, opens his window and presses the flag down before reaching for the card inside the mailbox. So this is it; the answer is right behind one simple envelope flap. A message from Jane that has been driving him crazy with a shoulder twitch and frog in his throat.

He taps the card on his hand while taking a few deep breaths, until a canine muzzle inches closer. "This one's for me," Wes says.

Finally, he slips the notecard out of the envelope. Jane sketched two clinking mugs on it, the steam rising from them in the shape of a heart. Inside, she wrote one brief line:

Oh Wes, it's simply Yes.

He reads it three times, folds the card and pulls his wallet from his regulation-trouser pocket to tuck it inside before driving away with a … wait. He glances in the rearview mirror. Okay, with a smile. Sort of. Maybe a half smile, but still.

twenty-seven

IT'S BUCKET NIGHT, GUYS." GREG elbows himself through the back door, arms folded around two brown bags emblazoned with red chickens. "Got the super deluxe dinner," he announces while walking into the kitchen.

Wes lifts the lid on a steaming pot on the stove and forks a few simmering green beans.

"Careful," his father warns, standing at his side. "They're hot."

So Wes cups his other hand beneath the forkful and blows gently on them before taking a taste.

All the while, his father watches closely. "Well?"

It's his mother's wise words that come to Wes then, the way she always said not to judge food instantly. Let it stew. So he nods while chewing the beans. "Comme ci, comme ça." He gives his outstretched hand a shake as he declares his judgment.

"It's been ages since I've heard that," Pete remarks.

"Just like Mom used to say, remember?"

"Oh, do I ever. Still miss her."

"Can't believe she's been gone ten years now."

"At least she got to see you in uniform, third-generation

196

with the post office." Pete pats Wes' shoulder. "Made her so proud, and I remember how she felt better that week. Didn't think the cancer was going to come back."

"Yup." What Wes doesn't say is that the post office isn't forever. It was always an interim thing, tiding him over between college and, well, *something* else. Someday. He chews another bean. "Few more minutes. Little too crunchy."

"You two sound like an old married couple." Greg sets the overstuffed bags on the kitchen table. "What's going on here?"

"Making green bean casserole for tomorrow. I'm teaching your brother." Pete lifts the lid and takes a taste for himself with Wes waiting, hands on hips.

"Is that really Mom's old apron you're wearing?" Greg asks. He pulls a large cardboard bucket from a bag.

Wes looks down at the navy polka-dot apron and touches the ruffle around the sweetheart neckline. "Got a problem with it?"

"Not at all. Looks cute."

"Hey. You try standing at a hot stove over boiling pots and see if you don't want to cover your clothes."

"Here." His father nudges him with another dripping forkful. "They're good now."

Wes takes the fork and samples the beans. "Okay, I'll drain them. You get the mushroom soup ready." He turns to Greg, who is setting out another loaded bucket and biting into a fresh-made dinner roll. "Chuck's Chicken takeout?"

Greg clamps the roll in his mouth, slips out of his wool coat and hangs it on the chair back. He nods while reaching for the roll and ripping off a hunk with his teeth. "Absolutely. Who feels like cooking the day before Thanksgiving?"

"Everybody's cooking today," Pete argues as he peels the top off a can of soup. "For the holiday. Hurry up with those beans, Wes."

"If you can believe it, Chuck's is pet friendly, too." Greg pulls a squeaky toy from the bag. "They sell their mascot as pet toys." He tosses a plush chicken to Comet, who catches it midair and brings it near the back door, gnawing on it already.

Wes gives the strainer a shake over the sink and pats the wet beans with a paper towel, then checks a pan on the stovetop. "The onions are nicely caramelized. Don't we mix them with the soup and cheddar now?"

"Pour the beans in this." Pete hands him a white casserole dish. "I'll mix the rest."

"That the best dish we've got?" Wes crouches to a lower cabinet and rattles through the pots and bowls there, finding a gold casserole dish with white flowers imprinted on the side. "Mom always used this one for the holidays. What do you think?"

"You're right," his father says. "She loved Thanksgiving."

"This deluxe chicken is as close to Thanksgiving as I'll get, after being in my scrubs, working tomorrow." Greg pulls two more buckets from the second paper bag, then sets out three plates and silverware. "You guys got it made. Still can't believe you're having turkey dinner at the Marches'."

"Why not?" Wes spoons the beans into the gold dish. "They're old friends."

His father, who had been hovering beside him monitoring the recipe, gets busy stirring the cheesy soup concoction in with the beans, so Wes sits at the table while his brother samples the bucket of corn niblets.

"What's going on with you two, anyway?" Greg asks around the corn. "You and Jane."

When Greg reaches over to straighten a ruffle on Wes' polka-dot apron, Wes swats his hand away. "We're probably going to start seeing each other."

"Are you serious?" Greg lifts the top off the bucket of mashed potatoes.

"Wes, let's go," Pete says. "Time to add those French-fried onions."

"Yeah, we talked about it," Wes tells Greg over his shoulder on the way to the counter. "Why?"

"Do you really think that's a good idea?" Pete asks while sliding over the bean dish.

Wes looks at him. "Why wouldn't it be?"

"I'm not sure you're thinking straight, after being left at the altar."

"It wasn't at the *altar*," Wes shoots back.

"Guess not. More like you got left homeless, at the curb," his father says. "*My* curb."

"And we don't need any more hearts broken," Greg says around a mouthful of potato, right as a shrill squeak sounds from Comet's toy.

"Hearts?" Wes turns to face him. "Jane's?"

"I *like* Jane." Pete reaches over to give the beans another stir. "And I'd hate to see her end up in your trail of destruction, after Sheila dumped you."

"What? What are you *talking* about? We'll go on a few dates maybe, no big deal."

"You're on the rebound, son. That's why I got you the dog, so you wouldn't be lonely and jump right back into something you might regret."

"And I thought you were going out west," Greg adds as Comet walks over and drops the plush chicken toy in his lap. "Why get involved?"

"That's just for a week," Wes tells him while sprinkling the French-fried onions on the beans. "So I don't have to listen to Aunt Connie and the gang grill me about Sheila every chance they get. It doesn't mean I can't date Jane."

"Shit, you get all the action. First you're getting married. Then you're *not* getting married. So you're on the market for, like, *one day*, and then you're taken. By a stunner, I might add."

"Ah, quit complaining, Scrubs. You get around."

In the quiet that follows—while Wes sets the pans in soapy dishwater; while Greg starts doling out potatoes and corn on the plates at the table; while Comet chomps into his toy bird, eliciting a squeal; while his father covers the casserole that they'll reheat tomorrow at the March house—it happens. Wes realizes why his mother loved being in the kitchen: It's the one room where worries are always set aside, at least for a while.

"Let's eat," Greg says, pulling his chair in close.

Wes lifts off his apron and hangs it on a wall hook. "See?" he asks his brother, motioning to his clean thermal-weave shirt and black jeans. "Not a speck on me."

Greg just shakes his head with a grin and pushes the bucket of chicken Wes' way.

⁂

On Thanksgiving morning, Jane maneuvers into a pair of black leggings and a tank top, then adds a black velvet tunic edged with gold studs, the bell sleeves accommodating her broken wrist for one more day. "Hurray!" she whispers, patting that cast on her arm. "Off you go tomorrow." But in the meantime, she adds her sister's snowflake sling to be festive.

"I like that the house is busy this year," Lillian says when Jane finds her at the dining room table. They collected pinecones from the yard to add to a collection of fat white candles for a centerpiece, around which they're arranging mismatched, antique china dishes. "And look! It's snowing!" She hitches her head to the big paned windows.

"So pretty." Jane walks around the black-painted table. She

pulls out each ladder-back chair to show the checked cushions, then arranges the silverware settings. "Hard to believe Dad was still alive last Thanksgiving."

"I know, dear. It was so sudden, the way he passed. But I feel at peace with it now, after all these months." Lillian opens the painted sideboard and gets out a serving platter and napkins embroidered with glittery oak leaves. "I *do* feel bad for Wesley, with everything that happened with that Sheila. It's hard to lose someone, no matter how it happens."

"I actually wanted to talk to you about that, Mom, before he gets here." Jane takes a leaf-napkin and lays it across a dinner plate. "Because, well ... I'm kind of seeing Wes."

Her mother looks up, platter held aloft, a strand of her silver hair falling loose from its chignon. "You mean Greg."

"No, Mom. Wesley."

"Wes? When did this happen? Wait, is that what all the birdseed and dog biscuits are about?"

Since being home, one thing Jane knows is this: Timing is everything. Like the first time she put up the red flag on the mailbox, all those weeks ago? It was pure cosmic timing that had her bump into Wes. And now? Timing again as the doorbell rings before she has to explain anything more.

"I'll get it," Lillian says, hurrying through the kitchen to the front door. "But we're not done!"

"Mom!" Jane calls after her. "Don't you say anything to embarrass me."

Lillian turns and tips her head with a small smile. "Me?"

"I see that twinkle in your eye, Mom. I'm warning you. If you say anything, I'll ... I'll ... Well, I'll go back to my apartment as soon as I get my cast off tomorrow!"

Just as the words come out of her mouth, Lillian opens the dodgy front door, which Jane holds in place so that her mother can take a casserole dish from Wes' arms. Pete follows behind, stamping his boots on the front stoop before coming in. When Wes moves aside in the hallway to let his father by, Jane closes the door behind them and the greetings begin.

"Happy Thanksgiving," she says to Wes as her mother and Pete walk toward the kitchen. "Let me take your coat!"

"Good to be here." When he pulls his arms from his parka sleeves, Jane reaches up to brush a few snowflakes from his shoulder. "Thanks," he says, slipping out of the coat, "and happy Thanksgiving to you. You look nice." He leans in to give her a quick kiss, except when he leans in, she thinks he's handing her the parka—and their hands get tangled, and the kiss does too, landing on her cheekbone.

So Jane steps back, a little flustered and wanting to fix that kiss, except there's that timing thing again. Right on cue, Lillian calls out to them from the kitchen, to come for a Thanksgiving champagne toast.

❧

No one can convince Wes otherwise. The best part of a holiday is sitting around the table after the meal's done. Candlelight flickers in the room, casting a glow on the wood paneling beneath the chair rail. Snow still falls outside the windows. The table's been cleared for coffee and lingering wine; chairs are pushed back; the talk comes easy.

"Easel Escapes is next week," Lillian mentions while refilling their wine glasses.

"That sounds interesting," Wes says. "Going somewhere?"

"They're painting weekends I lead throughout the year. Fall in the Berkshires, summer in Nantucket. Very setting-oriented, so we set our *easels* in scenic locations."

"Your students go with you?" his father asks.

"The trips are open to anyone, actually. Chloe coordinates

202

the excursions through the travel agency. I'm trying to convince Jane to come on this one, to the White Mountains in New Hampshire, since her cast will be off. We'll be taking a lantern-light stroll through a quaint village, and, well, a Christmas-cookie tour, too, through the different inns."

"I don't need convincing, Mom. Chloe's already reserved my spot."

"Terrific!"

And then, a lull. But one of those sweet holiday lulls when wine is sipped, when Pete walks to the window to check the snow, when Jane looks over at Wes, that smile reaching her eyes.

"It's been a wonderful day here," Pete says with a double take at the wall clock, then at his wristwatch. "But I think the time is off on your cuckoo clock."

"That silly thing's been acting wonky lately," Lillian explains.

"I can tinker with it." Pete eyes the ornate brown clock. "Point me to a stepladder."

"There's one in the broom pantry," Jane tells him. "Off the kitchen."

When his father excuses himself to retrieve the ladder, Wes asks Lillian if she has a shovel. "The snow's letting up. I'll clear your walkway outside, work off some of this great dinner."

"You fellas are awfully helpful. If you don't mind, the shovel is right on the back porch. I'll warm the apple pie in the meantime."

❧

As if he minds, as if this hasn't been the most comforting day he's lived in months. Shoveling is the least he can do in return.

It's easy to forget that good days like these happen, especially when someone decides to walk right *out* of those days, the way Sheila did.

Wes isn't sure how much time passes outside in the evening dark, until it happens. Until a motion catches his eye as he lifts another shovelful of snow. It's Jane, standing on the back porch steps wearing her poncho, a thick scarf and a crocheted cap with a pom-pom on the top. She gives a mittened wave.

"Snazzy hat," Wes says, leaning on his shovel.

"I came out to supervise while your dad adjusts the cuckoo clock. That little bird keeps chirping and flying in and out of his house. It's quite a scene in there."

"I'll bet." Wes starts up shoveling again. "Be done in a couple minutes." He slides the shovel beneath the snow and tosses it aside, working his way toward the carriage house when something hits him square in the back. He turns to Jane, whose one good hand joggles a snowball. So he drops the shovel and bends to scoop up his own handful of snow.

"Now you wouldn't throw a snowball at a girl with a broken arm, would you?" Jane asks.

He pats his snowball while slowly walking closer. "Why not?"

"I'm at a disadvantage."

"Didn't feel it a minute ago when you nailed my back."

"That lil' ole fluffball?"

Wes tosses his snowball in one hand, stepping closer and extending his other empty hand. "Give it to me."

Jane backs up, the smile never leaving her face, snowflakes lacing her eyelashes.

"Come on, deliver the goods." Wes stops in his tracks. "It's for the snowman."

"The what?" she asks, tipping her head, her brown eyes twinkling.

"Snowman."

So she gently places her snowball in his hand, and the building begins. By the time he's rolled the third snowball for the snowman's head, he hears Jane say something from where she's been leaning against a tree, watching.

"Huh. I believe this is number six."

"Six?" Wes asks as he finds a long twig, snaps it in half and pokes one on either side of the snowman for arms.

"On the list. My *I Insist List*. Wow, I can't remember the last time I made a snowman."

"*You* made a snowman?"

"It did start with *my* snowball."

Wes walks over to her now. "Cold?" he asks. When she nods, he takes her loose scarf and wraps it snug around her neck, touches strands of her hair, then pulls her close by the scarf ends. With the snowflakes falling lazy around them, he kisses her, right in front of the snowman.

"Want to go inside and warm up?" Jane hitches her crochet-cap-covered head toward the carriage house, and he motions for her to lead the way.

⌒◯

"My mother spent the last year working with contractors to rebuild this." Jane turns on a lamp just inside and slides the planked barn door closed. "The original carriage house burned down in a terrible fire."

"I remember that," Wes says as he walks into the spacious room. "It was all over the news." He takes in the ceiling beams, and a farm table set before a wall of windows off to the side, and plaid throws draped over the backs of a sofa and chair, and the stone fireplace Jane is headed to.

"I think my mother installed a gas fireplace," she says as

she hits a switch and the fireplace flickers to life, "to convince me to move in here."

"What about your apartment? And your job?"

"It's a short commute to Cobblestone, very doable." As Jane says it, she turns to the fireplace again, rubbing her hands together to warm up. "Come here," she says then, nodding toward a staircase. "I want to show you something."

They walk up the stairs to a cupola loft, stopping in a breathtaking round room of windows. The windowed walls give a panoramic view of the country fields outside. Snow lightens the night landscape, so they can see the bare trees, outlined now in white, and off in the distance, a silver glimmering ribbon of the Connecticut River.

"Look." Wes points toward the river where a seemingly mere shadow glides through an opening in the trees. "Is that a deer?"

Jane steps closer to the window, nodding. "We get deer out there all the time. I love this glass room," she says. "Tonight it's like we're standing in a snow globe."

"You know, Jane," Wes tells her. And like watching a mesmerizing snow globe, that falling snow outside quiets them. "Today took me *totally* by surprise. Actually, the past month has been taking me by surprise. It's not what I thought it would be, with my wedding called off …" He brushes back a wisp of her blonde hair, his fingers tracing along her face. "And with you." He reaches into one of his parka pockets. "So I brought you something."

She smiles in the dark space, the snow falling outside the window behind her. "Let's go downstairs, by the fire."

They settle in front of the stone fireplace, on the sofa. Wes pulls the plaid throw off the back and drapes it over their laps. "I was buying the green beans at the grocery store and saw this, and, well … I thought of you." He hands her a card in an envelope. "Open it."

Jane pulls out a Thanksgiving greeting card showing a pale yellow farmhouse set on a snowy slope. "Down the old country road," she recites before even looking at the verse inside. But she stops when those beautiful brown eyes tear up.

"And through the covered bridge," Wes whispers.

She opens the card then, and reads the entire verse:

> *Down the old country road,*
> *and through the covered bridge.*
>
> *Round a curve and continue on*
> *to the old farmhouse on the ridge.*
>
> *The air is crisp, the day is bright.*
> *Home again and all is right.*
>
> *Happy Thanksgiving*

"It's my card," she says. "I made this last year."

Wes takes it from her and flips it over to the back. Beneath the Cobblestone Cards logo, *Paved with nostalgia*, it says: Designed by Jane March. "I knew it was yours before I even saw your name. I recognized your house, on the front."

"You did? That's amazing. And I'm so glad to know it works."

"Works?"

"Yes. It's the artwork on the front that gets people to pick up a card."

"But the verse," Wes says, "well, I saw myself in it. Your words describe exactly what I see whenever I drive through that bridge onto Old Willow Road, with the mail."

Jane nods. "The picture catches the eye, but the message sells the card. Or so I'm told."

Wes looks at the farmhouse watercolor painting on the card again. "And I don't know how to tell you *this*, Jane, but this whole day has been like a Jane March greeting card, literally." He puts his arm around her and kisses the side of her head.

They sit close, watching the fire, the card still in Wes' other hand. He feels her head lean on his shoulder as the flames crackle before them.

"I'm going to a little Christmas party, Wes." Her voice is soft while they watch the flickering flames, while the snow taps at the windows. "At the community center. It's the fire department's annual shindig, mostly for the kids. Santa will be there, played by my brother-in-law, Bob. There'll be food, a few drinks. Would you come with me?"

He reaches to her face, hooks a finger beneath her chin and kisses her. "Yes, I would." He kisses her again. "Just let me know when. My calendar's open," he says with a slight wink. "But I think I better finish clearing your mother's walk right now. The snow's coming down pretty heavy again."

By the time Jane shuts off the fireplace and they close up, Wes sees that his father beat him to the shoveling. So they wind through falling snowflakes back to the farmhouse, past the dogwood tree where the snowcapped bird feeder hangs; beside the snowman that Wes obliges with his own scarf, wrapping it around the snowman's neck; before moving toward the house where windows are golden with lamplight, and the aroma of sweet apple pie surely awaits.

twenty-eight

THE *TING-A-LING* GETS HER ATTENTION. Jane looks outside from her window seat at Whole Latte Life just as the red-and-green Holly Trolley jingles past the coffee shop. One day after Thanksgiving, and Addison is in full Christmas mode. The pretty little streetcar chugging by is outlined in white twinkling lights; swags of holly crisscross its interior; shoppers fill every seat while it scoots them through the snow-covered town.

That Holly Trolley is so going in her New England Village card line. Jane pulls off her pom-pom cap and moves her left arm up and down. "It feels funny to wear a full sleeve without my cast."

"And isn't it nice to use your good sweaters again!" Lillian reaches over and pats Jane's now-castless arm.

"Gosh, Mom. My arm's finally better ... I'll be going back to my apartment, and to work, in a few days. So why am I feeling sad?"

Lillian sips her mocha latte, then loosens the plaid scarf wrapped around her neck. "I know why *I'm* sad." She points to her brimming mug. "Here today, gone to-mocha. You're *leaving* next Wednesday, and I'll miss you."

"Me, too. Even though I'll still be close by, I don't know. Being only twenty minutes away almost makes it worse. Because I'll be *so* close, but still *not* here."

"I think I'll make a big pot of homemade chicken soup, and freeze some for you to take to your apartment. Comfort food to help you settle in?"

Amidst the happy chatter of Black Friday shoppers—shopping bags at their booted feet, mittens on the tables—Jane lightly touches the cottony faux-snow tucked into the café's framed windowpanes. Outside, colonial lampposts around the town green have wreaths draped over their tops, with red velvet ribbons fluttering in the wintry breeze.

Lillian squeezes Jane's hand, and Jane sees it, the way she's trying to be brave and not hold her daughter back. "Since this is your last weekend home, I guess it's time for me to place that ad in the *Addison Weekly*," her mother says. "I really need a boarder in the carriage house, to help cover the expenses of that big old property." She pulls a piece of paper from her handbag. "Can you give this a last check? It's the ad you wrote for me."

Jane reads the paper and remembers it clearly: her words about stargazing in the country cupola, and making sweet family memories, and having loving chats. "Bliss."

"Pardon me?"

"That's what whoever moves in there will find." She slides the paper back across the table. "Bliss."

"Oh, Jane." Her mother skims the ad. "I do think you're getting your jingle back. This is perfect."

"I *have* been feeling jingly when designing, and I think your *I Insist List* really helps. It gives me this Christmas clarity." Her cell phone rings and she checks the caller ID. "Of all things, it's work, Mom. Cobblestone!" She puts the phone to her ear.

"Jane-o! Rocco here. Just got out of a meeting."

"Uh-oh. On Black Friday?"

"Trying to wrap up end-of-the-year loose ends. One of which is you."

"Me?" she asks cautiously. She looks across the table at her mother and gives her a sad thumbs-down. "But I had my cast removed this morning, and I'll be in the office at Cobblestone full time, next week. I promise, Rocco."

"Hold your horse-drawn carriage and hear me out! Because your latest designs? The cards with ice skaters on the pond, near a cocoa shack? Picturesque New England, especially the ones with deer close by, covered in snow. Haven't seen that old-fashioned charm in years. Say it with me, Jane."

"Say what?"

"The verse, that wonderful verse … May the, well, let me hear your lovely voice recite it!"

Okay, so now she can't fight the smile spreading across her face as she remembers that Christmas card's very special verse:

> *May the enchanted season*
> *of snow deer*
>
> *And the warmth*
> *of cocoa cheer*
>
> *Always be near.*

"We want more, Jane."

"I beg your pardon?" She shrugs at her now-worried mother.

"You've changed. Being home is working its magic on your designs. So here's the deal we ironed out at the meeting.

211

If you can keep the cards coming, then stay *right* where you are—do not budge—until the New Year."

"What?" With tear-filled eyes, she puts the phone on speaker so her mother can hear.

"Listen," Rocco explains. "We have limited office hours until Christmas. Then we're closed for a week at the holidays. You continue working from Addison until the New Year, Jane. And … with a bonus if you can keep these designs coming, and fast! I want them for next year's Christmas line. Can you do that for us?"

Jane holds the phone between herself and her mother. With a nod, they both answer Rocco together. "*Yes!*"

When the waitress later drops off a slice of red velvet cake for Lillian, and a frosted gingerbread cupcake for Jane, Lillian forks hers and clinks it to Jane's. "I am so thrilled to have you home for a few more weeks! Cheers?"

"Oh, Mom. A few weeks?" She lifts her cupcake and winks. "I have an even better idea."

⁓○

The truck tires spin when Wes pulls away from practically every mailbox. Sheesh, a little bit of Thanksgiving snow and everything's out of control. He's lucky he doesn't get in an accident, fishtailing like that. It's bad enough slipping and sliding to each mailbox, but getting around the Black Friday bumper-to-bumper traffic makes it worse.

Then there are the packages piling up, now that the Christmas season is officially here. When they don't fit in the mailbox, his canine assistant personally delivers them to doorsteps.

"Run it!" he orders Comet, pointing to each house's front door. The dog jumps out of the mail truck and bolts up

212

winding walkways, head held high to keep the bagged packages from dragging. One thing Wes notices is that now when Comet drops a parcel on stoops, he often stands there, watching the door and wagging his tail. Just a couple biscuits from random folks and he expects one at practically *every* stop—until Wes gives a sharp whistle and the dog returns to his postal-patrolling position in the back of the truck, keeping a watchful eye out the front windshield. "I saw you waiting for a treat there," Wes tells him at another stop. "Don't you be going diva on me!"

The only thing that salvages the snowy, sliding, bogged-down day is rounding the curve on Old Willow Road and seeing the Marches' red flag flipped up. Jane must've left him a note before her appointment with Greg to have her cast removed. He pulls off his beanie and reads her card right there, idled at her mailbox. Something about tomorrow's fire department holiday party also featuring an ugly sweater contest, so he should be sure to wear his *best* worst!

Ugly sweater contest? Wes shrugs, then rubs his knuckles along his unshaven jaw, wondering about *that* now, until Comet gives a quick bark behind him and plants a lick across his face.

twenty-nine

OKAY, SOMETHING'S UP. WES SUSPECTS it when he gets home from work Monday evening. It's not the aroma of simmering chicken soup that does it; it's something else. He knows for sure when he heads through the kitchen, Comet at his heels, and first notices the Santa Claus place mats on the table, then the soft music coming from wherever his father is. He turns the corner into the dimly lit living room, dim because the only illumination comes from white lights twinkling on a Christmas tree near the stone fireplace.

"You like it?" his father asks, taking a step back from stringing the lights.

"Well, sure." Wes walks closer. A tabletop radio plays Christmas carols, melodies about home, and longings, and peace. "But I thought we weren't doing a tree this year, since I'm going away and you're going to Connie's."

Pete talks while fussing with the branches. "I want you to have Christmas here, *before* you go. And it's too early for a real tree, so I brought this one up from the cellar."

Wes eyes several taped cartons set on the threadbare Oriental rug. He pulls open the flaps on one box. Nestled in the soft artificial garland is a pair of deer, the antlers on the buck swirling elegantly, the doe's expression gentle. His father whittled them years ago, spray-painted them a pale gold and gave them to Wes' mother for Christmas.

"The first pair I made," Pete says quietly. "Love deer."

Wes runs a thumb over the wooden deer, thinking of the full-sized pair his father had progressed to for Wes' wedding. "They sure are, Dad." He sets one on either end of the mantel. "Yup. A doe and her buck."

After tucking the garland around them, Wes sets out a snow village on the built-in bookshelf. "Chicken soup smells good. You made it?" he asks while arranging the little chapel and general store.

"Lil dropped it off Saturday night when you were with Jane at that fire department Christmas shindig."

"Don't remind me."

"Why? What now?"

"Nothing, it was fine." Wes stands two miniature pine trees in the village. "Just something embarrassing happened, with that worn-out cardigan of yours that I wore. The one with the shredded cuffs."

"That's from whittling, where I rest my hands on the table edge."

"I know, but there was this contest … Oh, never mind." He plugs in the lights of the Christmas village. "So Lillian brought the soup?"

"Made a batch for Jane to take back to her apartment, and saved some for us. Helped me pack some orders for Near and Deer, too." Pete carefully hangs old red and gold glass ornaments on the tree.

And while his father reminds him how busy Near and Deer has gotten; while Wes suggests maybe he should retire from the post office and whittle full time; while his father argues that he loves his job; while they hang quilted patchwork stockings and handcrafted ornaments; while Comet noses open the flaps of boxes; while they arrange their collection of vintage black lanterns on the hearth and a model train set beneath the tree, the chicken soup wonderfully simmers. And suddenly, the room transforms into the exact replica of every one of Wes' childhood Christmas memories in it. With all the nostalgia the decorated room evokes, it's like he's watching a home movie.

"I'm glad we did this now, Dad. I'll be so busy these next weeks, first helping Jane move."

"When's she leaving?"

"Wednesday. I took the day off, so don't wait for me at the cove for lunch. Then I'm planning my trip west, researching the job market out there, packing." On his knees, Wes snaps together the last piece of train track beneath the tree. "It should be pretty warm in California," he says after a few minutes.

But when he stands and looks around, all he sees is the fully adorned room, the lighting low, the golds glimmering, the stockings hung by the chimney—and not a sign of his father.

So he walks quietly down the paneled hallway, past the dark banister, toward the kitchen. Up ahead, he can see the paint chips still lining the kitchen chair rail, a dozen house colors propped against the wall. He walks past the coat closet with the loose knob needing fixing. Moving to the side of the hallway gives him a wider view into the kitchen—a view of Comet sitting motionless on the floor, beside his father, who *doesn't* realize Wes is watching him.

Doesn't know that Wes stops in the hallway, silent, while his father stands in front of the wall calendar, first blotting his cheek with the threadbare sleeve of his sweater, then slowly tapping his finger on each calendar square as he counts the days until Wes leaves.

thirty

JANE DID THE MOST SHE could. Wednesday morning, labeled boxes line the back porch after she semi-lifted, mostly slid them out there. Keeping a secret, one she's about to spill, makes the minutes tick by slowly. She grabs her cropped puffy jacket and hurries down the steps when Wes' pickup truck pulls into the driveway.

"Over here," she calls, motioning for him to drive the truck to the back of the house.

Wes is dressed for moving; she can see that when he gets out wearing heavy boots, jeans and a buffalo-plaid flannel shirt. He pulls off his beanie and scrutinizes the boxes while walking over. "Doesn't look too bad," he says, then veers closer to Jane and gives her a quick kiss. "You ready to do this?"

"I really am! I'm anxious to get settled in again."

"Your mom's not here to see you off? I know she's going to miss you."

Hmm, is now the right time? No. Jane squints a little and eyes Wes. "She's at the community center. Lots of last-minute plans for the student art exhibit."

"Oh, that's too bad. Well, at least it's a nice, sunny day for a move," Wes remarks as he bends and picks up a carton.

He has no idea, and Jane can't wait to see that half smile of his when she stops him. As he approaches his pickup carrying the box, she calls out from the porch steps, "Wrong way!"

He stops and looks over his shoulder at her.

"Wrong way," she says again.

"What?"

"You're off by a few feet." She points to the carriage house, its copper weather vane catching her eye.

"Here?" He sets the box down on the leaf-strewn, snow-caked driveway.

She nods, grinning.

"You're moving here?"

And there it is, that half smile that she wishes she had a word for; it reveals more than he realizes on his whiskered face. It's a smile that has been showing itself more and more these past few days, even at the Christmas party—when he was *so* embarrassed to win the ugly sweater trophy.

"What about your job?" he asks.

"It's a twenty-minute commute, no problem. So this is it … Home sweet home."

It has to be the fastest move he's ever completed. Several boxes stacked on his hand truck, then wheeled across the driveway to the carriage house, and by late Wednesday morning, the job is pretty much done.

"I can't believe you're moving here." Wes folds back his flannel shirt cuffs. "What about the furniture in your Eastfield apartment? And dishes, pictures?"

"Mom and I will get the small things, in one trip." Jane

heats hot cocoa on the stovetop in the kitchenette. "We hired a moving company to handle the rest."

Inside the carriage house, sunlight streams in the windows near the farm table, and shines down from the cupola. The walls are painted a soft gold; tall candlesticks stand beside a vase of dried hydrangeas on a console table; a framed Lillian March painting is displayed on an easel in the living room. As Wes finishes unstacking the last of the moving cartons, Jane tells him how Cobblestone suggested she work from home until after the holidays.

"But it was mostly rereading the ad my mom was going to run, hoping for a renter, that convinced me to move in here. Because you know something?" she asks while glancing up at the sunbeams dropping in through the cupola. "I actually got *jealous* imagining someone else living in this beautiful space! And I'm so happy to stay in Addison," she says while digging through a carton on the kitchen countertop, then pulling out a piece of paper and flattening it gently. "Everything I love is here."

It's the way she says it that gets to him. Or more it's the way she stops fussing with the paper and looks at him directly, just before saying those words. It gets him to walk to her as she attaches the newly found paper to the refrigerator with a painted-cow magnet. It gets him to stand behind her and slip his arms around her waist over her soft blue sweater so that she turns within his hold and faces him. He gently moves a strand of her long hair behind an ear, touching her pearl earring as he does, then bends in and kisses her. His hands cradle her face as she leans against the refrigerator. And when he feels how she smiles beneath his kiss right as her fingers hook his belt loops to pull him even closer, well, damn if he doesn't almost choke up.

Because he never once dreamt he'd have a simple kitchen

kiss that means the world. No longer believed that anyone would stick around, for him. When he kisses her two small kisses, then tips his forehead to hers, there it is, that smile in her eyes that says it all. And to think that it took getting nearly *married* to someone else, just to find Jane's smile.

"What do you say?" he whispers after a glance at the *I Insist List* she just clipped to the refrigerator. "Dinner and number four?"

Jane turns to see what number four might be. "The tree lighting on The Green?"

"It's Friday," he answers from behind her. His arms reach around her hips and his head is beside hers, so close her blonde hair touches his cheek as they consider the list together.

"I'm going away for the weekend." Her hands cover his on her waist and she leans back into him. "Easel Escapes, with my mom. Up north, remember?"

"Right." He studies the list over her shoulder. "So let's pick another … Have you ever seen Derek's Deck the Boats Festival?"

"No, but I've heard a lot about it."

"Well, how about dinner and number seven, then? Saturday, of next week."

thirty-one

IT'S NOT THE BUSY DAYS that are weighing on Wes. No, it's something else. Something that has him turn on the radio and find a good, woe-is-me tune, sung by some lonely cowboy keeping the beat with spurred western boots, his deep voice delivering the blues one plaintive note at a time. Because while leaving envelopes brimming with holiday cheer in each and every mailbox, Wes is also wondering about Jane. She's been back from Easel Escapes for two days now, and he hasn't heard a word.

Not that they have many ways of communicating those precious words. So far, it's only through red-flag delivery, via her mailbox. Maybe it's time they exchanged cell phone numbers; even a brief text message would be nice. Then again, maybe not. It would just give him one more thing to fret over, checking for messages.

Instead, after worrying about quiet Jane, and getting in and out of the truck to run packages to doorsteps because now there are too many for Comet to bring up himself, he's had it. It's time for a popcorn break.

"Wes, my man," Derek calls out when Wes' black hiking boots—non-regulation, but comfortable for delivering mail packages—hit the creaky wood floors of Cooper Hardware Store.

Wes throws him a wave and turns to the popcorn machine. As he fills a paper cone with freshly popped-and-buttered kernels, he hears the rest.

"Still basking in the winner's glow?"

Without turning around to face Derek, Wes rolls his eyes and slightly shakes his head. But eagle-eyed Derek must see it.

"What?" Derek asks. "You better have that ugly sweater trophy displayed front and center. Right on that table beneath the photos of three *generations* of Davis postmen your old man likes to show off."

"Listen, Coop," Wes says, turning around with as much of a glare as he can muster over the lingering embarrassment. He tosses a handful of popcorn in his mouth and walks over to Derek at the counter, just as Derek resettles his baseball cap—brim behind—on his head. "So sue me. So I didn't *really get* what an ugly sweater party was."

Derek leans back, arms folded in front of him, head tipped. "We know."

"Shut up," Wes says, brushing off the subject. "Listen, you have any backpacks?"

"Wait. What's going on with you and Jane, anyway?" Derek squints at him now. "You two a *thing*?" he asks, air-quoting the word.

"A what?"

"A thing. You know." He raises an eyebrow, watching Wes.

"No. I mean, well ... We're kind of seeing each other a little." When Derek nods and starts to say something, Wes interrupts. "I'm really behind schedule, Coop. About those backpacks?"

"For what, like hiking?"

"No. Canine backpacks. For Comet."

"In the pet row. Might be a few left, they sell for Christmas. Folks like them for their dogs on trail walks."

"Okay, thanks." Wes turns toward the pet aisle.

"Going hiking somewhere?" Derek calls after him.

Wes turns around, walking slowly backward as he talks. "Nope. My dog's got a job delivering mail with me."

"No kidding."

"Yeah, keep it under your hat," he says, pointing to Derek's baseball cap. "I'm sure it'll get me good and fired. But Comet delivers packages right to front doors."

"How do you like that? The townies must love it."

"Comet's in the truck now. I'll have him deliver your mail tomorrow."

Wes finally settles on a blue—regulation color—backpack. In the rear of the truck, he straps the dog-pack over Comet's back and fills the two pouches with rubber-banded envelopes as they continue their route in the business district. They walk side by side into Wedding Wishes, and the bicycle shop, and the florist, and he's never seen the German shepherd happier, patrolling the town on paw. Maybe it's the friendly head pats he gets, and ear scratches, and even dog biscuits from a few shop owners. But it's clear Comet loves this new work duty when Wes feels a sloppy lick on his hand as they stride along the sidewalk returning to the mail truck.

"That's enough of that," Wes admonishes while shaking off the dog-kiss. He lifts the truck's rear door and Comet jumps in, tail wagging wide as he hurries to his post at the far end of the cargo area, patrolling as they drive.

❧

The thing is, it was all a ruse that nobody saw, all of it: buying the doggie backpack, hanging with Derek for a while, delivering the walking business route mail ahead of schedule.

And saving Old Willow Road for last. It was his way of giving Jane time to maybe, possibly, send a red-flag greeting. But when he and Comet round the bend in the road, her flag is down.

"You know what they say, buddy," Wes grumbles to the dark muzzle inching closer beside him. "Out of sight, out of mind."

So when Comet nudges his arm as though he wants to deliver a package to Jane and say hello, Wes takes the hint. "Okay, okay. But I'm only writing a mailbox message, and you're so *not* delivering it." He pulls a shiny sleigh bell as well as a notepad from his black duffel, and scrawls a line saying that he found the bell at Snowflakes and Coffee Cakes the other day. *Maybe it'll help get your jingle back?* he writes, then gives the bell a chiming shake while looking over at the dog. Once the note's folded, he opens his window, but suddenly unfolds the paper to add one more thing, just to be sure. *P.S. Still on for Saturday dinner and number seven?*

It's the perfect opportunity to jot his cell phone number so she can confirm. But he doesn't. Because the last thing he wants to do is wait for a phone call, too, one that might not ever come. So he simply folds the paper, leaves it in the mailbox along with the silver sleigh bell wrapped in red tissue paper, and drives on, accepting that he won't know her answer until tomorrow.

"Don't stay up too late, dear." Lillian sets a cup of hot chamomile tea on a coaster beside Jane.

"Thanks, Mom." Sketches spill from her worktable, three screens are minimized on the computer that now has Wes' silver sleigh bell sitting beside it, and Jane's never felt more inspired.

"You'll lock up when you head over to the carriage house?"

"Definitely." Jane glances to her mother. She's been so busy designing, it feels like that's all she's had time for: brief glances and short phrases. "You sure you don't mind me finishing this project here, taking over your sunroom?"

"Absolutely."

"Oh, Mom," Jane says, sipping her tea. "I am *so* glad to be living in the carriage house."

"Me, too. And hey, I really like that one," her mother says, looking at a watercolored sketch of a little wooden footbridge running over a snowy stream. At the far end of the footbridge, a jaunty snowman keeps watch, a beanie on its head, a familiar scarf tossed around its neck.

"Recognize it?" Jane asks while adding green shadow to the snowy branches of a fir tree beyond the snowman.

"Not the footbridge, no." Her mother leans closer in her robe, reading glasses perched on the end of her nose. "But I recognize that snowman, especially the scarf. He's the one you and Wesley built?"

Jane nods. "What I discovered at Easel Escapes last weekend, Mom, is that surprisingly, I'm most inspired by *home*. The part of the weekend that gave me the best ideas was when we got off the highway and drove through Addison's nooks and crannies."

"I've always felt the same, Jane. There are endless sights and stories to be captured in a painting ... right *here*." She gives Jane's shoulder a squeeze before heading to bed. "And of course, everything looks different when you're in love."

It takes a minute for her words to sink in. At first, as Jane adds red bows to the footbridge, she thinks her mother was referring to Edward, Jane's father. But as she puts the finishing touches on a pretty doe peering out from beyond a birch tree, she suddenly stops and spins around in her seat. Because now, as she sits swamped amidst Christmas card designs, so much so that she hasn't had a spare minute to write Wes a note, she wonders … No! It can't be. Was she insinuating that Jane and *Wes* are in love?

Just as she's about to call out to her mother climbing the stairs, Jane changes her mind. Because she knows exactly how her mother would answer a question about whose love she's referring to. Yes, she'd answer with that darn twinkle in her eye that says it all … without saying a thing.

Well, Jane's way too busy to think about that now. Yet all this thinking about love has her remember something. She brushes aside her pile of designs to find Wes' latest mailbox note; she cannot keep him waiting and let *another* minute pass without answering it. Opening his paper, she writes across the bottom: *I'll be at your place at five.*

Later, on her way back to the carriage house, she first walks in the silvery light of the moon, down the long driveway to the curb. And she can't help but wonder: Is her mother right? When Jane told Wes last week that everything she loves is in Addison, did she mean him, too? Beneath the endless starlit December sky, she carefully tucks his note inside the mailbox and flips the red flag up.

thirty-two

IN THE KITCHEN, A POT roast simmers in the slow cooker, so Wes swipes the tiled countertop with a damp rag, then dries his hands on the polka-dot apron he wears before hurrying into the dining room where the table is set for two. "Oh, shoot!" In a near panic, he searches for the gold-sleigh centerpiece filled with fresh greens—finally spotting it on the built-in cupboard. After arranging the sleigh on the table between two candlesticks, and giving a quick pressing to a wrinkle in the red-and-green plaid tablecloth, all's good.

Except for the front stoop. He rushes to the door, puts on the porch light and steps outside, checking the street for Jane's car. With minutes to spare, he pulls matches from his apron pocket to light the candles in two black colonial-style lanterns set on the porch for atmosphere, then returns inside.

When Jane rings the doorbell moments later, everything is done. Except, he realizes right while greeting her, the apron—which is still tied around his waist. So what should he do first? Take her hand and lead her in? Give her a kiss, touching that beautiful hair as he does? Ask for her coat and scarf? Or whip off the apron?

Jane breezes in to the old Victorian, sparkling just like the

Christmas lights and bringing a hint of cold air. "Hey, Wes," she says, stepping aside while he closes the front door, apron still on. "Mmh, something smells good!" She slips off her pea coat and red scarf. "I still love that dinner and number seven meant *you* were cooking dinner."

"Jane." He stops in front of her, turns up his hands and clearly looks down at his apron, then smiles and places his hands on either side of her face and *does* kiss her. To hell with the apron. This is better. Then he runs a hand down her left arm, over the soft fabric of her snowflake-print sweater. "You were okay driving? With your arm healing?"

"Definitely. It feels good to be using it again."

Then, nothing. Not that they seem to mind. Quiet seconds tick by before Wes motions for her to follow him to the kitchen. He turns and walks down the dimly lit, paneled hallway, wondering if she sees the old house as neglected and dark, or as authentic and charming. Wonders until she tugs on his hand.

"Wait!" she says, a little breathless.

He stops when she veers off into the living room. In the dusky light, the Christmas tree glows with glimmering ornaments; the burgundy Oriental rug is worn in just the right places of comfort; white twinkly lights frame the outside of the bay window and illuminate the lace panels inside; his father's burnished-gold love deer adorn either end of the mantel.

"What a beautiful room," Jane murmurs. She takes in every detail, including the three framed photographs hanging over an antique console table against the side wall. Which is where she stops, her coat hooked over her arm, her eyes on the portrait images of Wes, his father, and his grandfather— all wearing their mail carrier uniforms. "Well, I'll be." She glances at Wes, then turns back to the table with its poinsettia plant and tall lamp, and his father's photo shrine. "I recognize you, and Pete, but who's this?" she asks, lightly touching the third frame.

Wes moves beside her, studying the faded photograph of a man in uniform standing on a sidewalk, necktie neatly knotted, leather pouch slung over his shoulder. "My grandfather."

"Really! Three generations of mailmen? And look at you!"

"That was when I got my ten-year pin." He touches the photo where he's holding a framed certificate, and points out the pin on his uniform's lapel.

"That is incredible. What a wonderful history you have here."

"I guess it means a lot to my father."

"You must be so proud, following in their footsteps. Literally!" she adds with a wink, then turns and takes in the softly illuminated room. "I could sit here by that tree all night and be happy."

"Well," he answers, reaching behind his back and untying the apron. "Let's eat first, okay?" He leads her to the dining room and pulls out a chair. "Have a seat. I'll pour us a glass of wine."

"What about your father? He's not joining us?"

Wes shakes his head. "He's working up a storm in his whittling shed. Nothing gets him out of there lately. I'll bring him a hot plate of food."

"Really? He won't mind?"

"He's got his TV there and will be plenty content eating dinner in front of it, believe me. Comet's keeping him company, too, along with all his deer."

"Well," Jane begins, tipping her head and squinting slightly. "Let me take out his dish?"

"Seriously?"

She nods. "I want to say hello and see how business is treating him."

"Okay." They walk into the kitchen, where Wes scoops a serving of pot roast onto a plate and covers it with foil. He opens the back door, then stops. "Hang on, you need your coat. It's freezing out." He retrieves her coat from where she left it in the dining room, holds it open for her to slip her arms in the sleeves, hikes it up around her neck, then gives her another quick kiss before she goes.

"I can't get him to warm up to the idea of working with me," Pete says. "Even though he's like a changed man recently." When he uncovers his hot plate, steam rises from the pot roast, potatoes and carrots.

"What do you mean?" Jane sits beside the wood-burning stove, Comet's muzzle on her lap, while Pete sets out his fork and knife. Several deer in various stages of completion cover his worktable—a doe grazing; a buck looking over its shoulder; a fawn curled in tall grass. A few marking pens sit atop loose pieces of sandpaper, and assorted pocketknives hang on the wall pegboard. But it's the floor that gives away how busy Pete is—it's coated with wood shavings. He slides a battery-operated, flickering black lantern closer to his food plate.

"Oh, Wesley tries to hide it, but I see things. Sure, he checks his countdown app all the time, like he wants to escape the clutches of family at the holidays. But the closer that California trip gets, the more he settles in here." Pete aligns a napkin with his plate. "I think he's confused since that girl left him. Doesn't trust his own feelings. Like the other night, he and the dog stayed up till all hours getting the tree decorated, just so."

"That's really sweet."

"It might be because of you."

He holds up his hand before she can argue, so Jane simply shakes her head.

"And he *used* to whittle a bit," Pete continues. "Had a real knack for it, too. But since the whole Sheila fiasco, it scares him, whittling. That wedding was his ticket out of here, at least to explore things, and now he thinks he's actually turning into me, and living the life I've had."

"Doesn't seem like a bad life to me," Jane says as she stands to leave, watching for a moment more.

Sitting across from Wes in the Victorian's dining room, Jane enjoys the pot roast while listening to stories about his mail route, and how families' quirks show themselves in their mailboxes. He thinks the post office could do a psychological profile drawing parallels between mailbox style and family personalities.

"Like, the guy who won the fishing tournament at the cove this summer? Yeah, his mailbox? A largemouth bass."

"Seriously?"

Wes nods. "Or, there's the bird-watcher with a birdhouse mailbox. Things like that. You can tell who's who by the box they choose."

Later, when they drive to Addison Cove for Deck the Boats, they pass Cooper Hardware with its white lights strung across the Christmas tree lot.

"Oh!" Jane says, seeing the rows of pines and firs and spruces leaning against railings. "There's number nine on my *I Insist List*! I need one of those for the carriage house."

As she looks wistfully at all the possibilities, Wes slows the pickup truck. "Derek's got the best trees around. But he and his family close up early today, to run Deck the Boats." He glances at Jane. "I can bring you another day, get a nice Christmas tree over to your place. You let me know when it's a good time." He's quiet then, driving toward the boat festival, but finally tells her, "Just put the flag up."

                                                  *

At Addison Cove, Wes inches the pickup past parked vehicles and around walking people to find a spot at the far end facing the water. After grabbing two hot coffees from a food tent, they settle comfortably in his truck. An announcement requests that all vehicle headlights be turned off, and the water procession begins in pure darkness, with Derek's boat leading an illuminated flotilla circling the cove. Wes slips out of his down vest and explains Deck the Boats as they watch from the warm truck.

"Back when he lost his daughter—it's been, oh, six years now—I didn't think Derek would pull through. It was awful, Jane. So sad. I talked him through some tough times. His little Abby drowned here right around Christmas, and he does this every December now, in her memory. He believes her spirit is here, and she sees it all."

Jane silently looks out through the windshield at the night view, watching Derek's boat glide across the dark water with a colorful Christmas tree mounted on the bow and swags of tiny white lights draped on the boat's sides. Anyone in town who owns a boat follows behind his, each vessel glowing with lights and trees and inflatable snowmen and Santa Clauses and reindeer, all in honor of Derek's daughter. The lights twinkle twice: once on the boats, and again reflected on the calm night surface of the cove's cold water. Jane's never seen anything so sad, while so beautiful.

When the boat procession comes to an end, they decide to wait out the traffic. Wes turns on the truck so they get heat as the line of cars files to the street, and as the boats linger in their own marine line, waiting to be towed out one at a time.

"Let me call my father, to see if he needs me to pick up anything on the way back. Can you grab my phone from the glove box, Jane?"

She drops the door open and squints through the darkness for his phone, which she hands to him. But something else catches her eye, too.

"What's this?" she asks, pulling out a small, semi-whittled rowboat.

Wes looks up from dialing his phone, then disconnects quickly. "That's nothing." He takes the rowboat from her and turns it over in his hand. "I kill some time every now and then. You know, at lunch I saw a rowboat docked one day here at the cove, and …"

So maybe Pete's wrong. From the looks of things, his son *still* whittles, and just fine, too. Jane shifts in her seat to face Wes, and reaches for the whittled boat. "Let me see, it's so pretty. You really made this?"

Wes nods.

Her fingers alight on the curves and edges of the wooden vessel, down its center, feeling cut marks along its side. "Show me how?"

"To whittle?"

"Yes." Jane considers the little boat, her hand feeling the gouges and imperfections in the unfinished piece of wood. Then she looks up at Wes, who looks away, then back at her. Who pulls his beanie off, tosses it on the dash and runs his hand through his hair.

"When?" he asks.

"Now."

"Here?"

"Teach me something. While we're waiting for the traffic to clear."

He glances in the rearview mirror at the unmoving line of headlights behind them. "There's a knife in the glove box. An old one I snagged from my father. Right there," he says, leaning across and retrieving the pocketknife. "You sure you want to do this?"

"I am."

So Wes switches on the overhead cab lamp, which throws enough illumination to see the rowboat clearly, and Jane leans closer. "Set your arm here, on the armrest, for stability," he tells her.

Jane rests her left arm beside him, holding the wooden boat loosely in her hand.

"Okay," Wes says as he turns back his flannel shirt cuffs, then spreads a rag to catch the wood shavings. In the hush of the enclosed space, he opens the knife. "You're going to use this small blade. It's a nice, simple cutting blade, good for details. Here, let's swap for a second." He gives her the knife and takes the boat. In the dim light, she watches how he runs his fingers over the length of it, feeling the wood. "A few areas can be smoothed out, especially on the bottom, where it has to be flat. Give me your hand."

She places her right hand in his, and he traces her fingers over the bottom of the boat. "Feel that?" he asks, his voice quiet, his hand guiding hers. "You're going to even out that ridge."

She situates the rowboat in her left hand, the knife in her right, then pauses and looks up at Wes in the truck cab.

"Two things," he says. "Don't rush, ever. Not when you're using a knife. And remember, *you* control the blade."

"Okay."

"You're going to do a paring cut. Use your thumb to stabilize the wood, then squeeze the blade toward you, like you're peeling a potato."

Jane touches the blade to the wood and lightly, slowly, pulls it through a thin layer.

"Even lighter," Wes says. "Here, watch." He takes the knife and boat, and positions the blade over the bottom of the rowboat. "Put your hand on top of mine." When she hesitates, he looks up at her so close, hovering over their impromptu project. "Come on," he whispers, hitching his head toward the wooden vessel.

Jane sets her right hand barely on his. As he talks, he begins using the blade, his thumb supporting the side of the rowboat as he pares. "It's detail work," he explains. "Just shaving off the thinnest slices, smoothing out the bottom so there's less sanding afterward, and the boat will sit straight."

His arm leans on the armrest now, the fingers of his left hand folded around the rowboat, his right hand moving slowly over the wood, her hand above his, shadowing the movement. The truck is quiet, the lighting soft, his voice subdued.

"Feel that?" he asks as his hand pulls the blade over a slightly elevated area on the curve of the boat's bow.

Her hand scarcely covers Wes', his skin warm beneath her fingers, and that's when it happens. She feels the carved rowboat as though it's afloat, as though she's lazily rowing on the cove, or on a calm, sparkling sea, maybe—a moment of life Wes' hand captures, beneath hers.

thirty-three

LOOK AT THAT ONE!" CHLOE stops in front of a brick colonial on Tuesday afternoon. With a touch of whimsy, a miniature old-fashioned sled hangs on its dark wooden door. Fresh balsam greens are tied to the sled with a plaid ribbon.

"Hmm. Jingle bell swell?" Jane asks. She snaps a picture for her inspiration file.

"Jingle bell what?"

"You have to rate the door, Chloe! It's Addison's Adorn the Doors competition. The winning door will appear on the December page of Addison's annual calendar? Sold by Vera at Snowflakes and Coffee Cakes?"

"Well in that case, what are my rating choices?"

"They're cocoa-cup ratings." Jane pulls an extra ballot from her puffy-coat pocket and puts it in her sister's mittened hand. "One-cup rating? Needs elf-help."

"No, this door's better than that."

"Two cocoa cups? Pretty as a snowflake."

"Maybe. What's three cups?"

"Jingle bell swell. That's what I gave it. The only cocoa rating left is four cups."

"Which is?"

"Fa la lovely!"

"That's it! The sled makes it so charming!"

They move on to the next houses, marking their cocoa-cup ballots as they go, checking off two cups for this one, four cups for that, Jane taking an occasional picture. There are snow-laced pinecone wreaths, and artificial snowmen with jaunty top hats keeping sentry, and stacks of gold-foil-wrapped gift packages—all in illuminated arched doorways and garland-lined porticos, beneath scrolled pediments as well as at simple painted-wood doors.

"I could use one of these gorgeous doors at my house. Especially for Christmas, with everyone coming over," Chloe says as they walk along Main Street. A cold breeze picks up, bringing a hint of winter with it. "Hey, you should bring Wes."

Jane reaches over and brushes a wisp of hair off her sister's rosy cheek. "He's going to California for the holidays, remember?"

"Still?" Chloe scrutinizes a door wreath made entirely of large jingle bells. "Three cups, jingle bell swell." She jots down her rating. "I thought that West Coast trip was pretty much a rebound thing."

"Apparently not," Jane says, stopping at a door with two birch-log deer standing beside it. "*So* fa la lovely. Four cocoa cups," she checks off.

"Aw, I guess you'll miss him." Chloe adjusts her cable-knit scarf around her neck, beneath her furry parka hood.

"I really will, Chloe. He's actually very sweet."

When they reach the Door Ballot box in front of the historical society, Chloe drops in their ballots. "I'll email you the Christmas menu later. Let me know what dish you want to bring, okay?"

"Sure, no problem. And don't forget to add what Olivia and Josie want from Santa, too." Jane snaps a picture of a pair of white ice skates hung on a burgundy door. She's taken enough photos to inspire an entire front-door greeting card series.

"Speaking of which, I have to pick the girls up from school." Chloe checks her watch and pulls her keys from her purse. "What are you doing the rest of the day?"

"Definitely uploading these beautiful door photos. Then, I'm not sure. I did ask Wes if he wants to do number eight with me tonight."

"What?"

"Number eight, on my Insist List!"

"Oh, *that*. For a second, you were sounding a little risqué!" Chloe throws a wink her way.

"Number *eight*, for your information," Jane says while slapping Chloe's arm, "is riding the Holly Trolley. I thought it would be romantic at nighttime."

"Did he call you to arrange the date?"

"Call? No. It's just that we use the mailbox … So, he'll put the red flag up."

⌒⌒

The trolley's nighttime route is different from the daytime. During the day, it bustles along downtown Addison streets, then through Sycamore Square, giving busy riders a lift to all the quaint shops and boutiques, with a nice stop at Whole Latte Life for a coffee and cocoa break.

But at night, the mood quiets. At night, the trolley moves through Olde Addison, jingling through the covered bridge and along snowy streets lined with the historic homes that make the town so special. There's a slight sway to the ride as the trolley rolls along the wide residential roads. Imposing colonials have a candle in each window; red ribbons flutter from balsam wreaths hung on paneled doors; garland drapes across white picket fences. The trolley, with white lights strung along the length of the red-and-green streetcar, makes its turnaround for the return trip at the cove parking lot. There, Vera's grand Dutch colonial steals the show with its wonderful widow's walk, illuminated with white twinkling lights and a rooftop Christmas tree, too.

The nighttime ride isn't all that's different. Wes feels it. Ever since their Deck the Boats date, with its one-on-one whittling session, something's changed between them. He sits beside Jane on the trolley, looking past her to see Vera's house.

"It's so beautiful," Jane says.

The trolley jingles its bells as it scoots by the Dutch and turns around in the parking lot. When Jane leans into him, Wes loops his arm around her shoulders. The stately homes, softly lit by candles and garland-wrapped lampposts, have a way of time travelling straight back two centuries as they drive along the side street exiting the cove.

"You must be getting ready for your trip," Jane says a block later, giving his arm a squeeze.

He pulls his cell phone from his down vest and scrolls to the California countdown app. "Let's see, today's December fifteenth. So nine days to liftoff."

She reaches over and tilts the phone her way, then gives him a quick smile. And yes, he sees it again, the difference. Sees how when she says he must be excited to go, her smile does not reach her eyes. Not one twinkle.

"What'll you do there? Have any plans?" she asks.

"I'll be staying with a college buddy. He's got his own business, something in real estate, so he'll sneak a little time off. We'll see a few sights, catch up." Wes takes a long breath in the sudden silence between them—wondering what sights can truly be finer than the decorated old New England homes outside the trolley windows. He slips the phone in his vest pocket, wishing now he'd never taken it out. It's warm on the trolley, so he pulls off his black wool beanie and folds that into his pocket, too. As he does, Jane reaches over and tucks down a piece of his wayward hair and whispers that she'll miss him.

"Well," he says, lifting her hand and kissing the back of it. Regretting that he even talked about his trip at all after hearing her sad words. "I'll just have to do more things with you from your list, before I leave."

She looks at him for a long second before snuggling against him in their cozy trolley seat, saying only, "I insist."

thirty-four

THERE'S THIS CONSTANT PUSH-PULL LATELY.
Stay, or go. East, or west. Like now: *Stay*—his father's voice
from the mail truck parked close beside Wes' truck. Or *go*—
the airline ticket laid out flat on the dashboard, held in place
with a clip. Hang around, or hit the road.

With his lunch spread before him on Thursday, all Wes
does is look from the airline ticket's LAX destination to the
cove water in front him.

"Why would I cancel my trip?" he finally asks out his open
window. "I've never been to the West Coast, Dad. And I'd
like to see California."

"But now?"

"Why not now?"

"Doesn't your friend there have family he'll be with on the
holiday?"

"Sure. I'll be checking in to my hotel on Christmas, not
spending it with him. We're meeting up a day or two later."
Wes puts the last of his ham grinder in his mouth. "He'll email
me the when and where," he says around the food.

"Nice." Pete swigs his bottled water. "Christmas in a
hotel."

"No, what's *nice* is Christmas Eve high in the sky, sitting back with a drink in hand. Far, far above any family aggravation."

"What's Jane say about this trip of yours?"

Wes drags a hand along his scruffy jaw before glaring over at his father, waiting for his answer. "Does it matter? I made these plans before I met Jane. And anyway, she understands why I'm going."

"Understands? That's hogwash."

"No, it isn't. She gets it, how I swapped my honeymoon flight for this one. But she did mention she doesn't want to *see* me go."

"Well, I'll *second* that. A lot of people don't want to see you go."

Wes bites into an apple, wiping his chin with the back of his hand. "Like who?"

"Me! For one. And Greg." Pete opens a sealed container of dog kibble and scoops some into a plastic bowl. "Comet, too," he says as he hands the bowl to Wes through the open window. "I forgot to give you his lunch before you left this morning. That dog'll miss you."

When Wes sets the bowl on the floor behind his seat, the German shepherd stands to lick it clean. "Yeah, well." Wes eyes the apple before taking another bite. "I see you guys all the time."

"What about Aunt Connie and the gang? And your cousins. You're thinking only of yourself."

Wes drops the apple core in his lunch bag and pulls out a wrapped slice of bread. He puts that bread in his coat pocket before lifting a cup of strawberry yogurt from the bag and holding it up for his father to see. "You pack this in my lunch?"

"It's good for you, and gluten-free, too. Got to stay healthy."

"Eh," Wes says, waving his father off. They're quiet for a minute, and so Wes finishes his yogurt, scraping a plastic spoon along the container bottom. "It's just that I thought I'd be in a different place this year, a newlywed with Sheila. So it's hard to be in those family situations, sitting around the table with everyone prying and being sympathetic and telling me it's for the best. After the holidays, they'll forget about my wedding-that-never-happened and leave me alone." He grabs a leash he keeps on hand, and slides his door open then, strapping on Comet's backpack when the dog jumps out. "Come on, Dad. Don't you need whittling wood? Let's walk over to the trees, maybe there's a branch we can snag. Got your saw?"

Pete takes Comet and holds him close on the leash. "This dog'll get you fired, the way you bring him on the job. Probably never should've gotten him for you."

"Heck, the dog only wants to do what he was trained to do: patrol. You should've thought of *that* before you took him home." Wes pulls on his wool beanie and turns up the collar of his parka, regulation today. The breeze is slight, faintly rippling the water. At the water's edge, he picks up a flat stone from the dirt parking area and skims it.

"Four skips," his father says, coming up beside him. "And look at that." He points to the two mallard ducks paddling toward the center of the cove. "They think you threw food."

So Wes pulls the wrapped bread from his pocket, gives a sharp whistle and tosses bits of it out to the returning ducks. When Comet tugs on his leash at the sight of them, Wes takes the leash from his father. "Let's find some wood. Near and Deer's supply must be depleted, the way you've been holed up in that shed."

His father walks with him toward the woodsy area at the far end of the parking lot. The ancient stone wall bordering it is clearly visible with all the leaves fallen now. Comet slows his pace, then whines sharply, which prompts Wes to stop walking.

"Look how he's always patrolling, Dad. He saw it before we did." Where the crystal-blue cove waters meet the edge of the woods, a lone deer steps out of the shadows to take a long drink.

"It's that same little buck we always see." As his father says it, the deer lifts its antlered head and looks directly at them.

"How can you tell it's the exact same one? You know how many deer live in those woods?"

Pete digs his hands in his coat pockets against a chill wind. "I'm telling you, it's the same one. White-tailed deer have a very small home range. They don't travel far, at all. Typically one square mile is it."

"Seriously? One square mile?"

"That's right. It's been documented that some have actually starved to death rather than venture outside their home range for food. They stick close to home, always, where everything's safe and familiar."

Wes moves a step closer to where the deer stands. Its white tail swishes twice before the buck resumes drinking. Comet stops whining and sits beside Wes, who is holding him close on the leash.

"You're just like the whitetail, Wes." The voice comes from behind, low and serious. When Wes looks over his shoulder, his father meets his eye. "Addison, all this," he says while motioning to the cove, "everything you do ... This is *your* home range."

His father takes the dog and heads to the wooded area then, where he cuts a branch into small pieces and places them in

Comet's backpack. The cove water ripples again beneath the breeze, and the distant trees stand stark against a blue December sky. The view, somehow, has Wes turn and walk backward a few steps, unable to stop himself from taking it in.

Finally he shakes his head with the home-range thought that his father conveniently did *not* finish. Oh, but he can hear the words that were insinuated: *Just like the whitetail, Wes. You'll never leave your home range.*

⌒⌒⌒

It's become routine now: The closer his trip gets, the more often Wes checks his email.

"Whoa, Comet, hang on," he says the next morning as he hefts his work duffel up on his shoulder, prompting the German shepherd to run to the back door. "Let me check before we go."

The dog follows him to his bedroom, where Wes quickly logs on and finds one email waiting, the one from California. The one from his college-friend-turned-realtor. The one with unexpected news, telling Wes how he's also been flipping houses the past year, and can hardly keep up with the business. The one saying he seriously needs a permanent business partner. Seriously.

You're the guy, Wes. It'll be that new beginning you've been wanting. And a booming opportunity. Here's the deal—you'll be my foreman on the job sites, keeping the contractors and renovations on schedule and under budget. Great work, and great money, too. Think about it, and give me an answer when you fly out.

Then comes the kicker.

SNOW DEER AND COCOA CHEER

It's just the thing to get you out of that one-horse town.

One-horse town. His home range. It's all the same ... and all he's been itching to leave behind. That one line stays with him the entire Friday morning, at each bungee-corded, and decorated, and tilted, and painted, and landscaped mailbox he fills with holiday greetings. At the historic sea captain house, where his goose pal awaits until Comet goes into patrol mode and shoos him off with a bark. At the Grinstead mailbox that has a cookie, and a dog biscuit, in it. At Mrs. Crenshaw's mailbox, where she has him double-check for her cable TV bill.

Here he is, the mailman. And his ticket out of this *one-horse town* was delivered virtually. No stamped-and-sealed envelope was left in his mailbox in front of a semi-shabby Victorian edged in curlicue trim.

No, this news is not a message that he can sit with in the recliner in front of the fireplace, near the Christmas tree, and slowly unfold from a California-postmarked envelope, a message he can hold in his hand while looking at the burning Yule log, a cold New England wind rattling the drafty house's windowpanes. Not a message that he can pull from his pocket at, say, a window table at Whole Latte Life and reread over a frothy cappuccino, the town tree twinkling on The Green outside the coffee shop. Not one he can unfold in his mail truck during lunch at the cove, and pass out the window to his father sitting beside him in his own truck, then talk about while walking along the shore and feeding the ducks. Not one he can prop up on the kitchen chair rail beside the dozen paint chips there, and consider from different angles as he walks past it.

And definitely not one he can jot a friendly note about on a piece of paper he keeps on the truck's mail tray, fold in half and leave in Jane's mailbox, flipping the flag up as he does. That's what he thinks when he rounds the bend on Old Willow Road and sees the March mailbox with its red flag flipped prominently straight up. No, he's not about to pull out his cell phone and show Jane the virtual words from California, enticing words that he's been waiting for.

Not about to watch what that one email does to the smile in her eyes.

He parks at the March mailbox for a long second that gets Comet anxious enough to step forward and plant a dog-lick across his cheek.

"Cut that out," Wes tells him as he wipes off his face, then reaches for the note Jane left. "Quiet now while I read this." He opens a card designed special for him, one with a watercolor fir tree on the front, its boughs dusted with snow.

Tomorrow's perfect to shop for a tree!
If you're free, and would care to come with me…

"Wes, Wes," he says to himself, looking at the lovely cursive of the woman who wants to decorate a Christmas tree with him. "How'd you get into this mess?"

thirty-five

ANY NEW ENGLAND VILLAGE HAS one, that endearing Christmas tree lot. Strings of white lights crisscross up above; wreaths hang on wooden racks. Then there are the trees: Fraser firs and balsams and blue spruces lean against railings, waiting to be stood straight up and tamped on the ground, their curved branches falling into place, a few needles dropping. That's the memory people hold dear, that snowy moment when someone puts a mittened finger to a cheek, trying to picture the tree at home with a lifetime of ornaments hung on each soft branch.

Jane decides this image is *so* being added to her New England Village Christmas card line. And the snow swirling down from the evening sky—delicate flakes spinning beneath the white bulbs strung across the tree lot at Cooper Hardware—makes it even better. She walks beside Wes, studying the green branches, the snow-dusted trees, the balsam fir he's lifting and tamping now, right as Derek walks up behind him.

"Wes, my man," Derek says, briefly putting his arm around Wes' shoulder and winking at Jane, too.

"Coop, what's the scoop?" Wes asks, shaking Derek's

hand while still holding the tree upright with his other hand.

"Busy as hell, I'm telling you." Derek hikes up his cargo jacket collar against the falling snow. "Last Saturday before Christmas, so the townies have been shopping all day." He points over to the tree-netting area. "Hot cocoa booth over there, on the house," he says. "Help you stay warm."

"Popcorn, too?" Wes asks.

"For you, my friend? Anything. Fresh-popped in the store," he tells him. "This tree for your place, Wes?"

"No, mine," Jane answers while pulling the fur-edged hood of her jacket over her head. "I actually moved into the carriage house, at my mom's."

"No kidding." Derek shakes the snow off his baseball cap, then resettles it backward on his head as he squints at her through the falling flakes. "Nice," he says. "I'll let Vera know you're sticking around, she'll be thrilled." A family walks past, eyeing the tree Wes still holds. "Got to run, guys. Cars are lined up to load their trees." Derek starts walking away, but turns back quickly. "Hey Wes, you still going to California?" As he says it, he discreetly motions his hand between Jane and Wes. He tries to hide it, but Jane sees the implication, the look questioning why he'd ever leave now.

"In a few more days, yeah. Christmas Eve."

"Too bad," Derek says, pointing to Wes. "You be sure to stop in before you leave. We'll hit up Joel's for a holiday toast."

"Will do." Wes waves him off and turns to Jane again. "We good here? This one work for you?" He gives the small balsam a spin.

If he only knew that any tree would work for her. She just can't say so. Can't say that if Wes, steadying a pretty balsam fir with his wool beanie pulled low, his face scruffy with whiskers, in his corduroys and snow boots and navy puffer coat—half unzipped and showing a plaid flannel shirt beneath—would simply *stay* in Addison for Christmas, she'd be happy with the scrawniest tree on the lot.

∼

"My parents bought these at the old Christmas Barn, way before Vera reopened it." Jane hangs the last of the delicately threaded snowflake ornaments on the edge of a branch. "When my mom was leaving for her student art exhibit tonight, she remembered them in the closet and gave them to me. For my own tree."

Wes steps aside and considers her decorated balsam fir. It's small, and they set it up on a low table in the cupola. Jane hung only those delicate gold snowflakes on the branches he'd first strung with white twinkling lights, then added one ornament from him: the silver sleigh bell he'd given her weeks ago, to help get her jingle back.

"What do you think? Do you like it up here?" Jane asks, her voice soft, her finger giving the sleigh bell a ring-a-ling.

The tree magically sparkles, the gold snowflakes seeming to dance beneath the shine of those tiny lights, just like the snowflakes outside the windows.

"Absolutely." But it's not just the tree Wes likes here; it's himself he's liking here, too. Which is a thought he hadn't considered until lately. Because the idea of standing in a carriage house cupola with beautiful Jane beside him on a dark night, with snow falling outside the walls of paned windows, a sparkling Christmas tree in the center of it all, well, a few months ago this would have seemed like a dream. Or a greeting card scene.

Not like reality, not for Wes, who also has received a job offer too good to pass up—far, far away from this home range.

Jane moves beside him and touches his cheek. "I'm so happy you helped with number nine on my *I Insist List*. But you seem quiet. Everything okay?"

"Well, I was thinking," he begins, glancing at her. "With your tree up and all, I did bring you a Christmas present."

"You didn't!"

He nods. "Just a little something, out in the truck. I'll get it for you."

When he hurries to the driveway without his jacket, the snow is falling, silencing everything beneath it. He grabs the gift bag from his pickup's back seat and turns around, the twinkling Christmas tree in the cupola catching his eye, first. Then a movement below gets his attention. It's Jane, in her black turtleneck sweater, jeans and fur-lined snow boots, standing outside the door with a thick wool scarf draped over her shoulders, watching him. So he walks over and sets her gift bag at the door, then takes her hand and leads her out into the snow, motioning up toward her festively illuminated cupola.

"Oh! It's so beautiful." She turns around, toward the main farmhouse, and that sunroom she's been using as her studio while finishing the New England Village card line. "Now how perfect is this? I can see my tree while I'm designing."

To Wes, the moment becomes almost magical as she looks up at her tree again. The only sound—if it's a sound at all— is the hush of the December night. Jane does a slow, silent twirl beneath the falling snowflakes, smiling, her head tipped toward the sky and its tumbling snow stars, her arms outstretched with one fringed end of the winter scarf in each hand.

It's only when she looks to Wes—the smile glistening in her eyes, her blonde hair glistening beneath snow crystals— that he reaches over and takes one of those outstretched arms, clasping his hand over hers. Then he folds his other arm around behind her and pauses, watching that smile gleam in her brown eyes as she rests her other hand on his shoulder. They stand still like that, pressed close together, wearing no coats out in the snow. He figures he can do one of two things: He can take off his heavy flannel that he wears over a long-sleeved thermal tee and drape it over her shoulders.

Or he can hold her close and dance.

With one adjustment of his stance as he brings his booted feet together, Jane seems to know, her smile growing wider. When he moves his left foot forward, she moves her right foot back. And it's enough. After the briefest of pauses, he moves his right foot to the side before closing both together.

The beauty of it is, she moves in seamless sync with him, and they waltz over the snowy driveway, past the snowcapped shrubs and glowing lamppost behind the yellow farmhouse on Old Willow Road. The illuminated Christmas tree far above glimmers in the carriage house cupola; the outstretched branches of trees in the yard are gloved in sparkling white; the snowflakes dance with them, whirling and fluttering down from the sky.

As the cold snow settles on Jane's scarved shoulders, the dance goes on, Jane close against him the entire time. He can't deny his awareness that each step is part of the waltz he'd secretly learned last summer, with a different woman in his arms. Steps he'd memorized, thinking they'd move along with his bride's, her white gown flowing around their legs. Never thinking that the first time he'd dance them it would be beneath a wintry sky, in the dark of a December night.

Never thinking—not for one second—that the dance would feel as genuine, and as beautiful, as his snow waltz with Jane.

thirty-six

"Y OU TOLD ME YOU COULDN'T dance!" Jane lifts off her damp scarf and drapes it over the coat tree beside the sliding barn door.

"I couldn't. At least not before last summer, when I took a few lessons. You know. For the wedding."

"You are a man of many secrets, Wesley Davis." She takes the gift bag he hands her then. "Come warm up near the fire," she says. "I'll open it there."

"That's okay, Jane. Maybe you want to leave it wrapped beneath your tree, in the cupola. For a decoration."

"Oh, no." She curls onto the sofa in front of the stone fireplace. "I want to open it with you here. Who knows when I'll see you again?"

Though it's not directed at him, he glimpses something. There's a slightest frown that she tries to hold back, even turning away so as not to let on. But sometimes the briefest expressions tell the most, and hers was filled with a sad regret. So he sits beside her on the sofa and leans forward, his arms on his knees, watching the fire dance now.

"I feel bad that I don't have anything for you, though." Jane sits with his wrapped present in her lap, her hands resting on it. "I didn't think we were exchanging gifts."

"I bought this on the spur of the moment." He looks from the gift to her face. "I just thought of you when I saw it."

She turns the small box over in her hands and rips off the wrapping paper. "I'm so excited to see what it is, Wes."

Which makes him feel even worse, somehow. When he saw the gift, it was all he could do to *not* think of her. But now, well, it doesn't even seem adequate.

She lifts the cover off the slim box and brushes aside the tissue paper. "Mittens!"

He nods while still leaning his arms on his knees. She moves closer, sitting up straight and aligning herself precisely beside him, their legs touching as she leans on her knees, too, mittens in hand. And he doesn't look away. But she's so quiet, he fears she won't even get it.

"No one's ever given me mittens before."

Drawing a long breath, he watches her silently. "Your hands, Jane. The thing is, they design these amazing cards, and so you have to take care of them. When I saw the mittens, well, they looked nice, and I thought they'd keep your hands warm, especially the one that just healed. In the winter months."

"I love them," she whispers.

He smiles briefly, and tucks her hair behind an ear, his finger touching a dangling silver earring as he does. It shimmers, and his finger brushes it lightly, moving it in the dim light beside the fireplace. He raises his other hand to her face, too, and kisses her. He doesn't intend it to be more than a kiss, but once he starts, his hands tangle in her hair and pull her closer. And when that smile, the one that usually reaches her eyes, instead fills her kiss, as those hands of hers unbutton his flannel shirt and slip it off his shoulders, what he notices is this: Even while taking one hand at a time off her face to slip his arms out of his shirtsleeves, their kiss doesn't stop.

Not until she whispers his name. Not until she takes his hand and leads him to her bedroom, where they stand and he holds her hips close, tipping his forehead to hers, before his hands lift her black sweater up over her head. When her long hair falls tousled and she returns the favor—lifting off his thermal tee and then placing her hands on his skin, softly stroking his sides, then his back—he can guess.

Yes, he can guess what he really doesn't want to know. Because knowing she loves him changes everything. Knowing might keep him *in* this one-horse town, might have him live the life he's been itching to leave.

No, if she *is* in love with him, it's better not to know, not to let her convince him. Not to let himself trust that he deserves this. So he backs away. But she tips her head and says his name again, her voice as light as the snowflakes swirling outside the window, her touch gentle while they undress in the darkness, then lie on the bed, her designing fingers toying with his hair and her smile toying with his heart. His kisses come slowly, with few words between them. There is merely his touch, her whispers, a down comforter keeping the world at bay on a wintry night. When he moves over her, her fingers draw a soft line from his neck, along his sides and up his back.

"Jane," he says then, the room hushed around them.

"What is it?" Her hand rises to his face, her fingers tracing across his chin, along his throat. Her eyes watch him as her hair fans the pillow, framing her face.

He touches a silky strand of it, then touches her face before kissing her cheek, her shoulder, her neck. "Nothing." He shakes his head. "No, I mean," he says while feeling the length of her body beneath his, feeling the curve of her hips with his hand. "You're so beautiful," he whispers, and that's all he can say. While icy snow crystals tap at the window outside, while only the shimmering glow of the living room fireplace reaches her bedroom, while kissing her deeply, while feeling her touch along his back, his shoulders, he doesn't dare say more, doesn't dare break her heart.

⁓

In front of the fireplace later, Jane walks to him wearing his flannel shirt over her jeans. She gives Wes a cup of hot tea. "This snowy night, tea for two," she murmurs as she sits beside him. "Me and you."

Wes takes the cup and holds it close, watching the fire. "Thanks. This is nice."

After a moment, she reaches over and her finger traces along his jaw, then stops. "Wes." As he sips his tea, she asks, "What's the matter? You really seem a little blue."

"It's nothing. I'm kind of tired, that's all." He glances at her, then back to the fire. "It's been crazy busy at work."

"I'm sure, especially this time of year. But what a great thing to be busy with! My hands might draw the holiday greetings, but *your* hands deliver them." She touches his arm, then cuffs his thermal sleeves the way he likes. "To *everyone*."

He smiles, that's all, just for a second, with a slight nod.

"Something else on your mind?" she asks. "Maybe thinking about your trip?"

There are moments, she can see tonight, when Wes struggles with his thoughts. This is one of them, and he sips his tea before answering.

"Little bit. My friend dropped me a line yesterday with an interesting offer."

"Really."

He nods again. "A job opportunity, actually. Which was kind of a surprise. He's looking for a business partner, and wants me to consider it."

"He's in real estate, right?"

"He is, but he's also been flipping houses in California. You know, buying fixer-uppers and renovating them for resale. Says business is phenomenal, can't keep up with it. So he needs a partner now."

"You?"

"Yeah. And it feels maybe like a chance I've been waiting for. A fresh start."

"But what about your job here? You'd stop being a mailman?"

"I'd have to."

"Oh." Jane turns and looks at the fire when quick, hot tears fill her eyes. "Wow. You'd do that?"

"I'm thinking about it. I want to hear my friend out. See what's involved."

"But the way you spend your days is so nice, being the bearer of good news, working with your dad, and hey, a third-*generation* mailman! And with a canine assistant now, too?"

"Comet? He'll probably get me fired as it is, which will make it easier for me to head out west." He sets his teacup on the table beside the sofa, then looks long at her while brushing the back of his fingers along her cheek. "I really have to get going. My father's so busy, he's been carving in the whittling shed every night until I kick him out."

"You see? Your dad maybe needs you around."

Wes gives her a smile. "He'll be okay, Scrubs is close by. But I did promise to help him pack orders tomorrow." As he stands, he checks his watch.

Jane follows him to the door, where he slips on his jacket. "What about your flannel?" she asks, tugging at the soft shirt collar around her shoulders. "You'll be cold."

"That's all right. You keep it tonight."

She lifts his black beanie from the coat tree and tugs it gently on his head. "I'll miss you when you're gone." She leans into him and gives him a soft kiss, then pulls back, feeling cautious. "Because, Wes?"

Wes touches her face, dropping his fingers to cover her lips while shaking his head. "No. No, Jane."

To his no, she nods back, because she wants him to leave here knowing. "Yes, Wes," she whispers. "Maybe you're not ready to hear it, I don't know. If it's too soon. But it's true."

He closes his eyes for a long second, one when he takes a breath before answering. "Don't tell me any more."

Before she might, he hooks his hand behind her neck and kisses her. It startles her, the way his hands cradle her face then; it seems he doesn't want to let go. And what he does is kiss her so deeply, she's left breathless when he suddenly slides the barn door open and hurries out into the cold night, leaving her only watching, her three words never said.

⌖

Nothing says *Merry Christmas* like red neon bells flashing in a bar window. 'Tis the season, if he only had a reason. Wes pulls off his snowy hat when he walks into Joel's Bar and Grille— walks straight to the bar with its miniature twinkling trees at either end, with its swags of garland strung above it, with rocking Christmas carols playing from the jukebox just past it. With Jane's unsaid words in his thoughts.

Walks straight to the bar to grab a stool and a good, stiff drink. But he's surprised at who's sitting there already, working on a drink of his own.

"Never thought I'd see you here," he says to his brother as he settles on the stool beside Greg. "No date on a Saturday night?"

"Nope." Greg sips some potent concoction.

"Come on, you must have someone waiting on the good doctor's arrival."

"Seriously, bro. I don't. It's another Christmas alone."

"No shit."

"What about you? Where's Jane?"

"Just came from her place." When the bartender approaches, Wes asks his brother, "What's your poison?"

"Whiskey sour."

"I'll have what he's having," he tells the bartender, pointing to Greg. He feels it then, his brother's piercing look, full of questions. But Wes just shoves his cap in his jacket pocket, hangs the jacket on the back of his stool and crosses his arms on the bar.

"Where's your flannel?" Greg asks.

"My what?"

"Your shirt. Your flannel shirt? It's like twenty degrees out, and you're wearing only a thermal?"

Wes fusses with the cuffs of his long-sleeved tee. "Jane's borrowing it, okay?"

"Is that right?" Greg raises an eyebrow at him. "What exactly is going on at the March place?" he finally asks. "You getting her all settled in at that carriage house?"

"Yup. Decorated her tree, gave her a Christmas gift."

"Really, now." Greg spins on his stool to face Wes. "What'd you buy her?"

"Mittens."

"Mittens?"

"Yes. But *nice* ones. Cashmere. Since her hand … Oh, never mind."

"Wait a minute. She's smitten, and you give her mittens?"

"Smitten? I wouldn't say that. It's just a holiday thing. Everyone wants someone around for Christmas." At least he can try to convince himself that's it: Jane's feeling sentimental at the holidays. He thinks of the words he would *not* let her say, even if it meant kissing her to stop them. She'd come so close to talking about love, a subject he doesn't trust anymore, and doesn't know if he ever will. "I guess I'll do for her."

And the thing is? He pretty much believes it. *He'll do.* Tonight was simply that kind of snowy night, one to snuggle up with somebody, some warm body. He's definitely not love material, not with his recent track record. "Anyway, Scrubs. I may not be sticking around Addison too much longer, so why get entangled?"

"What? What are you talking about?"

"Might be leaving this one-horse town." The bartender sets down his drink and Wes takes a long swallow. "*Permanently* leaving."

"You?"

"That's right." He tells his brother about the email offer to partner with his old college buddy. "What a break, man. Shit, I never even saw it coming, a chance to go into business for myself. Suddenly here it is, mine for the taking."

Greg downs the rest of his drink and pushes the empty glass away. "You're such a fool."

"What?"

"A God damn fool, leaving a good thing behind for the holidays, and maybe longer than that."

Wes sips his drink. "Jane."

"That's right. I'm actually jealous of you."

"Of me?"

"Damn straight. Two years running now, the girl of my dreams slipped away, right at Christmastime. Last year, Vera. This year, Jane. She's a wonderful lady, and only has eyes for you, bro."

"But I *have* to go to California. You realize how well I can do with that business? It could be the opportunity of a lifetime."

Greg stands and lifts his wool coat off the back of the stool, slips his arms in the sleeves and slowly buttons it before looking Wes straight on. "The opportunity of a lifetime is right in front of you."

thirty-seven

A MISTY DECEMBER MOON HANGS low in the sky, barely visible behind thinning clouds. Lingering snowflakes fall from those clouds, waltzing to the ground. Fir trees, their boughs heavy with snow, glimmer with colored lights. The night seems to pause right at this moment. Two deer stand side by side at the edge of a thicket, watching a man and woman hold each other close, dancing beneath the snowflakes.

Sunday morning, Jane sits back, brush in hand, and contemplates the painting. There's a wistfulness to the scene. More than likely, it comes from what she's actually seeing in her own life, too: a farewell that she wishes wouldn't happen.

"Mom!" Jane calls over her shoulder. Her mother's been fussing in the other farmhouse rooms, weaving garland on the staircase banister; filling clear jars with strings of shiny beads and tucking white candles in them. "Mom, can you come here?"

"What's the matter?" Lillian asks, hurrying into the sunroom, a Mason jar in one hand, a string of gold beads hanging from the other.

"I just have to ask you something." Jane dabs the tiniest

drop of water on the moonlight to make it even fainter.

"Oh, now *this* is stunning!" her mother says from behind her. "Very evocative. But a little sad?"

So Jane's broken heart *does* show in the painting, now that Wes has a California job offer luring him away. "Do you like it?" Jane asks.

"I do." Lillian puts a bead-draped finger to her face, contemplating the image. "But I'm not sure it's for a Christmas card."

"I'm still working on it, Mom. I'll get it there." With that, she picks up a thin brush and dabs the dark green paint.

"Your Christmas tree looks charming in the cupola, by the way. Did Wesley help put it up?"

Jane nods while painting. "We decorated when you were at your students' art exhibit. How'd it go there?"

"We had a good turnout, for closing night. Even sold a few paintings as Christmas gifts."

"Speaking of Christmas, that's what I want to ask you about."

"What is it, dear?" Lillian sits in the seat beside her and reaches up to tuck a fallen wisp of Jane's hair back into its low twist. "You seem quiet. Is it something with Wes?"

"Yes, actually. Can you call Pete?"

"Pete? Pete Davis?"

"You must have his number, right?"

"I do. I got it back at Coveside Cornucopia, when we made our Thanksgiving plans."

"Good. Because I really need to talk to him and don't want to call his house. You know, with Wes being there. Can you ask him to stop by for a coffee?"

"Today?"

"Yes, today."

"Well, I think he works with Wes on the weekends,

packing up deer orders. Why? What's going on?"

"This." Jane motions to her snow-waltz painting. "I'll explain more later, Mom, when Pete's here. If you can just invite him over, for a little while. Maybe say it's for Christmas … to wish him some Christmas cheer before the holidays." Jane points to the two deer in her painting. "And to thank him for donating those beautiful carved deer to decorate your exhibit this month."

"He calls them his love deer. Imagine? He made them for Wes' wedding."

"I know." She looks at her mother beside her. "So you'll call?"

"Right away."

⁓

Early that afternoon, a door slams outside, and Jane looks out the window from the carriage house. Pete's vehicle is in the driveway. Her mother stands on the back porch, motioning him to come into the house, and Jane gives them a few minutes alone before heading over. She tromps through the fresh-fallen snow and stamps her boots on the porch steps; inside, her mother and Pete are in the kitchen. Coffee aroma fills the air, and her mother is arranging a plate of sliced sandwiches on the wooden table, right beside a flickering pillar candle nestled in an evergreen centerpiece.

"Jane, good to see you," Pete says.

"Same here, Pete." Red-and-green plaid place mats are set out, with a snowman mug at each one. Jane grabs the coffeepot and fills the mugs, steam rising from the fresh-brewed coffee.

"I'm so glad you were able to stop by," Lillian says to Pete, nudging the plate of sandwiches his way.

Jane puts the coffeepot down and sits across from him. "But I'm afraid my mother got you here under false pretenses."

"Is that right?" He lifts half of a ham and cheese sandwich off the platter and sets it on his dish.

"Well, not entirely, dear," her mother tells her. "I *did* want to wish Pete a merry Christmas, especially with everyone going their separate ways for the holiday." She turns to him then. "Hard to believe a month's gone by since Thanksgiving. Coffee cheers?" Lillian asks, raising her snowman cup.

"Absolutely." Pete tips his mug to hers, takes a sip, then bites into his sandwich. "My family will be split up for this holiday, with Wes leaving soon."

"Which is what I wanted to talk to you about." Jane holds her mug close. "I'm going to get right to the point, Pete. I have to ask you something."

"Shoot. What is it?"

"I don't want to impose," she begins, then hesitates. When Pete turns up the cuffs of his cardigan sweater, fine wood shavings cling to the fabric. "I know you're *very* busy, Pete. That Near and Deer is taking all your spare time. But I'm in a bind."

"You? What's wrong?" He clasps her hand briefly across the table. "Though I might have an inkling."

Jane gives him a smile. But there's a sadness there, and the way it rises straight from her heart, it *must* be visible in her smile, too. "And I'm sure your inkling is correct, so you'll understand. I've helped you a bit with your marketing, and this time, I'm afraid I really need *your* help."

"Anything. Anything at all, Jane."

"Oh, I'm so relieved." Jane sips her coffee. "It *is* about Wes leaving."

"We kind of thought Wesley had something to do with

266

this," her mother says.

"I know he recently came out of a difficult situation, with his cancelled wedding and whatnot," Jane explains. "But things have happened between us. And I *think* he thinks so, too."

"I'm happy to confirm that for you," Pete says before finishing off his half-sandwich, then reaching for another from the platter. "He's a changed man since you two started cavorting."

Jane looks long at him. "Honestly?" she asks, feeling tears fill her eyes.

"Let's see how I can explain it." He looks to Lillian, then back to Jane. "Now don't get me wrong, but lately he's even *more* tormented with his life, or should I say, with his impending trip. He's brooding, skulking around at all hours."

"A trip which now includes a solid job offer," Jane whispers, because it's the only way she can talk without crying.

Lillian turns to Jane with concern. "I didn't know this! And a job could make the trip permanent?"

"It *could*," Pete explains. "But I think he's tormented because of you, Jane."

"Tormented because of Jane?" Lillian asks.

"That ticket to California was his ticket to a new life, to lick his wounds after being jilted. Which he took pretty badly. Now the *last* person he trusts, especially with matters of the heart, is himself. So," Pete says, pausing to sip his coffee, "as much as he cares about you, he doubts himself too much to believe you'd feel the same way."

"Me?"

Pete nods. "He just doesn't believe that someone as special as *you* would walk into *his* recently pitiful life, as much as he wants to."

"When is he leaving?" Lillian asks.

"Four days. Right on Christmas Eve," Pete tells her.

"Unless …" Jane says.

"Unless?" Pete sets down his mug and raises an eyebrow.

"That's why Mom invited you here. I have an idea," she explains, "of something I'd like to do. To convince Wes to stay … in Addison. Can you help me put it into action?"

thirty-eight

DON'T LOOK."

After work on Monday, Wes measures a piece of candy-cane wrapping paper over a small box. The kitchen table is covered with gift tags and rolls of giftwrap and a bag of bows. When he reaches beneath the bows for the scissors, Comet's muzzle nudges his arm. "I said, *don't look!*" The dog backs up a step and tips his head, ears standing straight. "Here." Wes bends down and grabs the squeaky chicken toy, then tosses it across the floor. When Comet runs after it, nearly falling over the stuffed bird, Wes asks the dog, "Don't you want to be surprised on Christmas morning?"

To which a chicken squeak comes in reply. So he figures it's safe to open the box and check the new leather collar he bought; it's as close to post-office blue as he could find. "It might help keep us out of trouble," he explains as he wraps it and puts a red bow on top. "If you ever get caught in my truck, at least you'll be wearing a regulation color."

Until now, it hadn't occurred to him that he'd be missing this part of Christmas: the gift exchange. His airline ticket to California is propped on the chair rail beside the half-dozen potential house-color paint chips. He glances at the ticket, then wraps his father's gift: a pair of postal-regulation wet-weather trousers with reflective trim.

"Won't be able to keep an eye on Dad if I take that job in California. Don't need him catching pneumonia, getting soaked and cold in the snowstorms," he tells Comet. It's what he *would* say to his father, if he sat near the tree with him on Christmas morning.

After sticking a bow on the wrapped box, he sets it aside. "You and Scrubs will have to keep him in line," he says when the dog carries the squeak toy back to the table and drops it at his feet. "And check this out." Wes holds up a cookbook filled with wholesome ten-minute meals. "If I move—and I don't know if you'd come with me, sorry—well, Scrubs can't be eating takeout all the time. At least when he comes here for dinner, I make him something good. You know, chicken, stuffed peppers." Wes pages through some of the recipes. "I got him this, too," he adds, showing the dog a pizza roller. "Scrubs loves pizza, but without me around to get some nutritious food in him, the doc has to make his own *healthy* pizza now. We'll wrap it in this." He unrolls a length of wintry woodland wrapping paper covered with a farmhouse scene—smoke curling from the chimney, two deer standing off to the side. "Looks like a Jane March greeting card, no?" he asks the dog when he tapes the giftwrap and puts a blue bow on the top corner.

And that's it. Everything's wrapped and another Christmas is only days away. Comet follows at his heels when he carries the stack of gifts down the hallway. The living room is dark, and he wonders for a second what's keeping his father. But then he gets to it, plugging in the Christmas tree lights and making the room festive one more time before his trip. Once he arranges the presents beneath the tree, he goes to turn on the flameless-candle lanterns nestled in greens, on the hearth.

And that's when he sees something tucked into his stocking beneath the mantel.

Well, now. It has to be from his father, because Greg hasn't been over for days. After pulling the gift out of the stocking, Wes can't stop his hands from peeling back the wrapping paper and turning over the box. From the shape of it, he knows just what's in it, and so he opens the box and lifts out a shiny, folding whittling knife. His eyes drop closed for a moment as he feels the weight of it in his palm. Then he opens the silver blades, touching an edge to his finger.

The top three whittling rules? his father taught him over time. *They're all the same. Be sure your knife is sharp, always!* When he turns the knife over, he notices a small gold strip that bears his engraved initials.

"He wants me to be his apprentice," he says to Comet, who follows him to a club chair and sits at his feet. In the dark room, Wes looks from the knife to the twinkling tree. The house is quiet, the knife weighing in his hand as his thumb glides over it.

The next morning flies by, with Wes busier than ever delivering stacks of holiday cards. There's no time to even look at his watch between the starts and stops at every single mailbox, all while ordering Comet to run gift packages up to decorated Cape Cod doors and wreathed Tudor stoops and swagged colonial porches. When he finally pulls into Addison Cove's parking lot for lunch and doesn't see a mail truck waiting at the water's edge, he instantly worries. His father *always* gets there first, somehow. It's only when he goes to call him on his cell that Wes remembers he took the day off, mentioning overdue Near and Deer orders to package— though Wes swears they'd completed them all.

"It's just you and me, pal," he says to Comet, the dog standing behind him in the cargo area. "Might not be doing this much longer, either." Wes pulls his airline ticket from his duffel and puts it on the dashboard. "Two more days and I'll be flying high. Going to see the Pacific Ocean, I guess." He fills Comet's small plastic bowl with a scoop of kibble he packed into his duffel. "I'll let you know how it is."

And then, nothing, on this last Tuesday before Christmas. Nothing except Wes facing the cove water, an airline ticket in front of him, the mail truck oddly quiet without his father in a truck beside him—opening and closing his window as he thinks of things to say. Wes picks up the ticket and reads the evening departure time, then sets it back on the dash. "Let's take a walk," he says, not really hungry enough to finish his sandwich. "Come on."

In the parking lot, he leashes Comet before they walk along the cove's shore. And all the while, it's there: the weight of the knife he'd dropped in his pocket this morning. "Winter's the best time to find whittling branches," he says to the German shepherd. "With the leaves gone, you can see those branches clearly. And *I'm* sounding exactly like my old man." He leads Comet to the edge of the woods and finds a piece of fallen birch limb that looks about right. Usually he'd ask his father: *Straight enough for you? Dry enough?*

But today he's on his own. After wiping the birch off with a rag, he settles in his truck and pulls out that new, engraved knife, opens a blade and shaves off one strip of bark. It comes off so easily, he removes another, then another, until the bark's all gone. After turning the raw wood in his hand and showing it to Comet behind him, he picks up a pen. The cove water ripples outside the windshield as a cold wind blows, swirling dry leaves over by the distant trees where they always see that familiar buck.

After a minute, Wes rough-sketches on the stripped wood the profile he'll try whittling, then cautiously makes the first rudimentary cuts.

❦

It seemed like a good plan to set his alarm clock an hour early so he could pack more the next day. Until the alarm goes off Wednesday morning and Wes feels the fatigue.

He hadn't counted on staying up until all hours the night before. Hadn't counted on moving to the kitchen table once his father went to bed. Hadn't counted on sitting with his knife and that one piece of birch, carving and shaping and tapering. But the more the deer took shape, the more he whittled. He'd even walked out to the shed in his robe and slippers, just to get sandpaper to smooth a couple rough cuts.

And wouldn't you know it? He ended up toying with some of his father's knives and trying their blades on the leaping stag. The whole time he whittled, he pictured the little buck at the cove—the one his father *insists* is hanging out in his home range, leaping over familiar terrain.

But maybe his father sees things wrong. When Wes packs both their lunches before work, he discreetly drops the wooden deer into his own duffel. Once in his mail truck, he squeezes Comet into the back and props the deer figurine on the mail tray. In his mind, its leaping stance mirrors his own stance—flying right *out* of his home range. Flying far from Addison and family questions at the holiday table, from a post-office career he never intended to be permanent, from memories of a wedding that never happened.

Tomorrow night, he'll *be* that flying stag. But for now, he's got a job to do. After yesterday's overabundant holiday cards, today's deliveries are light—so light that Comet doesn't even need to wear his backpack. It happens every year, this brief lull before the extremely last-minute cards hit right on Christmas Eve.

"Save your strength," he tells the dog. "You'll be running lots of packages tomorrow."

The neighborhoods are quiet now, too, as people simply wait for the arrival of Christmas. So today he has a chance to admire the decorations on homes he'll be leaving behind: two black planters stuffed with birch branches and pinecones sit on the steps of a tiny Cape Cod; small wreaths hang on each of the many paned windows of an imposing stone colonial; swags of snow-dusted garland drape across porch railings.

In the pre-Christmas hush, every now and then he steals a ten-minute break in an office parking lot, and once at the cove. During each break, he whittles a little more, careful to go with the grain as he tapers and rounds the antlers on the leaping deer, its front legs tucked beneath it, mid-jump. While pulling the knife blade through the wood, he listens to the radio for tomorrow's weather, especially for his flight's late-evening departure time.

Finally, Leo Sterling announces his mini-forecast on the half hour. "On Christmas Eve, folks, that reindeer's red nose will be glowing bright … because light snow will be falling all through the night!"

Wes switches off the radio, sets the deer on the mail tray and continues with his route. "You'll have a nice white Christmas," he says to the muzzle inching more and more into the driver area. "With Dad and Greg. It'll be pretty outside. All that snow …"

It's when he rounds the curve on Old Willow Road that a sadness hits and he's not sure why. But there's a sudden hard lump in his throat. It could be that he'll miss his family after all; or that he'll miss seeing that Connecticut white Christmas;

or that further ahead, the red flag is raised on the March mailbox. Because who knows? This might be the very last time that flag is turned up by the beautiful greeting card designer who lives there—flipped up with a special message, just for him.

So does that red flag explain his unexpected blues? Was what he had with Jane merely a blip? A number on her *I Insist List*, as fleeting as that first snow only weeks ago at the covered bridge? Or does she really love him?

He eyes the March mailbox at each stop before it, wondering what Jane's message will be. Never expecting to open her mailbox and find a gift bag tucked inside. Clouds of red and green tissue paper spill from the top as he takes the bag and holds it for a long moment before flipping down the red flag. Comet steps closer, his neck stretched and his muzzle sniffing at the bag as Wes looks inside it.

"This one's for me," he tells his dog while moving the tissue paper aside and pulling out a Christmas sweater, to which he gives a low whistle. It's a navy Fair Isle sweater with a pin-dot pattern, except for the geometric snowflake motif across the shoulders. "Only the best," he says to Comet. "Only the best from Jane." He thinks of the ugly sweater trophy he won a few weeks ago and smiles at the memory. Now he carefully folds his new sweater back into the bag, feeling bad that he's got nothing to give her, even though she liked her mittens. As he sets the gift bag down, though, something catches his eye.

Could he? He reaches for the leaping deer he's been secretly whittling, trying out the new, sharp-blade knife from his father. The stag's not done, and is far from perfect, that's for sure. He turns it over in his fingerless-gloved hands. "Hmm. What do you think, Comet?"

The dog whines and wags his tail, seeming uncertain as

Wes pulls his knife from his pocket. He puts a few panicked finishing touches on the rear extended legs of the leaping stag.

It was just a practice piece, not one intended as a gift. At least not yet. He looks up at the farmhouse, and down at the almost-complete deer in his hands. The wood is rutted in spots and has a few rough edges.

No, the stag is definitely not perfect, and not done. But sometimes … well, the thing is? Perfect or not, it's ready.

With that, Wes wraps the whittled deer in some of the tissue from his gift bag, leans out and opens the March mailbox, sets his leaping stag inside, closes the mailbox and flips the red flag up.

thirty-nine

WHITE-TIPPED PINECONES ARE TUCKED INTO the soft boughs of the balsam wreath hanging on the wooden door. The wreath's plaid bow flutters in a winter breeze. On the wall beside the door, twinkling lights edge a tarnished-gold barn star. Evening shadows grow long, falling on the greens and birch twigs brimming from the antique milk can beside the door. To help light the way home, candles flicker inside mismatched black lanterns lining the side of each step leading to the front porch.

While considering her latest greeting card design, Jane rolls up the cuffs of Wes' flannel shirt that she wears over a green turtleneck sweater. She didn't think it possible, but here it is, early Christmas Eve morning and she's meeting her deadline, sending off the last of her holiday card collection to Cobblestone. This one was painted from memory as she pictured her own farmhouse front door. Beside her, steam rises from a cup of hot cocoa with a mini candy cane hooked over the mug's edge. She takes a long sip, squinting at her scanned door design on the computer screen, then turns in her chair and looks out the windows.

"Home, home," she whispers. "It's got to be about coming

home." Silver glass ornaments hang in the sunroom windowpanes, and outside, snow is lightly falling. Two cardinals perch on the bird feeder that she and her mother have been filling with Wes' black-oil sunflower seeds all season long. But it's those tiny flakes spinning down from the sky that inspire her.

Turning back to her work, she uses the photo editor to add a snow filter to the image. Suddenly her wreathed-and-illuminated Christmas door waits behind a gentle snowfall.

And she promptly adds the perfect verse to the card:

There's snow place like home…
Merry Christmas

Done, and in the nick of time! A couple clicks at the keyboard, and Rocco will receive not only his snowy New England Village series, but now her Christmas Door series as well. With crossed fingers, she lightly taps the two whittled deer on her worktable for luck, then sits back, sipping her hot cocoa. The notched leaping stag from Wes stands beside the gentle doe she'd bought from Pete at Twinklin' Pumpkins, and somehow, the two seem like a perfect pair.

When her cell phone rings, she takes it with her cocoa to the window ledge.

"Mom?"

"How are things there, Jane? Are you getting a lot done?"

"Yes, I miss you, but I did finish the last of my designs."

"Wonderful! Oh, and by the way, Chloe's reno is fabulous. It's like a new home here."

"I'll bet Josie and Olivia are excited for Christmas."

"Are they ever. I just finished hemming their shepherd robes for the living nativity tonight. The stable is all set up beside the church, with a pony and a few sheep in there."

"That is so sweet," Jane says.

"And they've got these old colored lights strung along the stable. It's simply charming." Lillian pauses a moment. "I passed it on my way to meet up with Pete at the coffee shop."

"You saw Pete already?" Jane's voice drops; she hasn't spoken to Pete since the other day when he brought over his carved love deer, which her mother helped finagle into place last night.

"I did! We had a quick coffee before he began his route. And Jane? It's all systems go. Pete took Tuesday off from work to arrange everything. And he says everyone *loves* the idea because, well, they love Wesley. Families on his route have all kinds of plans today. Wait till he sees."

Jane takes a long breath, watching the two cardinals at the bird feeder. Snowflakes float down around them. "Mom? What if he gets mad?"

"At you? Mad?"

"Sure. He can get a little testy sometimes, after what he's been through. Or what if he doesn't like it, and tells me I should mind my own business?"

"Jane. Wes doesn't admit it, probably because it really scares him, but Pete thinks his son loves you as much as you do him. So it's important that Wes knows how you feel."

"But I'm afraid he'll just drive right by our house, after all this. He'll see my red flag up, and keep on going."

"Shhh. Don't you fret. And it's too late, anyhow."

"Too late?"

"Yes, dear. Because Operation Wesley has already begun."

⟡

"I'm all packed and leaving tonight," Wes says as he settles into the driver's seat, pulls on his fingerless gloves and fastens his seatbelt. "You better behave yourself next week, when I'm gone." As he says it, he clips his airline ticket onto the dash, in clear view while working his last shift before heading west.

Comet sits very still in the mail truck's cargo area, leaning toward the front seat, his big black dog ears tuned to Wes' voice.

"Dad won't bring you to work like this, because he does *not* want to lose *his* job. But me?" Wes shrugs and puts the truck in gear. Tiny snowflakes fall from the low gray clouds, so he sets the windshield wipers to mist. "It's an okay job, I guess. I don't mind it, really."

Since the town shops will close early today, Wes delivers their mail first, walking the business district alongside Comet. Afterward, they drive through Addison's center, out toward his residential route. On The Green, garland wraps around the colonial lampposts, and the town tree glimmers beneath sparkling lights. At Whole Latte Life, pieces of cotton— meant to look like snow—are tucked into the corners of the coffee shop windows. Inside, folks linger with their holiday mochas, relaxing now, on Christmas Eve morning.

"Get ready, Comet. Their shopping's done, and they mailed those packages for you to run, pronto."

The dog gives a short bark and stands in his designated cargo spot, watching out through the windshield. At Wedding Wishes, crystal snowflakes hang in the display window where a tall mannequin wears a fur muff, with a white cloak draped over her long gown. As the truck approaches Brookside Road, they pass the white-steepled chapel with a wreath on each of its double front doors. Off to the side, a pony gazes from a makeshift stable outlined in colored light bulbs.

"Hey, look at that," Wes says, slowing the truck. "Maybe next year, you can be in the living nativity." He glances at Comet in his rearview mirror. "Dad would have to arrange it, though. Because who knows … I might be moving to California."

As Wes leaves the town center behind, snow continues falling. But that's not what annoys him when he makes the turn onto Brookside to begin his home deliveries. "Oh, swell." It's really hard to believe that this many people have last-minute cards to mail. "Are you serious?" he asks under his breath while pulling off his wool beanie and setting it aside. Every mailbox, as far as he can see, has its red flag flipped up. Every single one. "It's going to be a long day, so get ready."

At the first house on Brookside, an English Tudor with candles in the windows, he idles the truck at the mailbox. "Come on," he tells Comet. "We've got a rush package delivery." Wes gets out at the curb, tucks the festively wrapped package in a plastic bag and gives it to the dog. "Run it, and hurry up."

The dog takes long, slow strides to the door, head held high, and drops the bag on the front stoop before turning and running back to the truck, all while Wes opens the mailbox at the curb, pulls out the waiting envelope and pushes down the red flag.

Once settled again in the truck, he checks the envelope he's about to drop in the outgoing mail tray. "Hey, it's for me," he says, holding it up toward his observant dog. "Wesley Davis. Imagine that." Inside the simple Christmas card, the message reads: *Wes, you're the best! Merry Christmas.*

"Well, that's nice of them. Dawson family, good people." He drops the card on an empty tray off to the side and approaches the next mailbox, where the red flag is also flipped up. After sorting through the family's bills and cards, he opens the box, pulls out the waiting envelope, puts in their mail and drops the flag down. Again, the envelope from the mailbox has his name on it, so he reads the message. *We'll miss you next week … Hurry back. Oh, and Merry Christmas!*

The image on the card is of holly sprigs tied with a gold ribbon. He holds it up for Comet to see, drops it in the tray, puts the truck in gear and advances to the next mailbox, this one in front of a shingled saltbox. Smoke curls from its chimney, and lights glimmer beneath the snow now dusting its shrubs. He thumbs through several envelopes, opens the mailbox and pulls out the waiting card along with a dog biscuit in a plastic bag, puts in the family's mail, taps down the red flag and looks at the envelope in his hand, the one with his name on it.

"Okaaay," he says as Comet inches closer into the front area of the truck. "Get back now, and here. Merry Christmas from the Cloutiers." He gives him the dog biscuit, then looks at the envelope again and slides out the card. *Wes, If we could croon, we'd sing a tune for you to come back soon … with Comet, too!*

One careful glance down the street makes it clear that every mailbox—some wrapped with red bows, some topped with Santa hats, some draped in evergreen boughs—does indeed have its red flag flipped up. He's not sure why yet, but something's definitely happening here.

And as he arrives at each Cape Cod, each ranch, each Dutch and Garrison colonial—wood-sided and stone-fronted and picket-fenced—each mailbox holds a message for him.

Happy Holidays, Wes. Have a safe trip, come back lickety-split!

Merry Christmas, Wes and Comet. Hope your sub doesn't mess up our mail.

Wes, The heck with the West Coast, we need you most!

At houses with balsam wreaths hung on the doors, candles lit in the windows, and reindeer glittering in the front yards, all of it sprinkled with fresh-fallen snow ... the messages don't stop, many including pastries and candies and dog biscuits, too.

Don't go, you'll miss the snow! Okay, and we'll miss you, too.

Suddenly, this stack of Christmas greetings, and his California airline ticket clipped on the dash, well it all feels sad, somehow.

No one else will deliver our mail, always on time, without fail.

"Listen to this one, buddy." Wes turns in his seat and reads the note in another card. "Comet and Wes, the finest team." He blinks back really surprising tears then, before continuing. "That would be you and me, okay?" He scratches the dog's head and hands him the biscuit that came with the card. "So it says, Comet and Wes, the finest team. You belong right here, it would definitely seem."

The dog acts uncertain about all this card reading and biscuit abundance, giving a little yip. But inside several more greeting cards showing Santas and sleighs, snowmen and snowflakes, silver bells and berries in balsam, it's all the same.

Merry Christmas, and lookie! For Comet, a cookie!

Come back soon, because on this mail route, no one else could be so cute!

Christmas in California, if you must. But it might be a bust! Hurry back.

By the time Wes gets to the old covered bridge, oh he knows. He knows precisely who's behind these jingles and rhymes and greetings. And so before he starts delivering the mail on Old Willow Road, especially to one yellow farmhouse in particular, well, he has to pull over. And he does, right outside the red covered bridge, with its twinkling lights lining the roofline and big wreath hanging at the entrance. He parks the truck at the curb and quickly wipes a tear off his cheek.

"Don't you tell anyone you saw that," Wes warns Comet. Then he pulls on his wool beanie, zips his regulation-blue parka and walks onto the bridge with his dog. A cold wind blows the snow now, and tiny ice crystals hit his face so that he hunches into his jacket and tips his head down. He stops at the bridge window overlooking a babbling brook, the same place he stood weeks ago, on a snowy day much like this one.

Really, there's nowhere else for him to go to collect his thoughts. To get a grip and not choke up if he sees one more person waving a wide, happy hello from their doorstep, or living room window, or even from oncoming cars. To stop the burning tears if he reads one more special Christmas greeting, right as he's about to leave Addison behind.

forty

WHEN THE CUCKOO CLOCK CHIRPS in the dining room, Jane brushes aside her flannel shirt cuff and glances at her watch. "Wes!" she whispers, looking to the wintry view outside the sunroom windows where fresh snow is accumulating on tree branches and shrubs, and capping the pretty bird feeder now, too. How did it get so late? She puts the finishing touches on the most important Christmas card she's ever designed, carefully writes a note inside it and seals the envelope upon which she writes Wes' name.

There's just enough time: first to set up a few decorations, then to change out of her work clothes and into something festive. Hopefully, it won't all be in vain. She rushes through the farmhouse to the living room, where a balsam fir Christmas tree stands in front of the paned windows. When she hits the switch, white lights twinkle within its soft boughs and glimmer on the glass ornaments.

At the temperamental front door, she swipes her key off the hall table, pulls on her fur-lined hooded parka and snow boots, then slips and slides along the walkway to the mailbox.

The mailbox where Pete's carved love deer now stand on either side. With a coating of fresh-fallen snowflakes on their backs, the life-sized wooden deer are magically transformed into two very beautiful, glistening snow deer.

At the curb, Jane checks the strings of white lights wrapped up and around her mailbox post, then switches on the battery pack. What happens next surprises her. She'd never expected the shine of all those white lights to cast a glow on the carved deer, but they do. It's such a misty light in the snow, the deer look absolutely real.

With not even a minute to spare, she squints down the street to be sure the mail truck is not on its way, because she still needs to light each and every lantern, each and every Mason jar.

But first, Jane opens the Christmas-decorated mailbox, sets her lone card carefully inside and gently closes the box.

Quiet seconds pass, with snow softly falling all around her. Then, and only then, she flips the red flag up.

Wes finally decides, while looking out at the snowfall from the covered bridge, that he'll save Jane's house for last. Because he knows. He knows his entire life will come down to whatever she's tucked into that mailbox of hers.

From the looks of things, people on his route might say he appears calm as he stops the truck at each mailbox, finding the red flag up at all of them, waving and calling out Christmas greetings to families who happen to be in their yards. Occasionally he has Comet run a package to a front door, but always, always, he pulls his own personal holiday card out of each mailbox. It gets to the point where he has to stop opening the cards or else he'll never finish his deliveries. At least, not without choking up on some random lump of emotion as he reads the heartfelt words people penned in the comfort of their homes, just for him. Two stacks of unopened envelopes now fill a side tray in the front seat of his truck.

And one airline ticket is clipped to the dashboard. Details memorized. Departure tonight, on Christmas Eve. Destination: California.

By midafternoon, his route is almost done. Comet lies in the back of the truck with a belly full of Christmas dog biscuits, and all the outgoing mail has been delivered, except for the homes on one block of Old Willow Road, where he's now headed.

He sees it as soon as the mail truck rounds the bend. Jane's mailbox can't be missed; hundreds of white lights twinkle on its post; a miniature wreath hangs on its handle; beside it, if his eyes aren't tricking him—and they could be, the way they keep filling with those damn tears blurring everything—stand two carved snow deer. Of course, his father would immediately and sternly correct him by saying they are *love* deer, made especially for Wes.

Because there's no way Jane pulled this all off alone. Surely, his father was in cahoots with her, helping to put her entire sad, vulnerable heart out there for Wes to see on every single stop of his home range.

But still, he needs time before reading whatever is in her mailbox. Time to bolster his own courage. So he delivers the mail before it and after it, then turns around and finishes the other side of the street before returning to the only mailbox on Old Willow Road that matters.

When he stops the mail truck beside it, a few moments pass before his hand reaches out, careful not to damage the elegant twig wreath hanging on the mailbox handle. The two full-sized, carved deer are covered with snow, snow that doesn't melt—oh, how he remembers Jane telling him that fact. Maybe that's when he knew she was special.

Wes finds one simple envelope with his name written

across the front in her flowing cursive. Every bit of Jane March's heart is tucked inside that envelope; there's no mistaking that now. This is the culmination of every rhyming, thoughtful message put into hundreds of red-flagged mailboxes on his route today. He has to tap the envelope against his other hand to buy time, to clear his throat, to not look up at her house.

Eventually, he pulls out the card Jane designed herself. It's a watercolor of a blue-painted mailbox on a wooden post. A twig wreath decorated with a sprig of greens hangs on its handle on a snowy day.

But it's the mailbox's red flag that gets him. That has him blinking back those tears again. Because instead of a red flag propped up on the side, a bright red cardinal sits in its place, its feathery crested head snowcapped, its face as serious and gosh-darned hopeful as can be. Beneath the mailbox, Jane had written part of her message:

Don't fly away...

He shakes his head, the tears streaking his unshaven cheeks, unshaven because when the day began all those hours ago, he never counted on this. It was going to be a quick workday, then off to the airport, whiskers on his face, suitcases in his pickup truck, a ticket in hand. Busy Wes, heading west.

He reads her words again. *Don't fly away...*

After a second, he opens the card and reads the rest:

Stay.

It's the shortest message he's ever received, in all his livelong life. He reads that one word again, whispers it, touches it, closes the card and sees the painted Christmas mailbox with its cardinal perched like a red flag. Then he opens the card again, before glancing in the rearview mirror and dragging his hand along his jaw. And clearing his throat. And reaching in his duffel for a napkin to blot his eyes. His hand brushes against his brand-new whittling knife, and he thinks of the wooden deer he left in Jane's mailbox yesterday, reluctantly because it wasn't finished. It was rutted in spots, and had a few rough edges. She obviously loved it just the same.

Because when he looks up at the farmhouse, he notices the candles. Up and down each step to the front porch, they glimmer in old-fashioned black lanterns, casting a soft glow on the snowy steps. And along the porch railing, Mason jars stand all in a row, filled with glimmering gold beads catching the light of the candles tucked inside them. The flames waver in the twilight snowfall of Christmas Eve.

In front of him, the airline ticket is still clipped to the dash, though it's harder to see in the waning late-afternoon light. He checks his mirror again and runs his hand through his hair, touches his face beneath his tired eyes.

"Comet. Let's go."

Christmas lights on the surrounding homes are coming on now: draped over snow-covered bushes, wrapped around lampposts, lining rooflines. Wes slides open his door and gets out, letting the dog out, too. Snow falls around them, small flakes spinning from the sky. And he stands there at the mail truck, fussing; reaching in for his wool beanie and pulling it on; looking down at his half-laced, non-regulation snow boots with his uniform pants tucked inside them; seeing Comet standing patiently at his side, waiting; looking back inside the mail truck and reaching for the airline ticket clipped front and center on the dash.

Taking it in his hands and neatly, calmly, tearing it in half.

"This is it," he says then to the dog. "You heel now, and behave yourself."

They walk side by side up the Marches' snow-covered walkway. Wes squints against the cold snowflakes blowing against his face as he approaches the farmhouse. In the paned living room window, a grand Christmas tree glows in that magical way when you just know it's the only illumination in the room.

Beside the temperamental front door where he first met Jane, annoyed, back in October, a vintage barn star shines beneath tiny lights. And those candles, candles everywhere: flickering in lanterns on each step he climbs, glowing in Mason jars all over the porch—on the railing, on top of the antique milk can where he begrudgingly left Jane her first batch of mail. All of it, every twinkling detail in the dusk of Christmas Eve, is the most beautiful sight he's ever seen.

If he's not mistaken, he's truly living the reality—with each step on the walkway, and each step up to the porch, and each step he takes to the front door, where a balsam wreath is dotted with white-tipped pinecones. Yes, he's actually living a Jane March greeting card, without a doubt.

"Sit now," he quietly orders Comet, and the dog does. He sits perfectly straight, his eyes glued to the door upon which Wes is about to knock. First, though, Wes clears his throat, presses out wrinkles in his work parka and uniform, pulls off his wool beanie, lifts his hand and pauses for a second or two. After knocking three raps, he backs up a few steps, his gaze cast downward while he waits for whatever is next.

In the hush that follows, shadows grow long and snowflakes twirl past in a wintry breeze. But moments later, golden light sweeps across the porch; Wes looks up just as the heavy wooden door is opening. As it does, he sees a potted red poinsettia sitting on a white bench inside, along the hallway wall. Across from it, garland wraps around an oak banister leading up the staircase. To the side, a cozy fire crackles in the stone fireplace in the dark living room, beside that grand, sparkling Christmas tree.

And finally, in front of him, with a glittering scarf looped around her soft sweater, with her long hair tucked behind an ear, a gold earring shimmering, with her voice softly saying his name, with tears lining her face, and with her gentle brown eyes—smiling the way they do—is Jane.

ENJOY MORE OF
THE WINTER NOVELS

1) Snowflakes and Coffee Cakes

2) Snow Deer and Cocoa Cheer

3) Cardinal Cabin

4) First Flurries

5) Eighteen Winters

FROM NEW YORK TIMES BESTSELLING AUTHOR

JOANNE DEMAIO

Also by Joanne DeMaio

The Winter Novels
(In Order)
1) Snowflakes and Coffee Cakes
2) Snow Deer and Cocoa Cheer
3) Cardinal Cabin
4) First Flurries
5) Eighteen Winters
—And More Winter Novels—

The Seaside Saga
(In order)
1) Blue Jeans and Coffee Beans
2) The Denim Blue Sea
3) Beach Blues
4) Beach Breeze
5) The Beach Inn
6) Beach Bliss
7) Castaway Cottage
8) Night Beach
9) Little Beach Bungalow
10) Every Summer
11) Salt Air Secrets
12) Stony Point Summer
13) The Beachgoers
—And More Seaside Saga Books—

Summer Standalone Novels
True Blend
Whole Latte Life

Novella
The Beach Cottage

For a complete list of books by New York Times bestselling author Joanne DeMaio, visit:

Joannedemaio.com

About the Author

JOANNE DEMAIO is a *New York Times* and *USA Today* bestselling author of contemporary fiction. She enjoys writing about friendship, family, love and choices, while setting her stories in New England towns or by the sea. Joanne lives with her family in Connecticut and is currently at work on her next novel.

For a complete list of books and for news on upcoming releases, please visit Joanne's website. She also enjoys hearing from readers on Facebook.

Author Website:
Joannedemaio.com

Facebook:
Facebook.com/JoanneDeMaioAuthor

Made in the USA
Monee, IL
13 January 2023